THE Beautiful LIFE OF BOYS

First Printing, 2019

ISBN: 978-0-578-45355-2

To those who live a beautiful life.

"What?" I hear Sid's grandmother question loudly from down the hall while I'm getting ready. "Brighton? Can you come here?" Her loud voice carries down the airy passageway. I quickly set my toothbrush onto the bathroom counter and rush to check on her. She has already hung up the phone by the time I make it to the doorway of her bedroom.

"Yes, ma'am?"

"Your mother, she's flying back today!" I enter further into her bedroom. "She wanted me to tell you she's going to see you and your brother later at school."

"Did she say why?" I question. Mom usually isn't one to be vague.

"These old ears don't work like they used to, but I can tell you, that's all she told me." She gives me a joking gaze.

"Tell Sid to hurry up and get ready. I can't have you boys being late on my watch!"

"Yes, ma'am." I walk back into the hall, knocking on Sid's door as I go by.

Sid is my best friend. He lives with his grandmother in an old rickety house, smack dab in the center of Los Angeles. I swear, it's like a time machine put

4

here disguised as a house, Doctor Who style. It's really a sight. All these big buildings surrounding this little old wooden shack. The inside is newer than the outside. Sid's grandma decorated it in a way that feels comfortable, like a home.

Whenever my mom worked late, or, for any reason, couldn't be home with me and my brother, Elliott, Sid's grandma always let us stay here.

To be honest, socially, I've always been a little bit of a misfit. I've never really had any of the latest trends in clothes or electronics. Sid was always the same. His grandma couldn't afford to buy him all the things the other kids at school had and it was something that bonded our simple middle school boy brains.

The school day is already half over. On my way to the cafeteria, I walk past Elliott's classroom and wave at him through the window on the door. He laughs when he sees me and I see his teacher look in my direction, so I quickly make my escape. I'm not a big glutton, but lunch gives me the opportunity to breathe again. The school is very aware of our family's financial situation, so Elliott and I get a lunch ticket each day for a free meal. No matter how gross the food is, it tastes better knowing Ma won't have to spend her money on feeding us lunch. Our money problems are already hard enough.

Making my way to the lunch table, Sid has his signature Hot Cheeto and Marshmallow Fluff sandwich on rye, which we all tried once and swore to never eat again. I love Sid like my own brother, but that boy's got a messed up tongue.

Corina has a green Tupperware container filled to the brim with who knows what. She always has something that's bright red and smells like chili peppers. She always smells like some sort of spice. It's oddly comforting. Her mom owns a Mexican restaurant that everyone knows isn't really that good, but we all try to convince our families to eat there anyway to keep her mom happy. We all know that when her mom isn't happy, Corina has it harder. Her mother has a spicy temper, almost as hot as the ghost peppers she puts in her salsa.

Lin and Concha are eating school lunch, like me, but they always mix everything together into weird concoctions to see if it tastes good. Today, it looks like they have taken the pepperoni off their pizza, cut them into little chunks with their spork and mixed it in with some applesauce. Lin and Concha are both in foster care, so they get free lunch like I do, but I think they think nobody knows about it. Honestly, I'm not sure if anyone else notices. When I'm in line, I always see them discreetly pull out their small pink tickets and hand them to the lunch lady. I silently relate but we haven't spoken about it.

"Bright! Come sit down, my man!" Sid gestures to me, patting the table bench beside him. I sit down and try not to look at his Hot Cheeto dust and marshmallow coated fingers. As I'm eating my pizza, my thoughts start wandering. I'm not thinking about anything in particular, just about how Elliott hasn't eaten yet and the pizza already looked dry, so he probably won't like it. Or how Lin keeps trying to dip his pepperoni-less pizza in Corina's mysterious pepper mixture.

I love watching my surroundings. We do live in Los Angeles afterall, the epicenter of all things goofy, funny, strange, raunchy and outright bizarre. I'm waiting for the clock to strike 11:23 A.M. There are these groups of students that come into the cafeteria singing songs from whichever musical they're putting on at that given moment. This time, it happens to be The 25th Annual Putnam County Spelling Bee. The group of kids comes in, of course, right at 11:25 A.M. I think that's when their rehearsals end or something, because the time in which they come in is consistent day-to-day.

They are singing what I think is the opening number to the show this time. I'm not exactly sure. What I am sure about is that the song is literally about spelling... and winning spelling bees.

"Will Elliott and Brighton Anderson please report to the office? Bring your things, you will be leaving for the day," chimes over the loudspeaker, interrupting the chorus of high school morons thinking they're in a teen movie. The call comes not a moment too soon. I stand up and quickly dump my tray. My friends are all waving, looking so thrilled, but also jealous that I'm getting to leave early.

My thoughts jump back to last week when Mom suddenly packed her things and left. She hasn't gone on a trip since she and my father were still together, so it's nice she got to go, even if it was for my great aunt's funeral.

I try not to think about my father, but small things remind me him. Mom leaving like Dad used to when he was trying to win Mom over again, making her beg for him to come back after his seemingly endless manipulations, just to end up cheating on her is one of them. When I was younger and Elliott was just a baby, things were different. We had new backpacks every year and would eat out one or two times a week, just for the fun of it. But when Dad left, he took everything. He was our bread winner. When he left we fell hard below the poverty line. Mom worked every day to try to make us ignorant of the obvious changes. For Elliott, it worked, but I wasn't so lucky.

I see Elliott walking ahead, almost to the front office. I run up behind him and grasp the office door above his head, swinging it open. He jumps back, startled, but tries to play it off. Mom's standing in front of the reception desk, signing our names out on many miscellaneous forms.

"Mom!" Elliott exclaims, hugging her.

"Hey," I say, grabbing Elliot's backpack from him, swinging it onto my shoulder over my backpack strap.

"Good luck, Ms. Anderson. Boys, it was great having you here!" the receptionist says to us as we walk out the doors to the parking lot.

"Ma? What was up with that? What was she talking about?" I question her as we get closer and closer to the car.

"Get in and we'll talk," Ma says, opening the driver's side door, slightly smirking.

When I get in the car, there are multiple suitcases in the back seat, not just the one's Mom took with her, along with some blankets and pillows crammed into the space between the floor and the back of her seat. There is barely enough room for Elliott.

"What's going on, Mom? Are we going somewhere?" Elliott asks, tugging on one of the suitcase handles.

Mom turns on the car. Usually, when the car turns on the radio is already playing softly, but this time, it wasn't. Mom drove here with no music. She told me when

I was little: "a day without music is a day I don't want to live", and I've felt the same way since.

"Boys, this might feel sudden to you, but trust your momma on this." She pauses and clears her throat. "I went to the will reading while I was in Connecticut, and your great aunt has left us her home and some of her savings." I could tell she was struggling to tell us what she wanted to. "The house is really nice!" She's suddenly excited.

"So we're going to Connecticut?" Elliott says with a matching excited tone.

"Yes, dear. We're going to be heading to the airport right now!" Ma says, looking into the backseat over her shoulder.

"So, when are we coming back? How long will we be there?" I ask, hoping it won't be for long. I mean, how long would it take to sell a house? Mom's first priority is always us not missing any school.

"Do we have to sign something? Why do we have to go? Kids don't usually help sell houses." I chuckle, grabbing my seat belt to buckle it.

"I must not have been clear," Mom says, clearing her throat. She looks me in the eyes, making sure not to break eye contact. "These are three one-way tickets to Connecticut. Your great aunt left us a house much nicer than our apartment here. We will be moving, indefinitely." She's trying to encourage me.

"No way! Sick!" Elliott exclaims as he jolts back and forth in his seat in excitement. Mom shifts gears in the car as we prepare to leave the school parking lot. I grab her hand over the shifter and stop it from moving.

"What do you think you're doing, Brighton? That's

dangerous!" she says as she tries to move her hand.

"Do I not get any say in this?" I say, looking down at Elliott and I's backpacks on the floor near my feet, purposely not looking at her. "I'm seventeen," I continue, "you can't just pick me up and take me places like a baby. I like it here!" I say, looking out the window at my school.

"Exactly. You're seventeen. I have made this decision for us, and you!" Mom says as she rips her hand out from under mine. I scream into the air, venting my frustration, kicking the backpacks at my feet and opening the door.

"Where do you think you're going?" Mom shouts as I get out of the car.

"Anywhere!" I scream into the parking lot of the school, walking away from the car.

My mind is racing with the thought of leaving L.A. I walk through the school hallways that I used to feel at home in and everything feels like it's being ripped away from me. Everything is out of my control. I hurry to the cafeteria but everyone is gone. I must have been in the car longer than I thought. I try to hurry and think of what classes everyone has right now.

"Sid, Sid, Sid," I whisper to myself, pacing up and down the rows of cafeteria tables. "Band!" Sid has band after lunch. I remember that he always complains about getting Cheeto residue on his clarinet. Are these the memories I'm going to look back on when I'm all the way across the country?

I walk up to the band room and see Sid sitting on the old couch, fussing about with his sheet music. Hesitant, I open the door and fast-walk over to him, trying not to catch the attention of other students. Now, of course, this is high school, and when you walk into a class you're not in, everyone thinks you're insane and stares at you almost immediately. I walk up to Sid.

"Hey, man! Forget somethin'?" he says, tugging his beanie down over his ears. He looks directly at me for the first time since I walked into the room and I can see his expression change.

"Sid.... man.... help..." I say, out of breath from walking halfway across the campus.

"What's going on, man?" Sid says as he puts both his hands on my shoulders and starts pushing me towards the door.

"I need somewhere to go, somewhere to stay. I don't know, man, you gotta help me, please!" I say frantically as Sid quietly closes the band room door behind us, trying not to disturb everyone's practice. Sid grabs me gently by the back of the neck and we walk across the hall into the boy's bathroom. I push the trash can in front of the door as Sid hops up on the sink counter, pulling a single, slightly broken cigarette and lighter out of this pocket and lighting it.

It was almost routine; me securing the bathroom so Sid can smoke without getting caught by a teacher. We've been doing it every day, without fail, since sophomore year. It was our little bonding time. He'd tell me about what girl he was trying to get with this week, I'd complain about something unrelated.

I sit down on the floor next to the trash can and tell Sid the events that just occurred. *Sid is so odd* I think to myself as he ponders what I have just told him. He seems to always have a single cigarette, a lighter, and, without fail, every day, he wears mismatched socks and, sometimes, even shoes. When I first met Sid, I wasn't sure about him. He was just the weird kid who had nothing to offer me. However, he is actually very smart. Some of the things he says, to this day, still take me by surprise.

"Got a piece of paper?" Sid asks as he slides his beanie off his head. I hand him a gum wrapper that I had in my pocket from earlier this morning. He pulls the tiniest nub of a pencil out from behind his ear and begins to write something on the paper.

"Here," he says calmly, snapping me out of the my daydream, handing me back the gum wrapper.

10821 N Westwood Blvd is written in his surprisingly neat handwriting.

"Lay low until school is out. The others and I will meet you there. Don't go back to Gran's, your mom will probably go there looking for you," he says as he puts his cigarette out in the sink. He slouches his beanie back onto his head. I nod as I move the trash can away from in front of the door.

Sid goes back into his band class and I hear the quiet notes of his clarinet fade as I walk out of the school. Westwood is pretty far from here, but not so far that I don't think I can walk there. I make my way to the house. It takes about an hour, but it's nice. It gives me some time to clear my head.

I walk up to a small one-story house with boards on the windows. It looks like something right out of a horror movie. There might have even been one that was shot here. It is L.A. after all. I walk up to the front door and it's locked. I see a small metal gate in the yard that seems to lead to a back garden area. There, I see what's left of a broken glass sliding door with some faded Looney

Toons sheets nailed up in front of it, acting as the door.

The inside of the house isn't much nicer. I flip the light switch and the light doesn't turn on, just as I was expecting. There are a few bean bag chairs scattered about the room and some cardboard boxes tipped upside down with some ashtrays placed on them. I look into the kitchen and notice a few water pipes and some empty beer cans sitting on the counters. The tile flooring is peeling up and cracking. I step in to investigate further and I notice a Babe Ruth baseball card at my feet. It's one of his rookie cards. I recognize it because I once gave Sid the same one. I wrote *you're my best friend, dude* on the back.

As I turn around to go back into the area where the bean bag chairs are, a pigeon startles me. Apparently, it had made a nest in the open cabinets. I drop the baseball card and rush into the corner of the kitchen as it flies out into the living room, eventually making its way past the faded Looney Toons sheets. Once the shock has faded and I feel comfortable enough to move, I reach for the baseball card on the floor, which, this time, was turned over from all the ruckus. I notice some faded Sharpie on the back.

I pick the card up and walk over to the bed sheet draped off the door to get some extra light. I want to try and make it out.

'Y....r.....my....b...es.....f........e....nd.....ud...'

I immediately realize that this must be the place Sid and his older college friends come to hang out when they have nowhere else to go. He told me about it around the time his baseball card obsession slowly turned into a "chicks like guys who play baseball" obsession. He once told me about the time he and his baseball buddies "scored" with a bunch of girls from the rival school freshman year here. They had a huge party and everyone got super wasted. I guess the cops were called and everything. Sometimes, I'm envious of Sid's crazy lifestyle. Other times, I wonder how he manages to keep up with it all at only seventeen.

"WHAT UP MY MAN!??!! HOW YOU DOING!?!?" Sid screams as he and his friends enter the house. I'm startled after sitting here in silence for a few hours. I can tell his friends were surprised to see me, almost as if Sid was a traitor for showing me this place.

"Sid, man! You said this was our secret fighting grounds," exclaims the tallest one of the bunch. I recognize him from school.

"Joker, man, you can't say anything about not keeping secrets," Sid retaliates. "Remember when you told me about your cousin and the spin the bottle in 6th grade?" he jokes.

"I told you that in confidence!" Joker shouts.

"And this is an emergency so we both have problems now, don't we?" Sid fights back.

"Where are the others?" I ask Sid as he walks past the kitchen into the hallway leading to what I assume were once the bedrooms, but are now rooms filled with piles of trash.

"Corina and Lin went to your apartment complex to scope it out, to see if your mom is home, and Concha went home to see if she can borrow her foster brother's Camaro for the night," Sid says as he lights what definitely isn't a cigarette. "You want a hit?" he asks when he notices me watching him closely as he loudly exhales a cloud of smoke.

I've never been one to be very adventurous. The riskiest thing I've ever done is sneak into a second movie after the movie I paid for finished in 8th grade. I watch as Sid deeply inhales the smoke and blows it out into the room, creating sort of a dream-like haze everywhere you look, and something comes over me. An urge to not be me for one moment. An urge to forget all of my problems. An urge to just let go completely in a way I never have before.

I stand up and walk over to Sid and he passes me the joint, making sure to place it between my thumb and index finger, unlike a cigarette. He begins to roll a few more joints from a small baggie of pot that seems to have magically appeared from inside his beanie. It makes me wonder if that crazy bastard had that in there at school, too. Everyone in the room stares at me, since I'm clearly new to this. I bring the joint closer to my lips, breathing in and holding the smoke inside my body for a few seconds. I feel warm. I feel fuzzy. When I exhale, it isn't as beautiful as Sid's. I choke and gasp for air as Sid pats my back and laughs. It felt like one of the worst things I've ever experienced. I couldn't imagine why anyone would want to voluntarily do this to themselves. It burns.

An hour or so goes by and a few joints gets passed around to me. I'm feeling good, but nothing like I expected. When I had heard Sid talk about smoking, I always felt like I would be very giggly, but I feel calm, almost as if I'm being warmed from the inside out by the sun on a nice summer day. It's getting darker and darker in the house as the sunset grows dim outside. We hear a car pull into the driveway. Sid and I walk outside, leaving his stoner friends inside to finish smoking what's left of the final joint. It was an enjoyable experience. I almost forget the whole reason I even came to this house.

"Good news!" Corina says as she raises her hand in the air. She is almost silhouetted by what's left of the sunset behind her. She's wearing a crop top that only barely reaches her belly button and when she raises her hands I can almost see under her shirt. I notice she has bruises right under her bra.

"Your mom's car wasn't in the complex and all your lights in the apartment were off," she shouts as Lin rolls down the backseat window to the Camaro.

"We will have to squeeze, but hop in!" he says. His voice gets quieter as he scoots away from the window. Sid hops in the passenger seat and I squeeze in the backseat, sitting on half of Lin's lap. He smells like cologne and slightly like coffee. It's really nice. Lin is the latest addition to our friend group. He's got a muscular physique and his jawline is very square-cut. When he moved into the same foster family as Concha, we didn't think twice about accepting him as our own.

The streetlights on the roads are turning on as the sky gets darker and darker. Sid and Corina are both having their own talkfest and Concha is focusing on driving. I hear bits and pieces of Sid and Corina's conversation over the sound of the loud Camaro engine, but not enough to join in. Concha slows down the car as we pull up to my apartment complex. The lights are still off as we approach our building and Ma's car is still gone. I'm slightly worried that she's not home, but doubtful she would actually go to Connecticut without me. I have no idea where she could be. As the car comes to a full stop, I hop out and head toward the front steps of my building. I see Lin through the car window. He scoots over and re-adjusts from having me sat on his legs for so long. Corina scoots over into the now empty space.

As I walk up the steps, I'm struck with emotion. The feeling of being alone. If I don't go with Mom and Elliot, then I really will be alone. I can't expect my friends to be with me all the time, even though I wish they could be. I reach down and get the spare house key from under a ceramic frog lawn ornament we have next to our front door. I left mine in my backpack in Mom's car, along with my cell phone and any spare change I had.

The inside of the apartment smells like home, like a fresh shirt just taken out of the dryer. I can see dishes, presumably from Mom's lunch, sitting in the sink. Everything feels untouched. As I look closer, I can see some things are missing. Ma's favorite throw blanket isn't on the couch and a chunk of Elliott's manga seems to be missing from the bookshelf next to the TV. Ma must have packed them in our suitcases this morning before she came to get us. I grab a grocery bag from under the sink and walk slowly down the hall to my bedroom, trying to take in every creak of the floor and crack in the walls, since I might never hear or see them again. I quickly change out of my sweaty clothes, throwing my pants and shirt onto the floor of my closet.

I grab a pile of somewhat clean clothes off the ground and shove them into the plastic grocery bag. I'm not sure what's going to happen, but I know that I don't want to leave my friends. I love them. All of them. That's not to say I don't love Ma and Elliott, because I obviously do, they are my family, but I feel like everything is falling apart. I hear a honk from outside. I must be moving slow, probably because I'm still feeling a little foggy from smoking earlier. I rush outside and join the others in the car again.

"We have a surprise for you!" Lin says while I hop in the back seat as he puts his arm over my shoulder. Corina pulls up her bright green corduroy Jansport backpack from our feet and pulls out a more than a half full bottle of vodka, and I see Sid in the front, holding up a bottle of Sunny D.

"There's no better way to forget your problems than to get so smashed you forget your own name!" Sid exclaims as Concha starts the car and drives out of the complex. I look back at the rows of apartments and junker cars in the parking lot. Corina is sectioning the vodka out into empty water bottles as Concha makes a ruckus from the front seat about making sure she's is not spilling in the car. Sid then adds enough Sunny D to top off the bottles and hands one out to each of us. I take a sip and it tastes weird, but familiar. The vodka burns my tongue and nose as I swallow, but the crisp, cold, orange taste of the Sunny D masks the brutal burn nicely. I look out the window and see that the sky is more overcast then before. I realize we're heading towards the ocean. I lean back and close my eyes, listening to the sound of my friends chattering and having a good time. I feel good. My troubles are slowly slipping away as my bottle begins to empty. I open my eyes to see some blurry lights in the distance out the front windshield. I rub my eyes to clear the view and I see a ferris wheel. The Santa Monica Pier is right in front of me.

"Surprise, man! We're gonna get wasted and ride rollercoasters 'til we puke!" Sid yells as he takes the last swig from his bottle.

The lights are bright as I exit the car, brighter than I have ever seen before in my life. The world is spinning faster than normal as everyone walks arm in arm down the pier. As we make our way to the roller coaster for our first go, I look out to the ocean. It's calm and peaceful, a stark contrast with the spinning lights being reflected on the water's surface from the various carnival rides. We ride the roller coasters as many times as we all could afford with what change we had in our pockets. My stomach is in knots, but the only one who looks green is Sid and that sick bastard is absolutely loving it.

We're all making our way to exit the pier because it's nearing midnight and everyone is leaving. Lin yanks me aside and pulls two ride tickets out of his pocket. We stumble behind the base of a palm tree to separate us from the others. We hide, ducked down, looking at each other for a few seconds. I can feel his breath hitting my face as he breathes heavily. His breath is warm and has a potent harshness from the vodka. We sneakily run to the ferris wheel and board immediately for the last run of the night. We sit across from each other, taking in the view of the beach. We can see Venice in the distance. People are walking around lit by only the streetlights.

"What are you gonna do, Brighton?" Lin asks as I look back at him from looking out at the ocean. I stare at his face. It's flushed red from running around the pier.

"I'm scared, man. I'm confused. I don't want to think about it," I say as I lean back, trying not to rock the ferris wheel trolley.

"I'll give you something else to think about," Lin says with a more serious tone. "You have a mother and a little brother. A family. Me? Sure, I have my foster sister, but she could be taken from us any day. My life is temporary, ever-changing. A roller coaster." he says, looking over at the roller coaster that has now gone dark. "If I had to make a choice like yours, to stay here and live like me or leave all this behind and have something permanent, I think you know what I would choose."

He stops talking as the ferris wheel reaches the top. We look out at everything. The lights of the city are bright and the people on the ground are so small. I can't make out where Sid or Corina are. Everyone is just a small, insignificant dot. I look at Lin, who, to my surprise, is staring at me. We make eye contact. He gently slides over to my side of the trolley and rests his head on my shoulder. I rub his shaven scalp with my hand, feeling each and every pointy hair as the ferris wheel jerks back into motion and we're slowly brought back down to reality.

We meet back up with Sid and the others in the parking lot. Concha is in the driver's seat, chugging some water in an attempt to sober up before driving back to The Stoner Shack.

Lin and I hop in the backseat with Corina. We buckle our seatbelts and take off into the now dark, but yellowy lit streets of Santa Monica. The roads are pretty calm compared to usual traffic. A few cars pass every couple of minutes, which is good because Concha is a still a little tipsy. Her attempt to sober up helped, but she's still not one hundred percent. Any other day, if I was completely in my right mind, I wouldn't have gotten in the car. Today, I don't have a care in the world. The ride back to the house is calm. It's almost serene. I feel safe, even though I shouldn't. We pull up to the house and my peaceful thoughts are suddenly the farthest thing from my mind. The house is surrounded by cops; at least three squad cars.

"Concha, go! Don't stop the car!" Sid yells as we pull up to the house. Startled, Concha stomps on the breaks right in front of the house. I see my mother's car in the driveway. In an instant, Concha is pulled from the front seat by a cop and we're all instructed to leave the vehicle with our hands up. I step out and I see my mom exit one of the squad cars. She has a very intense look on her face, one I have never seen before. The angriest I think I've ever seen her is when I got a C- on an advanced chemistry exam.

"That's him! That's my son!" she shouts in the direction of the police officers. I'm pulled aside by a cop who smells like stale cigar smoke.

"Now, ma'am, your son is seventeen. The only reason he won't be booked is because we're relinquishing him into your care," the policeman says with an overly stern voice. The smell of a cigar is way more repulsive than the scent of the weed earlier. I see Sid and Lin getting handcuffed out of the side of my eye . Lin looks good, even from a distance. My mom runs up to me and hugs me, wrapping her hands around my head. I shove her off me and turn away.

"Don't you ever do anything like this again! Don't you ever!" she says over and over as her words slowly fade out.

"Don't force me to move."

"Why can't you understand that this is the best thing for us all?" my mother is screaming at me at this point. "Our apartment is falling apart. Your brother's ceiling is falling in. I didn't even want to go back there to look for you. You're lucky I did, though, or I would have never found this." She holds up the gum wrapper Sid wrote on earlier.

"Our kitchen is so small I have to wash our dishes in our bathtub. We've replaced the stairs on our porch over five times. I'm done investing money into a shoebox that can't stand on its own." She keeps going on and on about how our apartment is in worst shape than the Titanic itself.

"Ma, I like it there. It's where I grew up! It's where I made all my friends. It's where you've marked Elliot's height over the past 14 years." I feel the need to stand my ground and express that I am not backing down.

"Brighton, let's think about this. Great Aunt Debra lived on three acres of land. Her house, when I was a kid, went as far as the eye could see. It's the sort of house that calls for a family to live in it." I can tell she's trying to convince me, still.

"Are you really gonna make me go?" I ask in a final attempt to convince her to stay.

"Is the sky blue?" She gives me an eye.

I look to see everything around me. Sid and Lin are in the back of a cop car. Concha is in cuffs, sitting on the curb. This is all my fault. Everything that happened today was because of my selfishness. But still, I don't want this to be it.

This is one of the longest car rides I feel like I've ever taken. I look over at my mother, then back to Elliott. All I want to do is scream at the top of my lungs. I feel like I'm being dragged against my will to a foreign country. It might as well be. I've never been to Connecticut. My family has never really had the money to travel, except one time when Dad was living with us, and we didn't even pay for it ourselves.

"I wish dad was here..." I say to break the silence.

"Brighton Anderson, what did you just say to me?" My mother slams on the breaks.

"I. Wish. Dad. Were. Here."

"You know what? Your father is probably out with his new lover. He doesn't have time to care about what's going in his sons' lives." I'm shocked. She never speaks so openly about Dad.

"Mom!" I shout back, shocked.

"Not this again," Elliott sighs awkwardly.

"Elliott, please don't," she tells him, sticking her hand into the back seat and placing it onto his knee.

"Brighton, you will not say another word until we

get to the airport."

"Word," I say, peering into her eyes intently.

Suddenly, out of nowhere, I feel a sharp cut of a ring on my cheek. My mother has backhanded me for the first time. I *am* being kind of an ass.

"You want to get smart again?"

"Screw off." I turn into the door, leaning against the window. My mind's racing. I can't keep my thoughts straight, probably a result of the alcohol I drank. I'm sure the pot isn't helping either. This isn't good. I have to get on a plane like this? I wonder, would they even let me on in this state? Could this be my out? Could this be my time buyer? I look over at Mom. I know this probably isn't the best idea but I abruptly say, "I'm drunk." I cross my arms, bracing for another slap.

"If you're smart, you really won't say another word this time." She doesn't even move her glance from the road.

It's going to take about 30 minutes to drive to LAX. The Stoner Shack isn't even that far from it, but that's L.A. traffic for you. I look out the window, taking all the sights in. I realize that this will be the last time I see all of this for a while. I never thought I'd enjoy traffic on the 405, but, at this moment, it feels like home more than anything else. Who would have thought the crazy drivers of L.A. were something I was going to miss. Who knows what this town in Connecticut is going to be like. Or what the people will be like. Will they be nice? The people in L.A. aren't. But that's what I like. I don't like people being fake to my face. I would much rather someone look me in my eyes and tell me they don't like my bleached hair instead of them telling me they like it because they don't want to make me feel bad. Sometimes it's better to be blunt instead of sugar coating things. That was one of the many lessons I learned from my father over the years.

We're about fifteen minutes away from the airport now, and I can't stand this. I've never felt a car ride take longer than this one. All I want to do is tuck and roll out of the car onto the highway. Death seems a bit more fitting than my current circumstance.

I've only ever flown once. It was an amazing trip. Mom, Dad, myself and Elliott went to Paris, France. It was a surprise for us boys. My parents got married when my mom was pregnant with me; partially for societal reasons, partially for love. Everyone knew that, but everyone also knew that Mom and Dad didn't have a lot of money. Dad had more than Mom does now, but we weren't rich by any means, so they couldn't afford a honeymoon.

Dad was a dentist. His parents made him go to dental school. They wanted "the perfect doctor son", but my dad wasn't into the whole blood and guts thing, so he took the dental route. It was a small clinic, very mom and pop style. Some of the other dentists in the practice and a few of my mom's friends pitched in and helped send us all on a trip to the one place my mother always wanted to go.

The flight from LAX to Charles De Gaulle is roughly 11 hours. Thankfully, LAX flies with Air France, so the flights were a bit cheaper. Flying over the ocean was terrifying. I just remember the overwhelming feeling of fear. I was scared the plane would crash into the ocean. I was worried we had gotten on the wrong flight. When you're flying over land, it's so cool. It looks just like how maps look. People in movies always make fun of how the land looks when they're above because looks like weirdly shaped squares and rectangles, but it's true. That's really what it looks like. My mind was blown. Elliott didn't care much for flying his first time around. He was only nine, so that could've been a large factor in it. I remember him screaming most of the flight. Rather than being cliche and sitting next to a crying baby, we were the the people with the screaming baby, but it was a crying, oversized child, instead. Overall, the flight wasn't great. It wasn't awesome. I think it'd be pretty much how you imagine an intercontinental flight would be.

Times were easier then. I really envy Elliott. All he has to worry about with this whole move is how big his new bedroom is going to be, and which seat on the plane he gets. Me? As always, I'm overthinking things. What's my new school going to be like? What's the house going to be like? Will it be big? Will it not be? Will it look like a horror movie set like The Stoner Shack? Will it look like the white house? I have so many questions. Will we be moving to a small town? Will mom find a new guy? Hell, who knows maybe that's what she needs. A nice man to show her a good time. That could probably do her quite a bit of good. Who was this Great Aunt Debra? Why is she important? Why have I never met her? Why did she leave this house to my mom? Also, when the hell did my mom even live in Connecticut? I seriously thought our family origins were based in Los Angeles. Come to think of it, Ma has never really talked about her family. Whenever any relative was brought up, it was always Dad talking.

I look up and my trance breaks as I notice the very large, iconic LAX sign. We've made it to hell, my hell, my slave ship, my one-way ticket to bullshit.

"We're here!" Elliott screams from the back seat, bouncing around. "When we went to Paris, I think I threw up on the plane. Didn't I, Ma?" Elliott leans into the front seat.

"Yes, dear, I think you did!" She chuckles.

"How long of a flight is it?" Elliott asks.

"About five hours, sweetheart. We have a layover in Dallas."

"It's not straight through?" I look over.

"No, I couldn't afford them."

"Half the fun of going somewhere is getting there!" Elliott shouts in my face mockingly.

"Dad could've," I regretfully say.

"Do you hate me or something, Brighton? Why must you always throw in my face that your father is better than I am? Huh? Don't you think I know he has more money? Don't you think I know his girlfriend is younger and better than me? Don't you think I know that your father thinks I'm just as good as a used tissue?"

"Mom... I--"

"Save it. We're here. Get out of the car." She throws the car into park and begins to unbuckle her seat belt.

"What are we doing with the car, Mom?" Elliott asks as he hops out of the back seat.

"I'm leaving it here. The airport will eventually tow it. Maybe I'll have a way of getting it to Connecticut. But as for right now, it's being left here."

"You can't be serious, Ma. We need a car wherever we're going." I'm trying to reason with my clearly insensible mother.

"What? Your dad wouldn't leave the car here?"

"Mom..."

"Like I said, Brighton, save it. Grab your suitcase and get your ass out of the car. Now. Our flight is in less than two hours." Ma turns away from me. I've never heard her speak to me this way. It's shocking. It's hurtful. Am I just emotional? Am I just drunk? Maybe I'm being a bit too rough on her. I just really hate the idea of moving out of L.A. I mean, I only just met and started to get to know Lin. He seems really cool. I wanted to go back to the pier with just him. When we were on top of that Ferris wheel, I felt like all the problems in the world dissipated.

"We're flying Southwest," Ma breaks the silence. "Terminal B, gate C15," she reads off her phone.

"When did you buy these flights, Mom?" I ask.

"Yesterday. We will be flying economy, so don't get your hopes up. It's not gonna be a luxurious flight. Nonetheless, we almost didn't get to board a plane at all today thanks to you being a pain in the ass."

"What do you mean?" I reply.

"Well, I had to change our flights to a later time because you needed to run off and get stoned." I'm surprised Mom could tell I had smoked.

"You smoked weed?" Elliott asks, intrigued.

"Sure," I answer him, annoyed.

"Now, can we go inside? I don't wanna miss our flights," Mother objects.

She always was the one to make sure whatever group she was with stayed on track. Getting through security is a breeze, given it's almost three in the morning at this point. Ma had to rebook for a red-eye to Dallas and a morning flight into Connecticut. We get to the gate and there's only one other person sitting there which is odd, especially for LAX. This is one of the busiest airports in the world. I would figure even a red-eye flight would have at least more than a dozen passengers. As time progresses and the flight gets closer, a few more stragglers approach the gate. I've been watching the ramp as agents fiddle with the plane as they get it ready. I was attempting to make a game out of seeing if I could find our suitcases when they were loading them into the cargo bin.

"Good morning and welcome to Los Angeles International Airport," a voice chimes over the intercom, "this is the boarding announcement for flight 34BA with service into Dallas Fort Worth. Would all passengers with priority boarding please approach the gate to board the aircraft."

"Gather your things, boys," Ma says quickly, "we'll be boarding soon. We're in boarding group A."

"Thank you. Now we will begin boarding for group A. I repeat, boarding group A. Welcome aboard," the PA system comes on once again. But this time, it's us.

We approach the desk agent as she scans the two passengers in front of us' tickets. She then scans my mother's, then Elliott's. Elliott high fives her as we board the airplane. I stare at my boarding pass for a prolonged minute. I let out the biggest sigh of defeat I ever have, then hand her my pass. She scans it and I continue to follow my mother and Elliott down into the plane. The aisles are small and cramped. The air is stale and has a smell I imagine an old folks home would have. I take my seat at the back of the plane. Luckily, I'm in the window seat so I can rest my head against the wall. My head is pounding at this point as I feel myself coming back down to earth. The seat's cramped and I feel my heart start to race. I'm not very good with small spaces, never have been. One time when I was little, I got lost in a McDonald's play place. The fire department was called and it was just a great big mess. I watch as everyone else boards the plane, sitting one by one in their seats. Luckily, it looks like the youngest person on the flight is Elliott, so I won't have to worry about a crying baby worsening my already pounding headache. Mostly businessmen are on the flight, and the mix of cologne and aftershave slowly fills the stale aircraft air.

The doors to the plane close after all the passengers have boarded. A quarter of the seats are filled and I feel myself getting more and more shaken. The plane starts to move and I feel my stomach move into my throat. The walls feel like they are crushing me alive. Everyone else seems so calm, but my body is telling me otherwise. The seatbelt light flashes on as a flight attendant tell us various safety procedures, but her chatter is muffled in my ears.

I can't focus and my vision is blurry. I can't get out of my seat and I start to feel queasy. My mouth is dry and my pounding head isn't making it any better. We're about to take off and the ride is getting more and more rough. The man sitting next to me is reading a newspaper and peering at me from the corner of his eye. My face must look like hell.

We're off the ground and I look out the window. Los Angeles is getting smaller and smaller as we get higher. I feel floaty, even more so as we reach peak altitude. My hands shake as I anxiously wait for the seatbelt light to turn off. I watch it as it blinks. The flashing orange light taunts me because I keep thinking it's going to turn off, but it doesn't. I try to distract myself by rummaging through my backpack from school.

My phone is in it, but it's dead and basically useless this high up in the air. I look back and the seatbelt light is off. I unhinge my belt and nudge myself into the aisle, making my way to the airplane lavatory. I open the door and before I can even close it, my head is in the toilet as I puke my guts out. It burns from the mix of alcohol and greasy cafeteria pizza. A flight attendant comes up behind me.

"Sir, are you okay?" she says faintly as she places her hand on the bathroom door. I scoot my legs in and grunt as I grab the door handle.

I wipe my mouth and flush. The smell is horrendous as I stand up and look in the mirror. My eyes are sunken in and my skin looks dry. Usually my face looks rather youthful, but right now I look a wreck. My hair is messy and it's starting to get slightly greasy I can't wait to take a shower when I get to wherever our new home is. I tousle my hair with my fingers, trying to make the wavy blond locks looks somewhat presentable. I fail miserably. I splash water on my face in a last ditch attempt to feel more human. It feels nice, but only lasts a few seconds before I go back to feeling like a living zombie. Opening the door, the lights of the plane feel even brighter than before. I walk back to my seat and pass out for the majority of the flight.

I'm woken up by a flight attendant shaking my shoulder gently because we have arrived in Dallas. I feel substantially better, but still not one hundred percent. I see Mom and Elliott standing at the front of the aisle, looking at me. I stand up, grab my backpack and exit the plane. We have about an hour layover in Dallas before we board

31

our final flight. I take a seat in the terminal a few seats away from Mom and Elliott since he is getting fussy and I don't have the energy to deal with it. I scan the airport, trying to people watch as entertainment to pass the time. A boy catches my eye. He looks about my age, maybe younger, and he is wearing a white button-up shirt. His hair is a reddish brown color and he might have freckles. I can't tell because he's far away, but he looks like the kind of guy who would have freckles. He is on a laptop looking deep in thought. I pan my view past his lap. His shoes look polished and expensive. Overall, he looks like he is from a different class of life than me.

"Would passenger Carter Hall please report to the ticket kiosk. Carter Hall, please report to the ticket kiosk." I hear the overhead click off. I've heard multiple announcements like this coming from other terminals, but this one is the first to be from our loudspeaker. I glance back over to where the guy was sitting and he is gone. My eye traces the room frantically to find him. His bright white shirt catches my eye at the ticket kiosk at the front of the room.

Carter Hall, I repeat over and over in my head as I keep him in sight. I see him step back and smack his fist against the kiosk desk. The situation seems hostile, but they're not close enough for me to hear what they are saying. He walks away from the woman at the desk, still saying something I can't quite hear, and walks around a corner of the airport. I lose sight of him and go back to people watching.

"This is the boarding announcement for flight 1322 with service into Bradley International Airport. Would all passengers please proceed to gate A15 for boarding," I hear over the intercom as everyone gets up to board. I stay in my chair for a while. I'm not waiting for anything, I'm just taking in my last few seconds on the ground. I stand up as I see the boy from earlier, Carter, come around the corner and line up for my flight. I wait for a few more people to get behind him and then head for the line. As we board the plane, I can't take my eyes off him. He has a presence unlike anything I have felt in L.A. before. He takes a seat and I'm secretly hoping nobody takes the one next to his. I approach him and snag the chair beside him. He looks at me for a few seconds. I see his eyes scan me up and down and then look back down at his phone. I grab my phone out of my bag and pretend to type on it for a few minutes, making sure to hide the black screen from his view. I look over at him, waiting for him to glance back over at me.

"Excuse me?" I say, trying to get his attention, "you wouldn't happen to have an iPhone charger would you?" I ask, trying to not sound as dead as I feel. He looks at me and then reaches into his bag and hands me a white cord.

I plug the cord into the USB port on the screen on the back of the chair in front of me. My phone finally turns back on and I have so many missed texts. A few are from Sid, updating me on how everyone is now safe at home and that they all basically just got a slap on the wrist. Lin texted me a selfie him and Corina took in front of the police station. I look closer and see Sid's bare white ass in the background, mooning the photo.

I laugh a little too loud and Carter looks at me. I smile and look back at my phone. I feel red from embarrassment. We are now taking off and I'm praying to

God my stomach handles this flight better than before. Luckily, it's pretty much running on empty now because I haven't eaten anything in over twenty-four hours. I look over at Carter and I notice him scrolling on his phone. I recognize a character on his screen. It's from a manga I've seen Elliott read before. This is my chance to spark up a conversation.

"Hey, sorry if I'm being nosey but I recognize that manga your reading. Is it Bleach?" I say, trying to sound confident in my answer even though I only vaguely know what the hell I'm talking about.

"Oh, um," he says as he fumbles with his phone in his hand, "yeah, it is. I actually just got back from a trip overseas. This stuff was so popular over there, I couldn't help but get immersed," he says.

"Yeah, my little brothers loves it. He is always going on and on about it. I don't really know much, but it looks super interesting," I say, trying not to sound too pathetic. I look him in the eyes for the first time. I was right, he does have freckles, and his face is beet red. I quickly realize that his demeanor has changed and his movements seem squirmy.

"Oh, I'm sorry. I didn't mean to disturb you," I say, trying to fix the situation.

"No, it's not that. Really, you're fine," he says, running a hand through his hair. "It's just...I'm not really one to be into something like this and hearing that over here in America it's something a little brother would be into has made me a little embarrassed."

"Oh, no! It's fine! My friend Sid actually reads this stuff as well. Nothing like this, though," I say, quickly realizing Sid doesn't read 'manga' but full on anime girl porn mags. It doesn't matter, though, because I can see that this has calmed his nerves a little. The plane ride continues without a hitch. We have a few casual conversations here and there, but nothing to get excited about.

"You know, this wasn't that bad," he says as I look over at him, surprised by the sudden conversation.

"What?" I say, startled.

"This flight. I've never flown coach before. My ticket got messed up and I had no choice but to take this seat, but I'm glad I did."

"Oh really? Why?" I asked, intrigued. This flight, from my perspective, doesn't seem all that substantial.

"'Cuz I got to sit next to a cute boy," he says, looking at me. I blush and look away, confused but somewhat excited by the interaction.

The plane lands and I say goodbye to Carter and Los Angeles. My new life begins right now.

My first steps outside of the airport bring fresh air and a slight chill, similar to being at the ocean past sunset, but more humid and not too muggy. My hair feels stiff.

"Connecticut," I say under my breath. Mom looks at me and smiles.

"Come on, boys, the lawyers said they would send a taxi to pick us up and take us to our house," Mom says as she grabs Elliott's hand, walking toward the taxi gate.

Our home. She says it like it's supposed to feel comforting, but it's not. Nothing feels right. Even the taxis look different than in L.A. They're a bit too clean for my taste. Call me weird, but I've gotten used to a certain way of life, and this isn't it.

The taxi smells like a new car, but not a genuine new car. The smell is coming from a pine tree air freshener hanging from the window. The radio is playing some sort of news program just quiet enough to annoy me, but not loud enough to actually make out what they are saying.

Elliott and I are in the backseat. Ma took the front seat as awkward as that is. The cab driver is sparking up a conversation with her with the small amount of English he knows. Elliott is slouched over, half asleep, tired from the long night's travel. Once again, I find myself jealous of how he is just gliding through this like it's nothing.

Looking out the window, all I see is trees, the occasional pedestrian and some shops, nothing really spectacular. It's nothing like Los Angeles, just as I suspected it would be.

"What's our E.T.A?" I ask, directing my question at the cab driver.

"We're about 50 minutes away, dear. Try to relax," Mom answers back.

"Perfect," I say as I lean my head on the window. I close my eyes and drift off to sleep.

"Bro, look at that!!" I'm awoken to Elliott sprawling out over my lap, looking out my window. I'm greeted by a large two-story house with dark wood paneling and loose shutters. It's certainly bigger than the apartment, but not better in my eyes. It's, overall, run down. We all exit the taxi and pile up the front steps to the front door. Mom knocks on the door before opening it. Elliott runs in.

"Hey! What's up, big guy!" A strange man says, putting out a hand as if to get a high five from Elliott.

"Mr. Christiansen, hello, I'm Cherie Anderson. We spoke on the phone. It's nice to meet you," Mom says, putting her hand out to shake the hand of the man who is still in high five position.

"Likewise Mrs. Anderson, you can call me Sequel. Mr. Christiansen is my father," he says. shaking her hand.

"Ms.," Mom corrects him.

"Ah yes, my apologies. And these must be Brighton and Elliott. Now, which one of you delayed this meeting by about," he looks at his watch, "sixteen hours?"

"That was my brother! He got stoned!" Elliott announces to the group.

"Elliott Philip Anderson!" Mom exclaims.

"Kids! Am I right?" The man brushes off Elliott and walks over to me.

"So, what's your deal, Sequel?" I ask the man abruptly, hoping to get this whole encounter over with so I can go back to sleep.

"Nice to meet you, son. To you I'm Mr. Christiansen. I'm the nice lawyer here to give your mom the keys to your new house," He says in a condescending tone.

"Here you are, Ms. Anderson. Your keys. I just have a few papers you need to sign." He and Mom go into the kitchen.

"Go look around, kids. Choose a bedroom, get comfy," she says as if to tell us to "get lost, grown-ups are talking."

As I walk up the stairs, they creak with each step. The smell is odd, kind of stale, but weirdly fresh in a way. There is not a broken exhaust pipe for miles The air going through my nose with each breath feels nice.

I count the bedrooms. I'm at four already. Why would we possibly need this many rooms? We could have just sold this place and moved to a nicer apartment. I reach the end of the hallway to a single door. I open it and see a single window and a rocking chair. So far, this is the only room I've seen with any furniture, so I take it as a sign and choose it as my room. I lay down on the floor. The roof goes up into a point and wooden beams span across the ceiling. I close my eyes.

I'm suddenly woken up by a gust of air banging a

shutter on the house. It's dark outside. I can hear Mom and Elliott downstairs and I smell something cooking. I get up and walk to my door. My suitcases are sitting in front of me. I scoot them aside and walk down the hallway. A door is open and inside there is a mattress and a stack of comics. Elliott's room. I walk down the stairs. Mom is in the kitchen at the stove and Elliott is on the floor rustling with a rather large box.

"Look! Mom bought us each a mattress!" He points over to a rolled up mattress in the corner of the room.

"Brighton, help Elliott take that up to your room after dinner, come and sit, we're having spaghetti," Mom says, gesturing with a wooden spoon to the breakfast nook that now has a few bar stools under it.

"What time is it?" I ask, rubbing my eyes.

"About 9:30. We just got back from the store. We didn't want to wake you," Mom says, dishing pasta out onto paper plates.

"You bought all this stuff?" I ask, looking around at the pots pans mom's using to cook. And the bar stools, of course.

"We needed the stuff to live, son. We couldn't bring anything from home, so we gotta start somewhere!" She says in an uncomfortably happy tone. handing me my food.

I scarf it down. I didn't realize how starving I was and, from the looks of it, neither did Elliott or Mom because we all basically lick our plates clean. Elliott and I grab the mattress Mom bought and carry it up to my room. I unwrap the plastic from around it as it slowly unfolds, flattening out onto the floor.

"Let's test it out!" Elliott screams as he jumps onto the mattress, jumping up and down.

"Be my guest," I say as I sit down in the chair in the corner.

"Mom says we get to go to a new school. The same school as you, like before, and we can see snow in the winter, and go camping, and did you know there is an ocean here? I didn't. It's just like home!" Elliott says, out of breath from jumping on the bed.

"Jesus, Elliott, shut up!" I say, yelling. Elliott stops jumping and looks at me. I can see his eyes tear up.

"No!" he screams, running towards the door.

"Elliott, wait, no, I'm sorr-" I'm cut off by the slam of my bedroom door. I get up and walk down the hallway to his room. I knock.

"Elliott? Come on, I'm sorry I yelled at you." I knock again. No answer. I open the door and the room is empty. I continue to walk down the hallway,

"Elliott?" I say, searching. I'm greeted by a set of pull-downstairs that was definitely not there earlier. I gently walk up the stairs. This house is old and who knows how sturdy it is.

"Elliott? Come on, man, you up there?" I say as my voice shakes. I've never been too good at dealing with spooky situations, and a dark, probably spider-filled attic is definitely on my list of spooky places. I make my way up the stairs to see Elliott sitting in the middle of the floor lit only by a flashlight in his hand. I see he is hunched over one of his Japanese comics.

"Hey, buddy, whatcha doing up here?" I say gingerly. Elliott is reminding me of a creepy character in a horror movie Sid made me watch when we were little.

"Mom and I came up here earlier to see if there was any furniture. When we saw it was pretty much finished, Mom said I could hang out up here if I want."

"That's cool, man. Hey, sorry for earlier. I'm just tired."

"It's okay," Elliott says with a smile, looking up at me.

"So, what you looking a-" I say, stepping forward. I'm interrupted by the abnormal jostle of a floorboard under my foot. I step back onto the unsteady board again.

"Are you sure it's safe up here?" I ask. He walks over to me on his knees, shining his flashlight on the spot my foot rests.

"Move your nasty foot," he says, flashing his light on and off on my foot. "Its fine. It's just old." Elliott goes back to his comic.

"This house really is a piece of crap. The floors aren't even properly attached," I say as I try to press my fingers around the edges of the wood. I pull the piece of flooring up and remove it, tossing it to the side.

"We'll have to fix this up, get some bean bag chairs." I sit down on the floor next to Elliott, picturing The Stoner Shack. I pat his head as he reads, looking off into nothing.

We head down to our separate rooms. Hours pass as I lay awake in bed. I did only wake up from a nap that was God knows how long few hours ago. My phone rings. It's a FaceTime call.

"Hey, bud!" Lin says enthusiastically.

"Lin, man, its 2 A.M. What's up?" I say happily, curious as to why he was calling.

"Oh, man, I totally forgot about the time

difference. Did I wake you?"

"Nah, I can't sleep. I must still be on West Coast time."

"Is that Bright?" I hear in the background as I see Sid's head pop onto the screen.

"How's my southern boy?" he says in a baby voice, puckering his lips.

"If you guys only knew the day I've had."

"I bet! I can only imagine!" Lin says in his usual tone. It comforts me.

"What are you guys up to?" I ask. It's rare for Lin and Sid to hang out, just the two of them.

"Now that I think about it...you're in Sid's bedroom, aren't you?" I ask, looking beyond Lin and Sid's faces to Sid's iconic Nirvana poster dart board.

"We also had a weird day," Sid says looking at Lin.

They go on to tell me all about how some jerk at lunch told Corina her mom's restaurant was gross and how she started a food fight, but when they got caught, Lin took responsibility for it and got suspended for the week. His foster parents were so mad that he didn't want to stay there tonight, which is why he is at Sid's. The sound of their voices as they argue about who threw what and who landed the glob of cream corn on the drama teacher's lap gets quieter and quieter and I, somehow, end up falling asleep.

4

It's been about a week since the move. People have been coming and going out of the house; some are movers bringing in furniture, some are lawyers for odd paperwork about the will and our inheritance. I've been told roughly how much it is and it makes me feel some relief. I just try to stay in my room until all the people leave.

It's Monday morning and Elliott and I are awake bright and early because Mom told us last night today today we would be starting at our new school. As much as most kids hate school, I'm surprisingly excited. Even though I'm not very keen on studying, I find myself always craving structure and uniformity. School is just that. Eight periods, each a set amount of time. Nothing changes from day to day, except for a few minor things that usually don't affect me.

"Come on, boys! I've got a meeting with a man about a dining table in an hour. It won't hurt you to be a little early on your first day," Ma yells from the kitchen.

"Coming!" I hear Elliott say as I hear fast footsteps

down the stairs.

"Brighton! Come on!" I hear as I make my way to the edge of the steps.

"Coming Ma, give me a minute."

"We'll meet you in the car, then!" Mom says, rushing Elliott out the door. My phone buzzes. It's a text from Sid.

Good luck today, Brighton. Show them everyone from L.A. really is a star.

I laugh and send a simple *:)* back and head out the door. Elliott and Mom wave me to hurry as I rush over to the car. The school is about a 15-minute drive away.

As we're driving, I think about how if we were to drive this far in L.A., it would take us over an hour. But the roads here are quiet. Before I know it, I'm pulling up to the school. It's huge. No other way to put it. That's something I'm learning about Connecticut. Since the population isn't as dense, they make everything so big. Houses, schools, even the supermarket is giant. Of course, this school is no exception. Out front are 2 large flag poles, one hoisting the American flag and the other the state flag. Honestly, it's the first time I've seen it. Dark blue with some saying on it in Latin. I'm familiar enough to recognize the language but the L.A. public school system never really enforced language class as a requirement every year. Sid took Latin in junior year, so I did too, just to be with him. It was boring, but I guess I retained some knowledge.

The school building is a mixture of brick and large white pillars. At the entrance, there are multiple doors. I see kids piling in and the cars they just exited are pulling away. They are all substantially nicer than the junker Mom is borrowing from some relative I have yet to meet.

"Okay, Brighton, this is you. Head to the office to get your schedule. Elliott, I'll drop you off around back at the 8th grade drop off."

Elliots jerks his seatbelt. I know he hates that he is in 8th grade. I mean, he is 14. He should be a freshman but, in 5th grade, the school suggested to hold him back a year because his reading wasn't up to par. Naturally, Mom agreed and it's been a sore subject ever since. I hop out of the car, sticking my hand through the side of the seat to tousle Elliott's hair. He looks back and smiles as I gently shut the car door. They drive off and I'm left here alone. It sinks in. This is my new schedule. My new normal.

Making my way to the front desk, it's already so different than my old school. It feels more like a hotel lobby than a school office.

"Hi, I'm the new kid," I say to the receptionist.

"Last name?" she says with no emotion.

"Anderson."

"Anderson, Anderson, ah yes, you must be Brighton. Here is your schedule. Your first class is in Academic Hall C, Sector 2 with Mr. Briggs." I look at her as I take my schedule in total confusion.

"If you don't think you can manage to find your way yourself, there is a young man currently speaking to the headmaster. You can have a seat outside his office and wait if you would like."

"Thanks," I say, stuffing the schedule in my backpack and taking a seat. My jeans look dirty and dingy compared to everything in this school. It's all so new and shiny. I can hear voices coming from the room. The door next to me opens and someone begins to walk out.

45

"Now, son, I'm glad to hear your travels were inspiring. As for attendance, try to keep that in mind next time." His voice gets louder as the two end up standing in front of me.

"Oh cute boy, we meet again." My head springs up to the words being spout in my direction in an oddly familiar voice. The older gentleman next to him clears his throat. I quickly stand up.

"You must be the principal. Nice you meet you." I put my hand out. "Brighton Anderson, senior." I shake his hand.

"You can call me Headmaster Hall," he says as he turns to the boy standing next to him.

"Off to class you go," he says, walking back towards his office. I look at the boy in front of me. Where have I seen him before? I'm unable to put my tongue on it.

"Carter, this is Mr.Anderson," The receptionist says, pointing at me. "Will you please show him to your homeroom. He will be in your class starting today."

"Sure thing, Ms. M. Looking great today!" he says in a confident manner as he grabs the sleeve of my shirt with his finger. "This way." I'm guided toward the door.

"Carter, Carter, Carter" I say under my breath. "AH-Airplane boy!" I say out loud, quickly regaining composure.

"Ouch, should I be offended it took you this long to remember me?" he laughs.

"Sorry. It's been a weird week," I say, walking next to him instead of behind.

"I would remember that bleach job anywhere," he says, flicking my hair with his finger. I flinch, readjusting my hair.

"Well, here we are, Mr. Briggs' first period English." He says as we walk up to a door. Carter opens the door and everyone looks at us.

"Mr. Hall, I'm glad you have decided to grace us with your presence? Where was it this time? Paris? Scandinavia?

"Tokyo, actually," he says, taking a seat.

"And you must be, let me see here..." Mr. Briggs says, slipping his fingers through a stack of papers on his desk. "Ah, Anderson, Brighton. Mr. Anderson, please take a seat next to Naomi."

A girl with ginger hair raises her hand. I make my way over and sit in an empty desk next to hers.

"Hi, I'm Naomi! Nice to meet you!" she says in a half-whisper as class picks up where it left off.

"It's not often that we have a transfer only a few months into the year. What's your story?"

"I'm from Los Angeles. I moved here for the family, I guess." I answered her, not really knowing what to say. I mean "I was basically forced here to live in a dead woman's house who I don't know and I basically hate it here" doesn't really roll off the tongue.

"I like you. Something about you feels...fresh!" she says, looking me up and down. I nod to acknowledge her but try to focus on the teachings. She doesn't talk to me for the rest of class, thankfully. I've never really been good at talking to girls. Concha and Corina are the only exceptions.

Second period. Free period. As a senior and overall an adequate student, I don't have a full workload here just like at my old school. Normally, I would be overjoyed to have forty-five minutes to do absolutely nothing, but honestly, I would rather be sitting in class than be left to fend for myself in this school. Wandering around, I make my way to the middle school branch. I have no clue why. It's not like I know what class Elliott is even in, but I'm craving a familiar face. It's early, only 9 A.M, so everyone back in L.A. is either asleep or just waking up for school, so texting them to pass the time is out of the question. Time differences suck.

"Brighton Anderson, please report to reception. Brighton Anderson." I hear my name over the loudspeaker. It echoes through the school. *What could I have possibly done now?* I think as I turn around and start walking to the office. I make my way there after taking a few wrong turns along the way to find my mother standing in front of the receptionist.

"What going on, Ma?" I say, resting my head on my hand and leaning on the front desk.

"I forgot to give you your lunch money!" she says, pulling me in for a hug.

"Lunch money?" I say, pulling away,

"I'm sorry. I shouldn't have interrupted your learni-"

I cut her off. "Since when can we pay for school lunch?"

"We don't need help anymore, Brighton. Your great aunt left us with enough to put you and Elliott through college, and some to live on."

"More than you thought? Enough to buy our own car?" I ask doubtfully. Mom nods her head.

"So I get lunch money now?" I ask, still doubtful. Mom her head again.

"Mom?" I ask, seeing her eyes well up.

"We are gonna be okay, Brighton." Mom's emotions suddenly enter me. I'm reminded of all the struggles we faced back home when it came to money: the gas being shut off randomly and having to heat water up in the microwave for our showers. It's all better now?

My ears go silent. Mom's talking to me and I can't hear anything. Am I dreaming? Did I not wake up for school this morning and this is all just a false reality? The bell rings.

"Ma, I have to go to my next class." Mom looks at me, confused

"Why don't you come with me to get the new dining table?" she says, standing up and grabbing my shoulders. I must have looked shaky.

"No, its fine. I have class. You go," I say, removing her hand from my shoulders. I walk away and feel the cold air from outside hit the back of my neck as Mom leaves the front office.

I pull my schedule out from my bag; gym. Okay, I have to find the gym. I stumble around the school in a state of joy, feeling a bit lightheaded. I can go to college and not have to worry about it? No more food stamps or lunch tickets? Thoughts racing, I brace myself on a pole and look into the distance. There is a large building with double doors that looks gym-like enough. I'm still not sure, considering everything here looks different. I stumble in the doors and see a sign for the locker rooms. I walk through and see unfamiliar faces. Most of them look my age, so I must be in the right place. Not knowing if I have a locker or even gym clothes, I walk over to the sinks. Looking at myself in the mirror, I look pale and a little sweaty. I didn't realize how much this move would affect my life and my future. I'm dizzy with excitement.

"We meet again." A voice comes up next to me. "Should I be worried? Two out of three classes we have together. Must be a coincidence." I look up into the mirror and see Carter's face reflected back at me. I can only think about how his freckles really compliment his red hair. I open my mouth to speak when, suddenly, a wave of nausea is brought over me. I turn around and run into the stall, ary heaving over the surprisingly clean locker room toilet.

"Whoa, you okay, man?" Carter says as he walks up behind me. I hear a commotion of people enter the bathroom area.

"Come on, back up, give him some space!" I hear Carter order as it gets quieter and quieter. I turn around and stand up. Carter hands me a paper towel as I wipe my face. I am embarrassed that I worked myself up enough to be physically sick, although it was probably a mix of first day nerves and excitement.

"You need me to ring the school nurse?" a boy says from around the corner. Carter looks at me. and I gently shake my head no. Carter responds,

"But can you please tell the coach I'll be a little late? Gotta find a new shirt for the new kid." I look down and see a streak of orange puke down the front of my shirt. Grossed out, I take it off and throw it in the sink.

"You make quite an impression," Carter says, walking over the lockers. He opens his and hands me a white button up shirt, similar to the one he was wearing when I first saw him in the airport.

"Sorry," I say, grabbing it and putting it on.

"No problem. You looked like you had just seen a ghost," he says, adjusting his gym shorts. I try to look away, but I find myself looking back.

"My mouth tastes like shit, man. Is there a vending machine around here anywhere?" I ask. His intrigued look changes to a look of thought.

"Hmmm, no vending machines, but there is a juice bar in the junior cafe. Shall I take you there?"

"Junior cafe? What is this school?" I say as we both start walking to the door.

"I was surprised to see you here this morning," he says, not looking at me.

"Surprised?"

"Well, how do I put this lightly? Most kids at this school don't fly coach," he says gingerly.

"Rich kid school. Got it," I say, looking at him and smiling.

"It doesn't bother you?"

I look forward and see a cafe sign. I walk a little bit ahead of him and turn around

"I'm from L.A. I'm used to it," I say as I turn back around, walking into the cafe. I mean, there is no point in telling anyone my past. He comes around the corner and leans in the doorway as I look at the juice bars selection.

"Oh?" he says, looking at me. I notice his eyes are kind of a greenish gray color.

"Well then, cute L.A. boy, I think you'll fit right in here," he says as I pour myself a glass of some odd looking green juice and take a sip. "Not good?" he says, smiling as the look on my face goes sour.

"Would have rather tasted puke," I say we both giggle. I throw away the juice and we head out of the cafe.

"Whaddya say we blow off gym all together?" He says, coming closer to me. His shoulder is only inches from mine. Our hands are even closer.

"I don't know. Where would we go?" I say, trying not to sound lame

"I know a few places." He slips his fingers between mine. Not even a second passes before I rip my hand away. We both step back.

"Sorry. I just thought mayb-"

"No, it's fine. I'm sorry." I cut him off and run down the hallway.

"Idiot. Idiot. Idiot. Why did I do that?" I think to myself, still running aimlessly. He probably thinks I'm this big jerk now. I was just caught off guard. I stop and realize my surrounding. I'm in the same middle school building as before. I see a few bathrooms up ahead and duck into one to collect my thoughts.

Looking in the mirror, my cheeks are red, possibly from running or maybe from Carter's fingers. They were soft, not rough like mine. I hear someone sniffling in a stall behind me.

"Hello? Anybody in here?" I say, thinking I had been alone until now.

Hello?" I hear a voice that I couldn't mistake.

"Elliott?" I say, walking up to the stall. A toilet flushes and the lock unhinges. A puffy-eyed and red-nosed Elliott stands in front of me.

"Rough day?" I say, rubbing his head.

"There was a schedule mess up. The office thought I was supposed to be held back this year and put me in all 7th grade classes. When they realized the mistake, an office lady walked me to my actual class where she

52

explained to the teacher loudly how I was held back and this was my class and not to give me a tardy."

"So did you get a tardy?" I ask, trying to make him smile. He doesn't.

"This school sucks," he says, rubbing his eyes.

"I think I have something that will cheer you up," I say, pulling out my phone.

I dial and bring the phone up to my ear as Elliott watches, confused.

"Ma, it's Brighton. Elliott's having a rough day and I puked in gym class can you come to get us?" He watches as I listen to Mom. I hang up.

"Let's go," I say, grabbing his arm

"Ew, gross, you puked? And where did you get that shirt?" He asks. I almost forgot I was wearing Carter's shirt.

"Don't worry about it," I say, laughing to hide my smile AS i think about Carter wearing this shirt; how it smells like him. We go to meet Mom.

"Ma!" Elliott exclaims as we get in her car.

"Rough day?" she asks, pulling out of the school roundabout.

"Not as bad as Bright. He threw up on himself."

"I was wondering why your shirt was changed," Mom says, laughing

"Ok, I didn't throw up on myself. It kinda just splattered," I say, embarrassed.

"Ew!" Elliott screams. We arrive home and there is a large white pull away truck in our driveway.

"Oh, great, we're moving again," I say in a smart-ass tone.

"Very funny, Brighton. Actually, that is our dining

table," She says giddily, like a child showing off their birthday gifts.

The door opens wide to the living room, where there is a sectional and a television nicer than ones we have had in the past.

"Home sweet home," Elliott jokes as he turns on the TV. I walk past him and go up the stairs. I stop at the top of the stairwell.

"Ma, are you gonna get us furniture as well?" I ask, looking down the hall into my open bedroom door.

Mom shouts from the kitchen, "I thought you would want to pick it out yourself!" I hear her coming closer.

"Here is what I bought you!" She hands me a wrapped box. "Elliott, come here. I have a present for you!" She hands Elliott a smaller wrapped box. I watch as Elliott rips his open.

"An iPhone!" he shouts, removing the shrink wrap from the box. Mom looks at me as a signal to open mine. I tear the wrapping paper from the center and see that it's a silver laptop with the big glowing apple.

"Surprise! I know you always wanted one and I figured it would help you with school!" I set the present down at my feet and reach over to Mom.

"This is really happening, isn't it?" I say, hugging her.

"How do I turn this thing on?" Elliott says as he inspects the phone in confusion. We all laugh as I grab the phone and set it up for him.

"I'm going to FaceTime Sid," I say, picking up my laptop from the floor.

"That will really surprise him!" Mom says as she

walks to the kitchen.

I go upstairs and open my laptop, plugging it into the wall. It glows as it powers on. It feels solid, like it's made to last a long time. I open up FaceTime and call Sid. No answer. I realize it's only noon here. Sid's not even out of 4th period yet. With nothing to do, I log onto my Facebook and look up my school.

I type *Saint Anne Cathedral High* into the search bar and pause, thinking back to school. I add *Carter Hall* to the end of my search. I click the first page that pops up and it's his. I recognize him right off the bat because of the freckles and eyes, but Tokyo tower in the background of his profile picture helped as well. I scroll through his pictures, stopping on ones that show his face more clearly. I go into his tagged pictures and recognize someone. It's the girl I was sat with in homeroom. I keep scrolling and notice that she's in a lot of his pictures. I click through to her profile and see more picture of them together. *Are they dating?* I think, trying to deny everything I've learned about Carter so far . Then it hits me: she has his eyes and freckles. I check her last name.

"Hall," I say out loud. How lucky am I? The only two people who talked to me all day at school and they aren't only siblings, they're twins!

My intense social stalking is interrupted by a friend request notification popping up on my screen. I slowly click on it, wondering if it could be Carter. I open the notification and read:

Elliott Anderson wants to be friends

"Elliott!" I yell, getting up and going to his room. I plop down onto his bed. his eyes don't budge from his phone.

"Welcome to the twenty-first century, dear brother., I say in an old time accent.

"Shut up!" he says jokingly.

"Just be careful, alright. Don't go talking to any strange men on here, even if they do say they have candy!" I say, gesturing to the phone.

"I'm not that much younger than you, you know. Stop treating me like a baby," he says, finally looking away from his phone.

"Sorry bud, I just have so much fun messing with you." I jostle his hair.

"Yeah, you and everyone else at school," he says with a serious look.

"Everything okay?" I ask, trying to fill the role of the worried older brother.

"I just wish I wasn't in 8th grade. I read just fine. Mom still thinks I don't understand anything."

"Moms always think their kids are still babies. Hell, Mom still thinks I'm a baby," I say, trying to make him feel better.

"Lunch is ready!" Mom shouts from the kitchen.

"You sure you're okay?" I ask, getting up from the bed.

"Yeah, fine," Elliott says as he shoves his phone in his pocket and walks to the door.

"Remind me to get you a case for that. And a screen protector," I say cringing at a brand new iPhone being shoved into his rough wrangler jeans. We laugh and head downstairs.

A house, A new city, money, TWINS. What is my life? I think as I lay down in my bed. My stomach is feeling full from lunch. Everything still feels like a dream. It's later now and Sid must be off from school. I open my laptop and give him a call again. He answers.

"Hey, my man!" Sid answers enthusiastically

"Notice anything?" I ask, miming my hands around the video window

"Oh sick! Nice HD. I can see every pore on your ugly face now!" he laughs.

We slip into old habits and talk about everything and anything. I tell him about how we're better off money wise, trying not to sound too excited. He goes into a Sid-like rant about how I better not let the money go to my head and that just because I can afford college now doesn't mean I should give up on trying for scholarships. It's another one of those times Sid surprises me with what's hidden up there in his head. I tease an idea in my head.

"Sid, I think I made a friend," I say, trying to stay calm.

"Yeah, who?" he says in a jokingly defensive way.

"A boy," I say, trying not to sound too eager to share.

"Name?"

"Carter."

"Age?"

"Same as us." I pause for a second.

"That's great, man. What's he like?" Sid says, breaking the silence. I'm quiet again. How do I word this without sounding like a total weirdo?

"He has freckles and green eyes," I say, looking away from the webcam.

"Cool man," Sid says, obviously half-paying attention at this point as his video has paused and he is playing on his phone.

"And he, um-" I pause abruptly.

"You still there my man?" Sid says, thinking I was cut off.

"All good, um, yeah he has a twin sister!" I say, changing my tone.

"Awwwww hell yeah! That's hot!" Sid says.

"Sid! Food's ready!" I hear Sid's grandma yell from the speaker.

"Gotta go, man. Good luck with the twins! Tell the girl one about how hot your friend Sid is back in Los Angeles!" he jokes and hangs up.

"And he, um, thinks I'm cute," I say under my breath. Why was it so easy to say when I'm not talking to Sid? I get angry and close the laptop, rolling over onto my back. I raise my hand up above my head and see my sleeve half rolled up. I bring it close to my face and catch a faint whiff of cologne; Carter's cologne. I take a deep breath in and inhale the smell. What the hell am I doing?

5

My brother Elliott. He was always just a little bit off. Not that it's a bad thing, but I've never quite been able to relate. Sure, I'm not normal either, but Elliott has been given the short end of the stick in life decisions.

As the oldest of two siblings, I was a test run. Because they weren't sure what they were doing, my parents tried their hardest to give me a good childhood. They researched the best preschool, organic baby food, the whole nine yards. By the time Elliott was born, they had grown tired of each other, Dad more than Mom.

The cheating started after Elliott was born, but before that, while Mom was pregnant with him, the air in the house became heavy with anger. Everyone was angry. But a baby would fix that, right? I think that's what everyone hoped.

He weighed 8 pounds and 2 ounces. He was a healthy child, which was all anyone could hope for. I was only 4 when he was born, so I was overjoyed: one, because I didn't get an "icky" sister and two, because I was finally a big brother. Sometimes I feel like, for the first few years, I was more of a dad then a big brother. Hell, if my name wasn't so damn long, Elliott's first word probably would have been Brighton.

Skip forward to when I was 10 and Elliott was 6, just starting elementary school. He was bright, but this was also the peak of dad's cheating. Elliott was smart, but "distracted", as his teachers would say at every parent teacher conference I was dragged to. Because I was 10 and finally starting to feel like a grown up, or at least starting to feel *things* that were grown up, and going through some deep shit about who was giving me those feelings, I stopped trying to be friends with my brother and shut him out. It didn't dawn on me until later in life that I was such a bad brother to him. But it could have been worse. I could have treated him like our father. It wasn't like my dad was violent, more like forgetful.

I was his boy, his first born. He tried to make sure the world didn't affect me. This left Elliott on the outside. I remember one morning before school, when I was 12 and Elliott was 8, he asked Dad if he could join the school choir. He was going through a big "I wanna be a rockstar" phase that most L.A. born kids went through. Dad threw a fit about how education shouldn't be wasted on the arts. I left for school and went on with my day, assuming Elliott did as well. I got home and Mom and Dad were sitting around the TV eating dinner and Elliott was nowhere to be found. I asked my mom where he was and she said to ask my father. When I did, he had no idea where Elliott was. I, a twelve year old, discovered that my 8 year old brother had gone missing. We began to search the house frantically. Mom wanted to call the cops but, as per usual, Dad played Elliott's emotions down. He assumed it was all a joke and that he was just hiding in the house.

I rode my bike around the neighborhood and, after a few minutes of trying to find Elliott, I found him sitting in the neighbor's rose bushes, carrying only a Rugrats blanket wrapped around a stick with a few Legos and a spare pair of underwear. His attempt to run away was cute, but looking back, it really put a knife between our parents.

Mom no longer trusted Dad with us kids. She took on all the carpooling and after school duties, like homework and bath time, completely ignoring her husband who had, by this point, moved on to younger and, in his word, sexier things. Soon after this, our parents split and we continued living on without our dad. Elliott turned 10 and was going into 5th grade and I was just a little thing starting high school, kissing my best friend on the lips. You know, the usual.

Elliott saw me growing and living life and I could tell he was jealous. Mom was working two jobs, stressed to the max trying to support us both in the best way possible while trying not to let things change with Dad gone. That's when Elliott started having trouble in school.

He didn't have any major issues. If anything, I would say he was still smarter than I was at his age. But Mom was in a panic over the whole thing. There were endless meeting with teachers trying to get his grades up so, when his reading teacher suggested he be held back a year to "catch up" to his "peers", Mom, somehow, under the stress, agreed. As I moved onto sophomore year, Elliott repeated the 5th grade and he was horrified.

I remember him screaming every morning about not wanting to go to school and Mom forcing him to go anyway. It's as if he stopped maturing right then and

61

there. Being surrounded by the kids who were a year under him his whole school career tore him apart, and the kids tore him apart as well. The bullying never stopped. I was so engrossed in my own teenage coming of age antics that I hardly noticed Elliott's trouble until I came home one day and found Elliott in the bathroom. He was crying and he had the door locked. Mom was at work and I was supposed to be taking care of him. He had filled the bathtub up with water and had let it overflow into the hallway. I ended up calling Sid, who came over and helped me bash the bathroom door down.

Elliott was on the floor of the bathroom, sobbing like all the life had been sucked out of him. He was wet and crying and he would only tell us that he didn't want to go to school over and over again. We called Mom at work and she rushed home. I was blamed for the whole thing, so I ended up going to Sid's house that night. I've never talked about that night with Mom or Elliott.

The bathroom door of the apartment stayed duck taped up from the holes we put in it trying to kick it down. They were a daily reminder of the day I saw my brother's inner demons, not only for me, but for Elliott as well. When the tape would start to fall off or get all goopy and gross around the edges, Elliott would always replace it, as if it was his job because he caused it.

He has always been a little bit off since then, a little more immature and closed off, like he's just one step behind everyone else.

My senior year. If you would have told me 4 years ago that I would be sitting here with no friends, eating lunch in the library. Well, I probably would have believed you, but only if you also told me Sid would be right beside me. The most unbelievable part would be that all this is happening in Connecticut and that I'm eating a lunch, that wasn't bought with meal tickets.

The school lunch here is weird. Mashed potatoes, sure, but they are "seasoned with white pepper and chives" as the announcement lady said this morning. The main dish is beef brisket with pearl onions. I don't know what a pearl onion is, but it seems like something we wouldn't have been able to afford before. As I eat, I pull out my laptop and browse online for furniture for my bedroom. Elliott already has all his furniture and Mom is already onto decorating her room, but I just can't wrap my head around spending all this money at once.

"What's up, boy toy?" I hear from behind. It's Naomi. She has a banana in her hand. Her hair is up in a ponytail and her lipstick is brighter than ever.

"Whatcha looking at?" she says, bending over and looking at my laptop screen.

"I'm looking for furniture for my bedroom, but no luck," I say, shutting it. Naomi's hand comes out of nowhere and slips between my screen and keyboard.

"Let me see that." She grabs the computer.

"Okay. Ooh this is cute. Oh yes," she says, adding things to my cart. "There," she says, handing me my computer. I look at my screen in awe. The things she picked are actually kind of my style. "Problem?" Naomi looks at me, confused.

"No. I mean, I love it. But is it all this really worth it?"

"Well, what do you already have? Maybe we can forgo something."

"Well, I have a mattress.....and a chair." I say, thinking if Ma has bought me anything else.

"That's it?" Naomi says with a blank stare.

"That's it," I say, shaking my head.

"That's it!" she says excitedly. "I'm coming over! I've gotta see what I'm working with." And suddenly I have my own personal home designer.

"Meet me in the student parking lot at 2:30 sharp!"

"Roger that."

Putting my laptop away, I get up and go to my next class. The rest of the day goes by as usual. Perfectly scheduled, just how I like it.

The school parking lot is paved. It's probably normal for most people to think of a parking lots as paved, but at my old school, it was dirt. Cars would get dusty, not like anybody cared because their cars were all junkers. It makes sense why they would care here. Any car in this parking lot is probably worth more than every car at my old school put together.

"Ready to go?" Naomi says, sitting in her car. As much as I imagined her sitting in a convertible, I never really thought she would have one. But there she is, right in front of me with the top down, shiny white body and grey leather interior. I hop in the passenger side.

"So, first up: the mall!" Naomi says, pulling away from the school.

"Okay, if you think we can really fit any furniture in here..." I say, looking around. It's a rather small car.

"Oh I forgot to tell you, you're my date for the senior's party tonight, and you need an outfit." She says smiling, obviously trying to compensate for her hint that my fashion isn't up to par.

"Date?"

"Well, I said I like you. You're fresh and clean!" She says as if that clarifies anything.

"I-"

"Don't worry! No commitment. silly. You act as if you've never gone out with someone before." She cuts me off. Technically, I've never been on a real date or even asked anyone on a date, but I think it's best to keep that to myself if I want to have any friends left at this school.

We arrive at the mall. It's obscenely large, but the shops are far and few between. Most of the shops are empty and have the metal gates closed.

"What's with this place?" I ask, looking around.

"It used to be a lot more busy, especially during the summer when all the tourist come, but our town is just too small all year to keep any businesses open," Naomi explains. I haven't really learned a lot about this town and the other people who live in it.

"Tell me about Guilford. What's it like?" I ask,

suddenly intrigued.

"Well, you arrived during the nicest weather. Autumn is great because it's not too cold and the humidity is bearable. Winter is hell. It snows a lot. Spring is my personal favorite because of all the flowers. And summer is intense. It's a tourist trap. All the beaches and shops are packed basically all the time."

"What about the people? Everyone can't be like they are at school." I'm intrigued.

"You mean swimming in cash?" she asks, laughing.

"Everyone who lives here has a deep history with the town. I bet even you do if you dig deep enough," she says, pulling me into a store.

She's right. I feel so disconnected from this place, but in reality, Mom has a family here. She is a part of this town, therefore I am as well. From the looks of the house, our family must have had a significant history with this town too.

"Go try these on," Naomi says as I'm handed a mountain of clothes.

"Yes, ma'am," I say jokingly, heading to the dressing room.

The clothes she picked remind me of her brother, form fitting but classy. They aren't too formal, but still left an impression of importance. I try on everything, but I'm drawn to a white button up with one pocket. It's just like the one Carter let me borrow.

"These. I like these," I say, leaving the dressing room and handing my outfit to Naomi. She looks at the items, holding them up to the light as if she wasn't the one to pick them out in the first place.

"Not bad, Brighton. You might fit in here after all," she says, walking to the register. The cashier tells me my total, blank faced. The amount is more than the food stamps the government gave me, Mom and Elliott to live off of for a month back home. I hesitate to pull out my credit card.

"Will that be cash or credit?" the cashier asks, obviously impatient.

"Credit," I say, swiping the card Mom had given me for "emergencies."

I walk out of the store feeling something I've never felt before. It's kind of like a feeling of doubt mixed with a floaty feeling in my stomach, like I've gotten away with something. I feel like I'm walking out of the store with things I didn't pay for.

"Okay, back to yours now!" Naomi says, grabbing my hand. Learning from the mistake I made with her brother, I don't freak out and run away like a total idiot. Playing it cool, I take the lead and walk her out to the parking lot.

"Well, here we are! My humble abode!" I say sarcastically as we pull up to my house. Naomi puts the car in park.

"Nice car! Is that your father's?" Naomi asks, pointing to my driveway.

"I don't know," I say, confused. There is a new, shiny black car in our driveway.

"You don't know whose car that is?" she asks, opening her door. "Let's find out," she says. I walk up behind her and follow her into the house.

"Ma? I'm home. You here?" I shout into the house. I hear footsteps coming from above and then down the stairs.

"Did you see it?" Mom says, walking down the stairs. She looks up and realizes I'm not alone.

"Oh, hello there. I'm Cherie, Brighton's mother," she says, immediately putting on a smile. My mother is always like this when I would bring girls over. She was like this when she first met Cornia, until she realized we were obviously not involved romantically and dropped the act.

"Nice to meet you Ms. Anderson! I'm Naomi! Me and Brighton are in a study group together!" she says, smiling. I look at her, confused.

"Oh how nice!" Mom says, smiling at both of us. "Well, if you're studying, how about I make you something to eat," Mom says as she walks to the kitchen.

"That's alright!" Naomi says, catching on to what she's up to.

"Yeah Mom, we're not staying. We're going to study at one of the other kids' houses tonight." Naomi looks at me and smiles.

"Alright then. You kids have fun!" Mom says in a lonely tone.

"Mind if I show Naomi around the house?" I ask.

"Sure sweetheart, go ahead. I was just tidying up upstairs, so perfect timing."

I grab Naomi's hand and guide her up the stairs, partly because I'm trying to get used to it, just in case Carter tries again, and partly because I knew my mom would get a kick out of seeing me do so. We enter my room and close the door.

"Once again, you surprise me. Nice job keeping up," Naomi says, plopping down onto my mattress on the floor. "Wow! You weren't kidding when you said you needed furniture." She looks around.

"Yeah, I really wasn't." I plop down next to her.

"Restroom?" Naomi says, standing up, taking her backpack off and unzipping it.

"Down the hall and to the left," I say, not getting up.

"Awesome! I'm gonna go get changed, fix my eyeliner, you know, the basics. You get ready," she says, leaving the room.

I take my shirt off and throw it on the floor and my pants quickly follow. My new shirt feels nice and crisp as it lands on my chest. I button it up and it feels snug. The pants, as well, feel like a luxury, which is good because they cost an arm and a leg. Once dressed, I realize I don't have a mirror in my room. I grab my laptop and search for a mirror. One quick Google search later and I find a full body mirror. It's my style; not too fancy but better then what I had back in L.A.

"Add to cart," I say out loud to myself.

"Those are the words I like to hear!" Naomi says, entering my room

"What did we buy?" she says, looking at my laptop.

"A mirror. I needed one" I say, smiling as I press confirm order.

"Well, for now, I'll be your mirror. You look hot! Stand up!" I stand up and do a little spin. Naomi smirks at me.

"Shall we go?" she says, linking our arms together. Elbows locked, we walk downstairs.

"Well don't you two look fancy for your study

group," Mom says with air quotations, clearly reading into this more than she should. I continue with the lie from earlier.

"Yeah, our friend's parents invited us to all stay for dinner. They are very fancy people," I say, nodding at Mom. She nods back as Naomi and I walk outside. Mom follows us.

"I almost forgot. Catch!" she says, throwing me something. I catch it.

"Why don't you take Naomi in the new car," Mom says. I look down and I have keys in my hand.

"No way! Seriously?" I'm ecstatic.

"Go have fun," Mom says, smiling.

"But wait, what about your car?" I ask Naomi

"I'll send someone to come get it later. Now let's break this baby in!" she says, dashing towards the car. I hop in the driver's seat and put the key in the ignition. Seconds pass but it feels like forever. *Is this even my life*? I think as I turn the car on.

"Where to?" I ask as I pull out of the driveway.

"The school back parking lot," Naomi says.

"Seriously?"

She laughs.

"Not exactly where you would expect a teen rager to throw down," I say in a grandpa voice.

"Trust me," She says, smiling at me.

I pull into the back parking lot and there is a single unmarked school bus. I look at Naomi and she seems calm, so I park and we both get out.

"Okay, what is this?" I ask.

"Just wait," she says, as we walk towards the bus. I hear music getting louder and louder.

"No way," I say, approaching the bus. The doors spring open and light shines out from the interior. The bus's leather seats have been taken out and replaced with a few couches and tables with various alcohol bottles on them as well as lights and a full DJ booth. 15-20 people's sweaty bodies press up against each other, dancing.

"Welcome to Guilford!" she shouts as she takes a shot from someone. I look at the person's face. It's Carter.

"Cheers!" Carter says, looking me in the eyes. He hands me a shot glass and we all cheers to what is probably the most exciting night of my life so far.

"I've never been to a party like this," I say, many shots later. "Whoa, it almost feels like we're moving!" I hear myself slurring my words

"That's cause we are, champ," Carter says, rustling my hair.

"No way! Where are we going?"

"You'll see," he says.

"You know, you and your sister do that a lot," I say, straightening my back.

"Do what?" Carter says, intrigued by my drunken chatter.

"Saying the same things. It must be a twin thing. Keeping secrets from me... Holding my hand," I say, leaning my head on his shoulder. "I'm sleepy," I say, closing my eyes.

"What's up!" Naomi says, hyper as ever as she sits down beside us.

"Brighton is just telling me how you two were holding hands," Carter says to Naomi with some pressure behind his voice.

"I'm sleepy," I say again, now resting my head on

Naomi's shoulder.

"Well, we can't have that," Naomi says, pulling something out of her shirt, probably from her bra.

"Naomi, really?" Carter says, batting her hand out of sight. She grabs my hand and places a small baggie in it.

"Calm down, Carter, it's just something to wake him up," she says, looking at me. I look at the small baggie in front of me, confused.

"Here, I'll show you!" she says as she pulls her hair back. She lowers her body to a small tray, puts one finger on her nostril and inhales, taking a line of powder..

"See?" she says, handing me the tray. I look at Carter to see his reaction. He doesn't seem happy.

"Is it okay?" I ask, still drunk and still sleepy.

"I, personally, don't mess with the stuff. It gives me killer migraines. But if you want to, go ahead, bud," he says, patting me on the back.

I lean into the tray and prepare myself, not fully sober but still very much aware that I'm about to do drugs. *Sid has done worse* I think as I inhale.

"Oh geez, it burns!" I say, sitting up from the tray and rubbing my nose.

"Naomi, where did you get this stuff anyway?" Carter says, passing the tray away to a random party girl.

"I don't know. It's just being passed around," she says as she gets up and walks away.

"I don't feel anything." I say, half thinking I would immediately turn into the hulk or something. Carter just pats my head.

"Everybody off!" Someone yells as the bus comes to a stop. Some people fall over and there are a few screams from drunk girls.

"Okay Brighton, we're here. Time to be my date!" Naomi says, grabbing my arm.

"What? Where?" I say, hyped up. I'm not sleepy anymore.

Naomi and I exit the bus arm in arm. String lights are strung from tree to tree and colorful lights shine onto the large lake that is in front of us. It's like our own private beach. Loud music plays over speakers.

"Where are we?" I exclaim as everyone exits the bus.

"Wadsworth Falls. Nice choice, sis," Carter says, walking up behind me.

"Figured the new kid would get a kick out of it," she says.

We all face a huge waterfall, lit by multicolored lights. The bass from the music is pounding in the background. I look at Carter, and he looks at me.

"Let's dance! You are my date after all " Naomi says, pulling me away.

As a *Panic! At The Disco* song plays in the background, getting drowned out by the rushing water of the falls, I dance with Naomi, somehow sweating even though the air is crisp. I feel alive.

The people around us are all from school, none of which I recognize. Some are making out, some are drinking, others are smoking. I am immediately reminded of Sid and The Stoner Shack.

"I feel numb," I say, flicking my tongue with my finger. Naomi laughs.

"Besides that, how do you feel?" she asks as we continue to bop to the music.

"I feel like I want to-" I pause to think.

"Like you want to do this?" she says, caressing my face with her hand. She pulls me in and our lips touch for what seems like forever. She steps back and looks at me.

"No. Not that." I say bluntly in my messed up state.

She laughs. Luckily, she is just as messed up as me at this point and doesn't take offense.

"What time is it?" I ask, now more aware of what's happening around me.

"I don't know. Probably one or two?" she says, looking at her wrist. She isn't wearing a watch.

"How far away from home are we?" I ask frantically.

"Calm down, Brighton, like a half hour. I'll get you home before sunrise, don't worry," she says, trying to continue dancing.

"Will my mom be okay with that?" I ask, standing still.

"Your mom thinks you're studying, remember? She will just think you fell asleep at your friend's house or something. Trust me? " She says, grabbing my hands.

"I'm thirsty." I pull my hands away from hers and walk towards an open cooler I saw earlier. I grab a bottle of water and chug it quickly.

"All partied out?" I hear coming from behind me. It's Carter.

"This is all new to me," I say, trying not to sound lame.

"It's okay. My sister can be a little over the top," he says, looking out to the crowd of people dancing.

"You're telling me," I say, thinking back to the kiss, trying not bring that up like I did with the hand holding.

"Hey, do you wanna get out of here?" Carter asks, resting his hand on my arm.

"But your sist-?"

"-Can get a ride back with the others," he says, smiling. I look out at Naomi dancing as we walk away from the party.

"How are we getting out of here exactly?" I say, looking around at the forest.

"I called a cab like ten minutes ago. They should be just up here," he says, grabbing my hand to guide me through the dark path.

"9283 North Ridgewood.," he says, getting in the cab. As we drive into the dark, my eyelids get heavier and heavier. I rest my head on the window and pass out.

7

"Morning," I hear as I open my eyes slightly. The lights from the windows hurt my head as I roll over.

"Morning." My voice sounds horrible. I open my eyes and laying next to me, shirtless, is Carter. He is sitting on his laptop with headphones in.

"Oh shit," I say, sitting up. "What time is it?" I rub my eyes.

"Early. Almost ten," Carter says, taking out his headphones.

"I gotta get home! My mom must be worried sick." I get out of bed. I still have my pants on.

"No need to rush, I talked to her."

"My mom? You talked to my mom?" I say, confused, searching for my belt.

"Not exactly. Your phone kept ringing last night so I answered it. She asked about a study group. I told her we fell asleep watching a movie after we finished studying and that you would be home right when you woke up," Carter says, putting his arms above his head.

"Oh thank God," I say, sitting down on the bed. My mind went mad there for a second, remembering how she was the day we left L.A. and found me after being gone for so long.

"Breakfast?" Carter asks.

"I should really be getting home." I get up and walk to the door. Carter gets out of bed.

"Do you usually wake up before 10 A.M on a Saturday?" Carter asks.

"Well, no..." I say.

"Then breakfast," he says, opening the door and walking out into the hall.

Carter's house is big, bigger than mine. It smells clean, like lemons. The smell is, honestly, making me a little nauseous because I'm probably hungover.

"Breakfast! Get up," Carter says, banging on a door in the hallway. Naomi opens the door a crack and pops her head out.

"Oh! Brighton! Feeling alright?" she asks, perky as ever.

"Head hurts, stomach hurts, so yeah, I feel just alright," I say jokingly

"Good. I'm gonna skip on breakfast. You two go on ahead!" she says, closing the door and going back into her room.

"Well, that was weird," I say as we continue down the hallway.

"She must have scored last night."

"Scored?" I ask.

"Jesus, what did you do in L.A? There was a guy in there," he says, gesturing back upstairs.

"Oh," I say, embarrassed.

Carter's kitchen is fancy and everything feels brand new. It's very clean. A full breakfast spread, almost buffet style, is laid out on the kitchen island.

"Help yourself!" Carter says, grabbing a plate for

both of us.

"This is amazing. Is this what you eat for breakfast everyday?" I ask, putting as much bacon on my plate as possible.

"Only on weekends. Mom has the staff prepare it for my father. If he wasn't here, Mom wouldn't bother at all."

"Your dad's only here in the morning on weekends?" I ask, eyeing a basket of muffins.

"Oh, I didn't tell you?" he says, laughing to himself.

"What do you mean?" I ask, confused.

"Follow me. You'll understand when you see my dad. He's is in here," he says, walking to the dining room. His parents are sitting down already and his mom is drinking what looks like coffee, or possibly tea.

"Dad, this is Brighton Anderson. I believe you have met." His dad puts down his newspaper and looks up at Carter, then at me.

"Headmaster Hall!" I say, surprised, almost dropping my croissant.

"Ah yes, the transfer student. It's nice to have you in our home," he says as he goes back to reading his paper.

"Mom, is it okay if we eat in my room?" Carter asks as I stand awkwardly.

"Sure dear. Just don't make a mess." We head back upstairs to his room.

"You didn't tell me your dad was the principal!" I say, throwing a piece of my muffin at him across the bed.

"Mom said not to make a mess!" he says, throwing a piece of his toast back at me.

"In my defense, I thought you would put two and two together... Carter Hall and Headmaster Hall..." he says, laughing.

"Hey, Hall is a very common last name!" I laugh. My phone rings from across the room.

"Is that your mom again?" Carter asks as I get up.

"No, that's not Mom's ringtone it's-"

"Hey man!" Sid says, energized.

"Hey! What's up, man?"

"Jeez you sound horrible. You sick?"

"Not exactly..." I say, not wanting to explain that I got drunk and did drugs in a forest last night.

"Well, I just wanted to say: surprise!" he exclaims.

"Wait, what surprise?!" I say loudly. Carter looks in my direction.

"Well, not yet. But in exactly one month, on your birthday, Siddy boy is coming to the big CT."

"No way! Wait, what? How?" I'm overly excited now.

"Your mom invited me. She even paid for my ticket," he says,

"That's insane!" I say, still way to excited. Carter looks at me intrigued.

"Sid, I'm actually not home. Could I call you back tonight?"

"No problem, buddy. I actually haven't slept yet, so goodnight!" he says, hanging up the phone. It sounds like he had a even crazier night then me.

"What's all the excitement?" Carter asks, looking to match my level of enthusiasm.

"That was my best friend from back home. He's coming to visit, like, next month," I say, sitting back down on the bed in front of my half picked apart breakfast.

"No way! I can't wait to meet your friend. Is he cute?" Carter says in a flirty manner.

"Um, I mean, maybe in his own unique way. The girls seem to really like him."

"What about the boys?" Carter asks, raising one eyebrow.

"The boys?" I ask, fiddling around with my fork.

"Were there any boys who liked your friend, or maybe who you liked?" he pries.

"Shouldn't I be asking you that?" I try to deflect the question back on him.

"I make it known who I like. It's not a secret, so feel free to ask anything," he says, smirking. I grab my fork and stab one of the sausages on my plate and hold it up.

"So would you say you prefer sausage or a warm buttered croissant?" I giggle.

"Too many carbs, sausage all the way," he says, as he puts his croissant on my plate.

"You?" he asks, eating a sausage.

"I just love breakfast," I say, stuffing my mouth.

"Getting rid of the cheesy breakfast metaphors, I'm gay." Carter says, smiling.

"What breakfast metaphors?" I play stupid and we both laugh.

"So this friend of yours, I take it he's a croissant connoisseur"

"Big time," I say with a little pressure behind my voice.

"I sense I'm not getting the whole story between you two right now. Am I?" I finish my last piece of bacon and my last sip of OJ.

"More like the whole novel."

"Well, let's get you home then." Carter says, taking off his shirt.

"Oh shoot, my car is at the school."

"Okay then, to the school." He slides on a fresh T-shirt.

"Can I borrow a shirt?" I ask, looking down at my still shirtless body. Carter pulls out a pink v-neck and throws it at me

"I think you suit pink," he says, turning away from me. We see a taxi pulling out of the driveway as we leave his house.

"Naomi's little friend's walk of shame I presume?" I say in a snarky tone.

"Have I got my wires crossed here or are you jealous?" Carter asks, starting his car.

"Not jealous, just ticked off. She made this huge deal about me being her date and she didn't even notice we left."

"That's my sister: out with the old and in with the new. She loves a good challenge, but once she's conquered something, she moves on."

My car is the only one in the parking lot as we pull up.

"Conquered, huh?" I question what she could possibly be thinking.

"She probably realized you're into guys and moved on. Don't worry about it, man," Carter says. I open the door.

"I'm not gay." I get angry. The words coming out of my mouth aren't like me at all.

"Okay, chill dude. I was just kidding," he says through the rolled down passenger side window.

"She must be freaked out since I, like, kissed her," I say, trying to make him angry and bending the truth slightly.

"You and Naomi?" Carter asks, revving his engine. I don't respond. I'm not really sure where I want this conversation to go.

"Anyways, I gotta get home," I say, walking away. Carter speeds off and I can't help but feel like we just left things in a really weird place.

Some of my fondest memories are from my brief week in France. Sure, I was young, but not so young that I couldn't appreciate it. While it felt like a last ditch attempt to magically solve Mom and Dad's marital problems, for me, it was a pure, innocent trip where I experienced my first "kind of" love. I say it like that because I was only thirteen at the time. Something about the streets of Paris makes you feel like you can feel any emotion and do anything.

Before Paris, I had thought about the girls at school. Sid was already my best friend and he was always trying to get a new girl each week, but I just wasn't that interested. I didn't think much of it. Honestly, I had a lot more to worry about then if Jenny from down the street "like liked" me. During the trip, though, I felt something I never had before: butterflies.

We stayed in a very small hotel. It was cheap, with multiple stories and shoebox sized rooms, but it was right in the middle of Paris. Elliott, Mom and I got to share a queen sized bed and Dad had a cot brought up for himself. The room was so tiny that we all had to use the bathroom before we went to bed because Dad's open cot made it so we couldn't open the bathroom door. This caused some horrible trouble with Elliott and a soaking wet sheet. That's a night I don't ever want to relive.

One morning, when we were heading out for the day, we ran into another family in the elevator. They had a boy my age. He had olive skin and dark features. His mom and dad started a conversation with mine. They bonded over the small hotel rooms and exchanged stories of the trials of traveling with children. We learned that they were from Italy, but would often travel to Paris to visit family friends. We ended up going to brunch with them and exchanging numbers. Our whole trip after that was spent as a big group with this other family. Their knowledge of Paris was very helpful.

Grand. His name was Grand. Once I learned his name, I tried really hard to remember it. It was a unique name, but it suited him. Our parents wanted to eat at restaurants and talk most of the time, and Elliott was young enough to go along with what Mommy and Daddy wanted, but Grand and I wanted to explore. I'm still shocked to this day that Mom let me and a random Italian kid wander the streets of Paris alone at the young age of thirteen, but I don't think they will ever know how much I needed that time alone.

Because I had just become a teenager, I felt like my thoughts and all my actions were policed, like they didn't belong to me, but to my parents. I could think whatever I wanted but, in some way, my parents were always in the back of my head, influencing everything. Of course, going into "that day" I didn't know anything was going to happen, but, at the end of the day, I had felt a release of pressure on my whole body.

He could speak French and it was mesmerizing. He would ask for anything I wanted: water, where the restroom was, directions. I felt my stomach go in knots every time he would open his mouth. His English was good, but not perfect. I liked it that way, though. We didn't have to speak to have a good time and to share our emotions.

Our day started out with a trip to see the Arc de Triomphe. It was spectacular. Normally, something like this would have been boring, like going to a museum for a school field trip, but something about being there with this strange kid and not being with my parent made me feel more mature, like I could appreciate my surroundings.

There was a dense crowd of people in line to climb the arc to get to the observation deck and I found myself getting separated from Grand. Without thinking, I grabbed his hand. He looked at me and I looked at him. Again, with no words, I felt connected to him. We ended up keeping our fingers laced as we climbed the steps to the top. Our hands stayed linked together as we walked around the observation deck and looked through the gift shop. We looked around in silence, hand in hand, not caring about anything.

We left for the Eiffel Tower, taking a cab with the last money we had from his parents. We spoke a little during the drive. He told me about his older sister back home, Isabella, and how she couldn't come because she was sick, and that she probably wouldn't come to Paris again soon because she couldn't handle a long train ride. I didn't have to ask what she was sick with. I could tell from his eyes that it wasn't good. I felt something for him; not only sadness but the need to cheer him up. I leaned over to him and rested my head on his shoulder. He accepted it and leaned his head on mine. Thinking back, the cab driver must have thought he picked up a couple of weird queer foreigners, but my simple mind wasn't thinking about gay or straight, it was simply a feeling of closeness.

I was planning on going to the Eiffel Tower with my family the next day, but it felt better to be there with him. The sun was setting and the lights had just turned on on the tower. We wanted it to be completely dark before going up, so we found a crepe stand and bought the cheapest chocolate banana crepe to share. We took a seat on a bench and watched the sunset. It was chilly, so we sat close. I hoped he couldn't hear my heart beating a mile a minute or feel how nervous I was as we shared the crepe. I made sure not to take bite that were too big because I wanted him to have most of it. After finishing our crepe, we watched as people entered the ice rink below the tower. My hand was still tingling from the feeling of him touching it earlier. I ached for his touch, not in a sexual way, but in a very innocent way.

I felt so small as we approached the tower. Our moms were coming to meet us at a bus stop nearby so, pressed for time, we hurried up the stairs, all 647 steps, before riding the elevator to the top. As we approached the viewpoint, I became awestruck. The lights from the city shined and the ground was so far away. It was freezing and Grand's nose and ears were red. He rubbed his hand together, trying to keep warm. As we looked out to the lights of Paris, I grabbed his hands. He looked at me, not shocked, but as if I had read his mind. As the air got colder, the tower cleared out. We were alone, aside from a few other groups of people. They were most likely couples occupying their own little space anyways.

I remember the next few seconds so clearly because I probably replayed them over in my head a million times. Grand dropped my hands and they slumped down to my side. My heart dropped. I felt sad but I could still feel his warmth in my palms. The smell of someone's perfume swept in with a breeze. Suddenly, Grand's hands were on my shoulders and he was looking me in the eyes. I looked back.

"Vorrei ascoltare il battito del tuo cuore," he said, coming closer to me. At the time I thought he was speaking French, but a later Google search revealed it was actually Italian and his words meant "I want to listen to your heartbeat." You can bet that when I googled it my entire body turned into jello.

He grabbed me and hugged me. I could feel his breath on my neck. I was startled by the sudden embrace. I felt like I was out of my body watching a movie, one in black and white and with subtitles, the kind I usually hate. I backed up from his hug, feeling very unlike myself.

"Is this okay?" I asked as I got closer to his face. My lips were close to his. They weren't touching but they were close enough to make me wish they were. Our eyes were locked, staring each other in the eyes.

"Potrei guardarti tutto il giorno," was his response. I went in for the kiss, closing my eyes.

His lips were warm and tasted like chocolate. His hair was curly and my hand had trouble gliding through it.

"I could look at you all day," were his words before our kiss. I didn't need to know what he said to know we both were feeling the same thing. He pulled away as a clock bell charmed in the distance.

"We meet mothers now, yes?" he said softly in his broken, accented english. We walked down the steps slower than we came up them, hand in hand.

As we neared the bus stop where our mothers were waiting, I didn't want to let go of his hand. It felt like our entire day together would be taken away from me if I let go. When the bus stop was just around the corner, he let go of my hand. We shared a brief moment of eye contact.

"How was your day sweetie? Have fun?" Mom asked.

"It was the best," I replied as we walked away from the bus stop. I turned around and Grand was looking at me. We shared a final glance and that was the last time I ever saw him.

Our last day in Paris was spent visiting the Eiffel Tower. Mom, Dad, and Elliott were enjoying it, but I was flooded with emotions from the night before. In the moment, everything was fine, but now, almost a day later, I was feeling guilty. Being back with my family brought me back to reality .It reminded me that Grand and Brighton was wrong. We were two guys, not to mention we were both so young. The rest of the day I found myself staring at my hand and remembering the feeling of his. I felt the guilt crawling up on me. These guilty thoughts wouldn't leave my mind. I thought I would die trying to keep my cool on the eleven hour flight with my family.

The trip ended without anyone knowing about

that night Grand and I shared. The flight was a long and hard for me and my brain. With Sid and all the pressures from society reminding me that being gay was wrong, I tried to forget about the whole thing. Everything looked the same as before, but just a little off. It felt like something had started to change inside me and I was terrified.

9

"Okay students, line up!" a teacher shouts in the distance.

"Let's go, Brighton!" Carter says, grabbing the back of my neck, gently guiding me towards the bus. A trip with all the seniors to New York City. I'm officially going from one way of life to the other. I never would have thought, me being from Los Angeles, that I would find myself in New York, ever, let alone in my senior year of high school.

We all load up onto a bus. It's not your average yellow bus, though, it's a white charter bus with airplane-like seats. The only time I've been in one before was when my school took a trip to Seaworld in 5th grade.

"You know, I'm surprised we're going to New York," I say, sitting down in a seat. Carter sits down beside me.

"How so?" he says, putting his bag at his feet.

"I would expect such a fancy school to, you know, fly us all to Rome or something!"

"You want to go to Rome? I can take you to Rome," Carter says nonchalantly.

"Nah, maybe Italy though," I say, joking back...

well, half joking.

"What's up, my two favorite guys!" A pressure comes from behind my seat as Naomi rests her arms over our headrests.

"Wow, packed light? How unlike you!" she says, gesturing to Carter's small duffel bag.

"Yeah, I was wondering about that. We're leaving for a week. Even I had them put my suitcase under the bus," I say.

"I shipped my stuff a week ago. I didn't want to have to put creases in my nice shirts," he says, as if it's normal for a seventeen-year-old to worry about that kind of stuff.

"That's my brother," Naomi says, pushing my shoulder. I push her hand back. Our hand's touch for a few uncomfortable seconds. Naomi smiles and sits back in her seat.

Things have gotten weird between me and Carter. He hasn't been the same with me since that morning in the school parking lot. Sure, he jokes and we talk, but it almost feels like he doesn't want to be alone with me. I mean, Naomi is basically with us 24/7 now. It's not that I don't like her hanging out with us. She's cool and I'm not opposed to hanging out with girls, but, even with my friends back home, Sid and I still had hangouts where it was just us guys. Maybe things are different with twins.

"A whole two hours to kill on this bus. What will we do?" Carter says.

"Truth or dare?" Naomi asks, obviously eavesdropping from behind the seat. We stand up and swivel our seats around. Now we're all facing each other. The girl sitting next to Naomi ignores us and puts her headphones in. A few weeks into going to school here and I don't even know her name. The twins have been taking up all my social time. Although, for these two hours, I don't mind them occupying all of it.

"Truth or dare, Carter?" I ask.

"Hmmm, dare." he says, biting his lip.

"I dare you to... oh this is good. Stand up and do a strip tease, right now," I request, thinking back to the time I made Sid do it at summer camp. It was hilarious and he never lived it down.

"If you insist." Carter stands up and claps his hands. He begins to unbutton his shirt, slowly taking it off and draping it over his neck.

"Fag!" comes from the back of the bus, assumably from one of the school's field hockey players.

"You like what you see!" Carter shouts back.

"Sit down!" I say, pulling on his pant leg.

"Hey, you dared me. You took it back which means you go next. Truth or dare?" he says, putting his shirt back on.

"Okay fine. Umm, truth."

"Hmm…..first kiss?"

I thought to myself for a second. "It was in Paris, on the Eiffel Tower."

"Oh, how romantic! What a lucky girl!" Naomi gushes.

"I don't believe it. It's too good to be true," Carter says.

"No, it's true. I met her on vacation. It just so happens that she was Italian," I say, almost slipping up on the gender of who I had been kissing.

"I believe him! Brighton seems like the type of guy

to take things like that seriously. Now my turn!" Naomi says.

"Okay, truth or dare," I ask, hoping she will choose dare. I really want to make her stand up and scream something horrible at the top of her lungs.

"Truth."

"Boring," Carter shouts.

"Okay Naomi, who do you think is better looking: me or your brother?"

"Well, since we are twins and I'm really hot, I should say my brother, but that's weird, so I'm gonna have to go with you!" She looks at me and smiles

"Okay! My turn!" Carter interjects.

"Okay, truth or dare?"

"Dare."

"I dare you to play chicken with Brighton," Naomi says, giggling.

"Chicken? Like the pool game?" I ask, completely oblivious.

"No, silly! Chicken! One person puts their hand on the other person's thigh and slowly moves it up higher and higher until one someone yells chicken. The first one to do so, loses."

"Immature as usual I see, Naomi." Carter looks over at me and moves his leg closer to mine. "I'm not chicken," he says, gesturing down to his leg. I put my hand right above his knee.

"Okay, do I start?" I say nervously.

"Whenever you want," Naomi says, laughing at the fact that we're actually doing it.

My hand starts to slide up his jeans, very slowly. Midway up his thigh I stop for a second and look at him.

His face is calm. I continue to move my hand up, trying not to look away from my own lap. Seconds pass, but it feels like forever. I press my lips together as my hand gets higher and higher. Right as I'm about to get too close for my own comfort-

"Chick-en!" Carter springs up from his seat, covering his junk. I look up and his face is bright red. I realize what's happening and I take off my jacket, handing it to him. He sits down and places it over his lap.

"Okay, so my turn now?" I ask, trying to draw away from Carter's... situation.

"Sure. Carter, I'll ask him since you obviously need a minute," Naomi says, choking back tears of laughter.

"Truth or dare?"

"Dare," I say, trying to delay the game as much as possible for Carter's... chicken's sake.

"I dare you to kiss me," she says, smiling.

"Ummm, pass," I say, looking at Carter.

"What? You're shy now?" she says, looking at me. "Carter knows you kissed me at the party, right?" I knew Naomi wouldn't tell him the truth about her kissing me if he ever brought it up because that makes her look good, but I didn't think she would bring it up to Carter in front of me. "Oh, and no passes. This isn't kids play." I think back to five minutes ago, when she almost made me touch her brother's you-know-what.

"Fine," I say, leaning into Naomi. I kiss her and then quickly lean back.

"Hmmm, it was better when you were drunk," she says, laughing.

Carter hands me back my jacket. "Okay, my turn."

"Okay, truth or dare?"

94

"Truth" he answers. Just as I expected, the last round must have spooked him.

"Okay, hmm. Oh, I know. Since you didn't believe my first kiss, what was yours?"

"Easy. Freshman year. Gym locker room. Very sweaty," he says, whispering.

"Oh, how did I not know this?" Naomi says, leaning in close.

"Well, because, my dear sister, this nice young man was deep in the jock closet and freshman year you couldn't keep your mouth shut about anything," he laughs.

"Is he on this bus?" I ask, looking at the boys in the back.

"Oh, no. He graduated a few years ago."

"You have to tell now!" Naomi exclaims.

"Trevor," Carter says abruptly

"Nooo! Trevor? Wannabe mustache Trevor?" Naomi bursts out laughing. I sit in silence as they talk, since this all this happened before I knew them.

A teacher stands up and shouts from the front of the bus that we will be stopping at a rest area in five minutes.

"Looks like we have time for one more. Naomi, truth or dare?" Carter asks.

"Hmmm, truth."

"Do you like Brighton?" he asks as if he already had it prepared.

"Yeah," she says as if she already knew the answer. "There is still time, so I'll go. Brighton, truth or dare?"

"Truth," I say, knowing we don't have time for a dare and I really do have to pee.

"Okay. Do you like me?" Naomi asks, point blank.

"Ummm," I pause for a second, thinking, "yes..." I say. I mean, I don't dislike her. She's sweet and very pretty. Sid would, for sure, try to go after her if she went to our school in L.A.

The bus pulls into the rest stop and the doors open. Carter and I both spring up out of our seats at the same time.

"Oh, after you," he says, letting me out into the aisle, not making eye contact. I quickly make my way into the restroom. Carter follows behind. He walks up to the urinal beside me.

"Thanks," he says, looking at the jacket tied around my waist. At least, I think that's what he was looking at.

"No problem," I say, sympathizing. I zip up my pants and walk over to the sink. Another guy walks into the bathroom and goes up beside Carter. I wash my hands slowly since it's the same guy who yelled at him on the bus.

"Don't peek!" he says, unzipping his pants. Carter walks away from the urinal and joins me at a sink.

"Ass!" I say to the guy who is clearly triple my size.

"Is that all you can think about, fag?" he says, not looking back at me. I take a step towards him.

"Brighton, it's fine. Let's go back to the bus," Carter says, putting his hand on my chest. I leave reluctantly.

"That guy was such a jerk. I can't believe people like that still exist here."

"It's not your problem though, right?" Carter says,

96

looking at his hands in his lap. We left before he could dry them, so they're still wet. I can tell he is upset. He thought I was gay. I've rejected him so many times. To be honest, I could be gay, but I'm not sure if I just don't want to be, or if I'm actually not. I mean, Naomi is really pretty. I don't know if I could be with her, but I can kiss her. I mean, I've now kissed Naomi the same amount of times I've kissed guys, and she wasn't bad. Am I just scared?

"Right," I say back to Carter, looking at my hands as well. I feel ashamed, but not ashamed enough to change my answer.

The bus takes off and we don't continue our game of truth or dare. Carter just reads some manga on his phone and I listen to music, trying to drown out my own thoughts.

"Ten minutes until we arrive!" I'm jerked awake by the hustle and bustle of kids grabbing their bags and teachers yelling. I, somehow, managed to doze off and my head had slumped over onto Carter's shoulder. I sit up, embarrassed, and look out my window to see the New York City skyline. I yawn and look over at Carter. He is drinking from a water bottle.

"Where did you get that?" I ask, parched from my nap. I feel like I probably had my mouth open, looking like an idiot.

"Here, have a sip." He hands me the bottle and I take a drink. "Indirect kiss," Carter says as he takes the bottle back.

"If that's true, Carter, then we have kissed a million times," Naomi says, chiming into our conversation. "We have nothing planned today after we check into the hotel; want to come to my room and have room service?" she asks.

Carter and I are rooming together and Naomi is rooming with some girl from her science class. The rule is guys with guys and girl with girls. It's as heteronormative as ever, I'm aware, but for most of the kids in my year, it's best that way.

"Nah, sis, I'm tired. I want to unpack and take a nap," he says, yawning. He must not have slept at all on the way here.

"I'm down," I say, because food is always a yes in my book.

"We're here! Everyone line up beside the bus for your luggage!" a teacher says as the bus comes to a halt.

"I'm gonna head up, guys," Carter says, taking his duffel bag. It's just me and Naomi. I grab my suitcases and she grabs two. I take one from her and pull it behind me.

"A true gentleman," she says, walking in front of me.

I follow her into the hotel lobby. I feel like I've been transported into an episode of *The Suite Life of Zack and Cody*, with a set of the crazy twins to boot. Bellhops are wandering about, luggage carts in tow.

We get to Naomi's room and take a seat on the bed. It's huge and her roommate isn't here.

"Oh, we have it all to ourselves for now," she says, taking her shoes off and sitting on the bed.

"I'm starving!" I say, searching for the room service menu. We're not allowed to leave the hotel until roll call tomorrow morning, so, for now, room service is the best we can do.

"Here it is!" Naomi says, pulling a leather menu

out from the side table. "Ohh, lamb," Naomi says, flipping through the pages.

"No no no, we're in New York, we have to go for the pizza!" I say in a very bad Italian accent.

"Molto bene!" she says back in an equally bad accent. We both laugh and fall back onto the bed. I grab the phone and call in an order for two cheese pizzas and a few bottles of sparkling water. "We know you have a thing for Italians," Naomi says, rolling over to face me.

"Oh yeah," I say, still laughing. We make eye contact.

"Yeah," she says. She kisses me. I roll over and she comes with me, now sitting on top of me. I look up at her and she's unbuttoning her shirt. *What's happening,* I think. My thoughts are racing. I don't know how I feel. My heart is pounding in my chest and my hands feel like they could start shaking any second. *Why am I scared?*

"Come on," she says, pulling my shirt off over my head. I follow along by undoing my belt. She takes her pants off and we both slide under the covers.

"Um?" I say, my voice shaking. Naomi gets up and runs over to her bag. It doesn't surprise me that she came prepared.

She gets on top of me and I feel my heart pounding. She kisses my neck and begins to rub her body on mine. I suddenly feel weird and claustrophobic. My legs flail as Naomi slides off me and rolls to the side of the bed. I stand up and grab for my pants.

"I'm sorry, I can't- I'm sorry!" I say, trying to put my belt on while walking towards the door. Naomi is hiding under the duvet.

I open the door and, as I'm about to step out, I'm

greeted by Carter, his hand raised, about to knock.

"I couldn't sleep," he says, walking into the room. I take a step back. He looks at me and then into the room.

"Whoa! Okay," he says, stepping out of the doorway. I walk back to my room, or should I say my and Carter's room, shirtless, without my suitcase, on the brink of tears. I couldn't do it.

I'm laying in bed, surrounded by darkness. The sun has set and I'm the only one occupying my room. Carter isn't here and I don't know where he is. I never got to eat my pizza and my body is too shocked to order food. I don't know what Naomi could be thinking, but my mind is thinking the worst. What if she and Carter are going on and on about how I'm just a loser virgin who couldn't get it up, or if they have come to the conclusion that I'm gay, which is what I've I've concluded. I didn't freak out because it was my first time or because I'm claustrophobic, I freaked out because I felt bad, like I was telling a huge lie. It didn't matter how much I wanted to be with her to prove something to myself, I just couldn't do it; and now I have to deal with the consequences. I know I don't like girls, and I know I've liked guys in the past. I mean, I always knew I liked guys, but now it seems so much more real.

I reach for my phone to check the time. It's 8 o'clock. Room call is at nine, so Carter should be back soon. His dad is the principal, so he must have some respect for the rules. Carter. He probably won't be very happy after walking in on me and Naomi. I mean, it's his sister. Even if he can relate to why I might have totally led her on, I still almost did something horrible to her. She likes me, and, to my knowledge, she thinks I like her in the same way. I have to tell her. She deserves to know, but I deserve privacy too. I don't want to talk about how I'm feeling with anyone. It feels weird to be having all these thoughts that I know not everyone has, but Carter must have felt like this at some point. His first kiss was with a guy freshman year, and even if it was a long time ago he wasn't born out of the closet. Am I seriously thinking about asking him about this? The New York pollution must be getting to me.

I hear the mechanical lock on the door click as a light comes in from the hallway. I see Carter's face and immediately feel a weird emotion come over me.

"Carter?" I say in a shaky voice.

"Why were you sitting in the dark? You scared me, you freak," he says, turning on the lights. He looks at me and rushes over. My eyes are teary and I feel my hands start to shake.

"Hey. Hey. Hey," he says, sitting on the bed next to me. "It's alright." He brushes my hair with his hand.

He smells like pizza. He must have been with Naomi all this time. I lean over and my head falls into his lap. I fall asleep right then and there. My emotions wore me out and Carter's warm aura made me feel like everything was alright.

The next morning I wake up and Carter is no longer in bed with me. He's in his own bed, still asleep. The sun is just rising.

"Carter?" I say, trying to wake him.

"Hmmm?" he says, half-asleep, looking in my direction.

"I'm going down to the breakfast buffet. Do you want anything?" I ask as my stomach growls.

"Sausage." He giggles and goes back to sleep

"A waffle it is!" I say, getting out of bed, my suitcase at my feet. He must have brought it from Naomi's room. Too hungry to change my clothes, I grab the room key and head down to the buffet.

It's a standard continental breakfast. A lot of kids from school are already down here because we have a tour around some museum at nine and everyone is trying to eat first. I grab a tray and put some scrambled eggs on a plate with some ketchup. I walk up to the waffle machine to make one for Carter and there is a group of guys surrounding it. One of them is making a waffle and filling it with random crap from the cereal bar. I recognize one of them. It's the jerk from the bus. He is waiting with a plate, I assume, to make a waffle as well. I line up behind him.

"You waiting?" I say. I want to make sure I'm in the right place.

"Yeah," he says. I wait a few seconds. "Why don't you go in front of me," he says, gesturing his plate forward.

"O-okay?" I say, taking a step in front of him.

"Didn't want the queer staring at my ass!" he says to his other jock buddies. They all laugh.

"What's your problem?" I shout, thinking that if they all decide to beat me up, we're in a public place and I probably won't die.

"Oh, did someone get in a fight with their boyfriend last night? All cranky I see," he says in an overly feminine voice. They all laugh again. I set the empty plate I had been holding down on the counter and walk away. Steaming, I knew I didn't want to go any further in that situation. I take my plate of eggs and head to the elevator.

"Oh, my sausage!" Carter says excitedly, looking at my plate.

"No sausage," I say, slamming the plate down on the desk.

"Whoa, what's wrong?" he says, getting out of bed. I take a fork full of eggs and shove them in my mouth as I take my shirt off.

"Nothing, nothing. It's just that, not only am I the new guy, but I'm also the new school queer!" I say with my mouth full, taking off my pants.

"Whoa, I don't follow," Carter says, looking at my plate to see that I really didn't get him any sausage.

"That jock from earlier! He seems to think that I'm your boyfriend!" I say, walking towards the bathroom. "I'm taking a shower," I say, slamming the bathroom door. Carter stops the door with his foot.

"What's so bad about that?" Carter says, walking into the bathroom. We're both in our boxers.

"Oh, what? You think I'm gay now too?" I yell as I grab my head. "I didn't ask for any of this." I want to cry but I'm too angry.

"It's fine, Brighton. Calm down," Carter says, grabbing my shoulder. I pull away.

"I know you know about what happened between me and your sister yesterday. I'm sure you guys made fun of the poor closet case for hours, huh!" I'm still yelling but my is voice getting shakier and shakier.

"Who do you think I am?" Carter raises his voice. I'm taken aback. "You think those guys don't get on my nerves either? You think I don't want to just throw punches left and right? I do. But we can't do that. It won't make things better." he says, his voice shaking now as well

"I'm not like you. I can't be. I can't. I can't." I slide down to the floor, hugging my knees. Words are spilling out of me beyond my control.

"Hey, come on now. It's not that bad," he says, meeting me on the floor.

"Naomi hates me," I say, looking at him

"No, you're lucky. She actually really likes you and thinks you just got cold feet yesterday."

"It wasn't cold feet..." I mumble, looking up at Carter.

"I know," he says. I kind of knew he did.

"Carter?" I say, standing up. He follows. "I don't know about anything right now," I say, looking him in the eyes. He leans in and we kiss. Seconds go by and I start to panic. "No, not now!" I say as I shove him out of the bathroom door and slam it closed.

"Brighton, I'm sorry," he says, knocking. I get in the shower and drown out the sound of his voice and wash the feeling of him off my lips.

Feeling calm after my shower, I open the bathroom door and go to my suitcase. Carter is sitting on the bed fully dressed, ready to go meet up with the rest of our class.

"I'm sorry, Brighton," he says.

"It's okay," I say. "I need a friend," I say, only partly telling the truth. To be honest, I could see myself liking him, but right now, I can't think past this trip ending and getting back home to Mom and Elliott.

"Okay. I can do that," he says, looking away as I get dressed.

"Carter, normal friends can get dressed in front of each other," I say as he looks back and sees that I had my boxers on under my towel the whole time. I laugh.

"Baby steps. Remember what happened on the bus?" he laughs. I blush. We head out the door and go down to the front of the hotel to meet up with our classmates. Naomi joins up with us and everything is the same as before. My life feels back to normal. At least, as normal as it could be.

A few days pass and we get to the last night of our trip. We are allowed to roam the city and do as we please. Carter, Naomi and I decide to go out for some greasy New York pizza. We all sit down in a tiny hole in the wall pizza joint and enjoy our cheap slices.

"You know, I was a little skeptical about $1 slices the first time I came to New York, but now I love them!" Carter says, taking a bite.

"I love these little red things," Naomi says, reaching for the hot pepper container across the table. She bumps my drink and it tips over, pouring onto the floor and all over Carter's lap and legs.

"Oh shit!" He jumps up.

"Oh, I'm so sorry! Here, let me help!" Naomi grabs some napkins from her plate.

"No. No. I gotta put water on them before it stains!" Carter rushes to the bathroom

"I'm gonna go help." I get up and follow him. He is in the bathroom, obsessively dabbing his pants with a wet paper towel.

"Are they that expensive?" I ask.

"Armani," he says, wetting his paper towel again, completely focused. He stops and looks in the mirror. "Looks like I pissed myself," he says, laughing.

"Yeah, that's unfortunate," I say, laughing as well.

"We should go back out there. Naomi is waiting," he says, walking toward the door. We both go outside the bathroom and I feel the urge to not be myself for a second. I grab him by the arm and kiss him, but only on the cheek.

"Baby steps," I say, running back into the restaurant. Naomi isn't at the table. We look around as she comes out from the corner we were just in.

"Bathroom. Hands were all greasy," she says, holding up her hands and sitting down.

We eat our pizza and continue on with the rest of our night. Carter and I decide to say goodbye to Naomi and head back to our room.

"Wait, Brighton! Stop!" Carter says as we walk up to our hotel room door. I see that it's open a crack. Thinking it must be the maid service, I take a step forward and open the door. I'm knocked back onto the floor by five or six large guys running out of our room.

"What the hell?" Carter yells down the hallway, walking over to help me up.

"You okay?" he asks as we walk into the room.

It's trashed. All my clothes have been thrown everywhere and the air reeks of paint fumes. I look over and see my suitcase emptied and flipped open with the word 'FAG' spray-painted across it. I grab the suitcase, drag it into the bathroom and throw it in the shower. I scrub and I scrub but the word won't come off.

"Brighton, stop, it's spray paint. Water won't remove it," Carter says, turning off the water. A knock on our door scares me. Carter goes to the door and answers it.

"Brighton, here." I hear Naomi's voice coming from the hotel room. She walks in and places one of her suitcases in my line of view.

"I'm shipping back my clothes and some of Naomi's, so you can borrow this, okay?" Carter says as I step out of the bathtub, my clothes now dripping wet.

"Thanks Naomi." I walk up and hug her. She pats my back.

"Did they take anything else, or do anything else?" Naomi says, picking up the phone in our room.

"Hi. This is room 302. I'm just wondering if you could tell me how many keys are out for my room?" She nods for a few moments then hangs up.

"Those idiots at the front desk must think all high school boys look the same. They basically just handed those jerks a key to your room."

"It just won't stop," I say.

"I'm sorry, Brighton. This is all my fault," Carter says, shoving a pile of clothes off the bed before sitting down.

"Should I tell father?" Naomi says, pulling out her cell phone.

"No!" I accidentally shout too loud. "Nobody needs to know about this. It was my stuff that was damaged and it's not a big deal." Honestly, I would like to make a big deal out of this, but the fact that this wasn't just normal bullying means it would be a very big deal and I would be in the spotlight for all of it.

"Okay, but your both sleeping in my room tonight." Naomi says, grabbing both our hands.

"Naomi, it's fine," Carter says, stopping in his tracks.

"No. Those guys have keys and they could come back. I don't want you to get hurt." We both head over to Naomi's room by force.

"I'm going to bed," Carter says, plopping down onto the couch in Naomi's room.

"Sorry for intruding," I say to the girl who was also assigned to the room, who sitting in the other bed. She just nods and smiles.

I sit down on the bed next to Naomi and we both play on our phones for a while. I didn't really want to play on my phone, but I am waiting for everyone to fall asleep.

"Naomi, come with me," I say, whispering as I grab her hand. I take her to the hallway and close the door behind us.

"Listen, I'm sorry about the other night. It's just-" My explanation is cut short by Naomi's lips.

"You were just nervous. I get it," she says, smiling but not looking me in the eye. I suddenly think about home. I don't mean the place I'm living now, but L.A, and how Sid would react in this situation, and how Sid never had fag spray-painted on any of his things. He is going to be here in a week and I can't have any of this get back to him.

"You know, I think I know why I was nervous," I say, already regretting the decision I have made in my mind.

"Oh yeah?" Naomi says, getting closer to me.

"I think I was just upset I didn't have the chance to tell you yet."

"Tell me what?" she asks.

"To tell you that I really like you." I say. The words sound forced.

"I really like you too," she says, kissing me again. "Okay, so when two people really like each other..." Naomi begins.

"Would you like to go out with me?" I ask, sounding more confident in myself.

"Yes, that would be nice, Brighton!" She says, hugging me.

Our New York trip comes to an end and we all wake up the next morning and ride the bus home. I gEt a text from Sid saying that he is already packed for his flight, which is, now, in less than a week. This trip left me feeling super weird. I almost lost my virginity, I kissed a boy and I liked it, and I got a girlfriend. Oh, and I gave Carter a boner. I can't forget that.

11

My best friend Sid, he sure is a special one. He's like a zebra without stripes. I've always been a little jealous of him. Not in a bad way, but the feeling has always been there. He is always one step ahead of me in life, knowing what he wants and where he is going.

The day I met Sid, or, as I was introduced to him, "Sidney", is so clear in my head. I think back to it a lot. We met in first grade. It was the second or third day of the year and I was still getting used to leaving my mom everyday in the morning. The class was silent as the teacher entered the room with a boy following close behind her. She introduced the new kid as "Sidney Walton." Everyone in the class laughed because Sidney is a rather girly name. Sid bit back.

"But you losers can call me Sid!" he said, taking a seat at the table behind me. I was fascinated. Because my name is Brighton, I was always made fun of for having a "rich name" when I clearly wasn't rich. I tried to get people to call me Bright, but nobody ever stuck with it, besides Elliott, and that was only because he was too little to say Brighton properly to begin with. Days passed and I didn't talk to the new kid. He was fitting in as well as a boy named Sidney could. Roll call would bring laughter but he just took it. He wasn't popular but he wasn't unpopular. Then the faithful day came, the one I'm so fond of in my memories. It was snack time, and the teacher put napkins with stacks of goldfish crackers on each of our desks. We all ate quietly as the teacher typed at her desk. Suddenly, I heard coughing come from behind me. It got louder and louder as I watched Sid stand up and walk to the front of the class. He's was holding his throat and yelling in a raspy voice, "I'm choking. I'm choking."

The teacher grabbed a bottle of water off her desk and handed it to him. The whole class was laughing at him as he gasped for air, sipping on the water. He went and sat down at his desk again, pacing himself, only eating one goldfish at a time. After that, nobody talked to him. He was the weird kid now because he had made a scene. Kids are jerks. But, on that day, for some reason that I can't remember, I started talking to him. I walked up and said, "hi."

"Hey, Brighton," he responded. I stopped him.

"Bright," I said confidently.

From that day on, he was Sid and I was Bright. He didn't have friends and I didn't either, so we became best friends. We weren't friends because we had anything in common, besides our pink lunch tickets and worn out sneakers, but because we both needed someone. I didn't realize, at the time, how much he needed me more then I needed him.

Fast forward to freshman year. Actually, it was more like half way through the year. With my trip to Paris already come and gone, I was feeling very weird around guys my own age, especially Sid. That year, he went from looking like me, to looking like he belonged in high school. Like I said, always one step ahead. He had started smoking weed, which I didn't have a problem with. He had other friends, which, once again, I was fine with. But the one thing I was never okay with, were his girlfriends. I would always say rude things about them to him. It was horrible, and looking back, I realize I shouldn't have been so jealous. But I was, no doubt about it. I wasn't necessarily attracted to him. I mean, he was always a little scraggly around the edges, but the thought of him being with a girl made me so angry. It was a bad time, for sure. But, to this day, I'm not sure if Sid knows just how weird my feelings for him were at the time. I know he knows they were there, though. I cringe just thinking back at how horrible I was to him.

It was during summer camp that everything came to a peak. The summer of our freshman year was the last time we were able to go. Sid loved it. He lived with his grandmother and she never really got out of the house, so he loved to go outdoors and be a man. I was indifferent about the whole thing but always went because of him. We had the same cabin in Big Bear every year. We'd always chose the one right by the lake, farthest from everyone else's, so we could stay up and talk without getting in trouble with a counselor. We were all sad that it was our last year. Some of the kids our age were there for training to become a counselor next year, but Sid and I couldn't afford to keep coming every year, so we decided to have one last hurrah.

It was the last night of our last day there and we were in our cabin. It was humid and the cicadas in the trees outside were loud. We were sitting under a blanket with a flashlight, telling stupid scary stories like we used to when we were kids. It was amazing and I was feeling good. Happy. It was strange. Sid was always happy. I don't think I had ever seen him sad. I told some stupid scary story that ended in me jumping up and scaring him. We both rolled over in the bottom bunk, laughing, laying on our backs. At that moment, I was taken over by emotion. I rolled over and laid a big fat one on him. My lips to his. He quickly rolled backwards and wiped his lips with his hand. I still remember his words.

"What the hell. man? Gross!" he said in a way I had never seen Sid act before. I laid there traumatized, unsure of what to do. Sid didn't look happy. It was the first time I had seen Sid without a smile on his face. It made me feel sick that I did that to him. I was disgusted.

"Just kidding, man!" I said, trying to recover from the situation. The kiss didn't feel good at all, so, in my mind I was thinking: *oh, thank god, I must not be gay.* In reality, the kiss wasn't good for so many different reason, many of which I didn't know at the time. It was mainly because it was Sid, but it goes far deeper than that. The summer ended and Sid and I went on pretending like nothing had ever happen .

The next year, sophomore year, was a big one for our friendship. We added a few new faces to our friend group: Corina and Concha. They were my first friends who were girls and it was very weird. Even though you would never guess it now, looking at how much they act like brother and sister, Sid and Corina dated. I was not okay with it at first, but I got used to it after seeing them together everyday. Corina and I were close. We both had some issues with our parents. Her mom was very mean, sometimes abusive, and she knew about my dad leaving my mom. We bonded over that. She and Sid still had a closer bond, though. I was always trying to get closer and closer to her, not to be spiteful or anything, but because I wanted to understand what Sid felt for her. That's when things got real; the realest thing I've ever had to deal with in my life.

One weekend, Corina and Concha decided to have a "girl's weekend" and, for some reason, they invited me. Looking back at it, I see why. We were staying at Corina's house. It was above her mom's Mexican restaurant and it always smelled like tamales. After hours of hanging out, Concha had to go home because the foster home didn't allow sleepovers, which was understandable. I was left with Corina and we continued talking. I felt like I was really getting to know her and that I could open up to her. We, inevitably, started talking about Sid, since he was the reason we were friends in the first place. That's when I opened a can of worms I really shouldn't have. Corina was talking about a time when Sid's grandmother walked in on them making out in Sid's room and how awkward it was. Trying to one up her story, I abruptly said, "I've kissed Sid," not thinking about how weird it might be to hear another guy say that about your boyfriend.

To my surprise, she said she already knew. She explained to me that when they first started dating, they were both a little insecure about how many people they had been with, so they both made a list naming all the people they had kissed.

I explained to her that this was a secret and that I didn't care that Sid told her but that she had to keep it a secret. Things got really serious after this. She kept mentioning the list. She said that her list was longer then Sid's but they never got around to going over her's. I could tell that she wanted to talk about it, so I kept the conversation going.

"Who was on Sid's list? Besides me?" I asked, curious, knowing Sid had only had about a hand full of girlfriend by this point.

"I don't remember any of them besides two," she said, not looking at me. I remember going over all the names that I could remember in my head. I could think of at least four he probably kissed, so it was weird to me his own girlfriend couldn't recall any. Things got more intense as she grabbed my hands. I remember the next few moments word for word.

"You told me a secret of yours today, right?" she said, gripping my hands as I nodded. "And you know I wont tell anyone?" she asked. I nodded again. "The names on the list; I only remember two because there were only two on it," she said, not looking at me. I was confused. I knew one of the names was mine.

"And who was the other one?" I asked, curious.

"Brighton, you can't tell anyone I'm telling you this, okay? Sid would kill both of us. I shouldn't even be telling you, but it's too much for me to handle." Realizing that the mood had changed, I got more serious. I crossed my legs and sat up straight. "All he had written on his list was Bright and Jay."

My heart stopped. The name sunk into me. We both sat in silence and I started shaking with rage. This was the first time I experienced a panic attack. Jay was the name of Sid's mom's boyfriend when we were in seventh grade, the same year Sid started trying to get girlfriends.

"So that means..." I said, calming down. Corina had tears in her eyes.

"Don't tell anyone. Don't tell Sid that you know," she said, crying. I understood everything in that moment. Why Sid lived with his grandma. Why he never talked about his mom. Poor Sid. I don't feel bad that Corina told me. This is a lot for a fifteen year old girl to keep all to herself, let alone the sixteen year old boy it happened to.

The story doesn't stop there. Sid and Corina broke up a couple weeks later and we all decided to continue being friends. I never found out exactly why they broke up, but I have a feeling it had to do with me. A week before the break up, I accidentally told Sid that I knew about what happened to him. It was one of the worst slips of the tongue that I've ever had in my life and, to this day, my body aches when I think about it.

It was just a random Wednesday after school. It should have been a normal night; a good one. I had just gotten my first phone that I had saved up for for months and Sid was excited to help me download all the apps he used and teach me how to use them. He tried to convince me to download a dating app because "my virginity was scaring off all the ladies." We joked around when I refused to download the app. The next few seconds haunt me because I feel like I was the worst kind of human: the kind who can't keep secrets.

"I've been with someone. Kinda," I said, thinking back to the kiss in Paris. Sure, it was just a kiss, but Sid didn't need to know that.

"Oh yeah? Who?" Sid asked mockingly.

"You don't know them," I said, trying to get out of

the conversation.

"Oh, is poor little Bright ashamed that I was his first kiss?" he said, puckering his lips, referring back to that night in summer camp.

"You're just mad that I wasn't yours!" I said, embarrassed that Sid would even bring that up.

"What do you mean?" he said as he stopped laughing. "How do you know it wasn't mine?" he said seriously. I attempt to change the subject. "No, wait. What do you know?" he asked, completely serious now.

I freeze. I can't think of what to say to stop this from happening. My hands were shaking as I began to speak.

"You, you know, your like, you were," I said in a shaky voice.

"I was what? Brighton?" he said, using my full name. It was so unlike Sid.

"I'm sorry, I just- Corina... you told her about us an-" he cut me off.

"Well, yes. That sick bastard felt me up when I was little. My mom never believed me and that's how I ended up here. You happy?" he said angrily.

"No, Sid, I'm not happy! I'm so sorry!" I said, realizing that I had just made the biggest of mistake of my young life.

"Don't apologize. You didn't do anything wrong." He looked at me.

"But I did, in the cabin." My eyes began to water.

"No no no, hey, no, none of that," Sid said. He hates crying.

"If I had known, Sid, I would have never kissed you. I don't even know why I did that. It was horrible. I'm so sorry!" I sobbed as all my emotions ran through my body.

"Do you know why I told Corina about this?" he said in a calm voice. "Because I wanted to make sure she would still treat me the same," he said. He sounded so mature. I was taken aback by how this goofy looking guy could be so put together.

"And that's exactly what I'm not doing," I said, wiping my eyes.

"If I'm not crying about it, why are you?" he said, half-smiling.

The rest of the night was weird. Sid wasn't completely normal and I was trying to overcompensate for my actions earlier that night. I tried to be too normal. Things slowly went back to how they were before. That's how Sid and I became not only best friends, but brothers. He's someone who, no matter what, will always be my rock and I'll be his. Sid and Bright.

Sid is arriving tomorrow. Naomi is coming over to help me plan my birthday party after school. There are a few things on my to-do list. The most important thing is to have the best 18th birthday ever, but, since Sid is going to be here, I don't think that will be a problem. Second, I have to tell Carter that I'm dating his sister. And last, I have to deal with those jerks at school. I feel like a horrible person, and I might be, but it's only temporary. I can't deal with Sid being here and those jerks at school. I just can't. Naomi can get those guys off my back. She's popular and pretty. I feel guilty, so I haven't been able to sleep. I don't lie, never have. It's eating me up inside. It's a type of stress that I can't seem to shake.

I'm sitting in class, tapping my pencil obsessively. Ever since the trip, I've been jumpy. I can't think straight. I feel like my guard is always up.

"Pre-party jitters?" Naomi asks as she grabs the pencil from my hand.

"Yeah, I guess."

"It will be fine! We're still thinking about having it at the old warehouse, right?"

"Yeah, I want to go all out!" I say, thinking purely of blowing Sid's socks off.

"That I can do, but it will cost you."

"I'm going all out. I'll spend as much as I have to."

"I wasn't talking about money. I was thinking more along the lines of you spending some alone time with me." She smiles.

"Or that." We both giggle. Carter looks back at us and smiles.

As much as I wish it could wait until after I eat lunch, I have to tell Carter or my heart might explode. Once I do that, Naomi and I are planning on going public and spreading the word to everyone. The bell rings and I run up to Carter.

"We're skipping!" I say, grabbing his arm.

"Yep, you're coming with us." Naomi grabs his other arm.

"I'm not objecting," he says, shaking us off. "Who needs chem anyways."

We go out to the parking lot and get in my car. We drive off so we don't get caught, but we pull over to the side of the road since everything is too spread out in this damn town to actually go anywhere.

"Okay, you tell him!" Naomi says giddily.

My heart sinks. I'm about to tell another lie. What if he asks me questions about why I like Naomi? Will I have to lie again?

"Carter, well, I-I'm going out with Naomi now." I grab her hand.

"Yep! He's all mine!" Naomi sticks out her tongue to Carter. *Weird,* I think. But Naomi's always weird, so I move past it.

"Oh wow," he says in a neutral tone.

"Yep." I say back in an even more neutral tone.

"Naomi, can I talk to your boyfriend alone?"

"Where am I supposed to go?"

"Stand outside. Please?" Carter asks. Naomi obeys.

"You're lucky you're the older twin," she says, getting out of the car and slamming the door, leaning up against the window.

"Am I just supposed to pretend you didn't kiss me?" Carter whispers.

"Carter, please, just don't." I'm shaking and he clearly notices.

"I just don't know what to do here, Brighton. This is a weird situation. She's my sister, and I get you're scared, but you can't do this to her."

"I'm not you, Carter. I can't just do this."

"You think I was born this brave? I was just like you once, but I was considerate enough not to mess with other people's feeling," he says, still whispering.

"I like Naomi," I say, still shaking, feeling my throat tighten.

"No, you like me," Carter says, no longer whispering.

"Shhhhhh!" I say, covering his mouth with my hands.

"Wow, really? This is how you want to spend your senior year? Afraid every second?" he says, ripping my hands away. "What's stopping me from telling her myself, huh?" He's whispering again.

"You wouldn't," I say, shaking my head.

"I could..." he says. I can tell he's bluffing..

"Gay scouts honor. You wouldn't," I say, trying to lighten the mood, or else I might start crying .

"So, you're gay when it suits you?"

122

"You know what I mean, Carter, please?" He looks at me with disappointment in his eyes. I feel myself breaking.

"Please, just 'til after Sid leaves. Please. Please! Sid can't find out. Please."

"Just 'til after your birthday? Then you will tell her?"

"Yes. Just 'til after my birthday." My voice shakes. I'm suddenly scared shitless of what I just agreed to.

"Fine," he says, not whispering anymore, "but if she asks me anything, I'm not lying."

"Deal," I say, knocking on the window to get Naomi's attention.

"Those guys at school have won, you realize," Carter says quietly as Naomi gets in the car.

"Jeez, guys, it's freezing out there. Let's head back," Naomi says, shivering in the backseat.

"Oh, I almost forgot! I updated my Facebook. Your turn." She pulls out her phone and shows me her screen.

I pull out my phone and change my status. Carter coughs to show his disapproval and I start the car and drive back to school.

Gym class. The one class I have with the idiot jocks of senior year. I have since learned that my lovely and most adamant tormentor's name is Jean. He is here on a field hockey scholarship. He isn't the most wealthy or smartest kid here, but he is the best player on the team and basically loved by everyone. I walk into the gym, expecting the worse. Carter's walking in front of me, keeping his head held high. My locker is right next to his and Jean's is on the other side. I hear him talking with his friends and my nerves are heightened. I hear his voice getting closer. I quickly slip my gym shorts on and change my shirt.

"Hey, uh, Brighton, can we talk?" he says as he comes around the corner. I look at Carter but he doesn't look back at me.

"Uh, sure?" I say, walking with him to his locker.

"Rick says you scored with the queer's sister."

"Well, yeah. I guess." I say, extremely uncomfortable with more than half the words he chose to use in that sentence.

"Hey, listen, thanks for not telling the principal about the spray paint."

I think about the fact that I didn't do it for them, I did it to keep my closet doors tightly locked.

"Yeah, no problem," I say, still extremely uncomfortable. I walk away and go back to my locker.

"Look at you go," Carter says, slamming his locker shut and walking out of the room. I feel like a horrible person.

Halfway through the day, Naomi texts me about party ideas. We decide on a DJ, a location, decorations, everything. Sid keeps randomly texting me to ask details about tomorrow like: will he have to sleep on a couch? What will he do if he wants to jerk off while he's here? Do flight attendants listen to you poop on the airplane? I just ignore all his texts. He is just freaking out because it's his first time flying.

The atmosphere at lunch is weird. I'm sitting with Naomi and Carter, but we're not talking. Naomi says some stuff to me about the party but I don't say much back. Carter's words keep playing over and over in my head; *those guys at school have won.* It makes me sick. I feel like they didn't win. I feel like we're all still playing this game and I just pressed pause. But, I see where he is coming from. I am hiding myself more because of them. In L.A, I never felt the need to date girls. No one questioned me for not talking about who I had a crush on. It was simple; if I wanted to talk I would, even if I was vague. But there weren't any bullies back home. Yeah, maybe people aren't waking around worshiping the rainbow flag, but everyone accepted that some kids were gay and moved on. Obviously, good old Connecticut is a little bit behind the times. The bell rings and my last few classes fly by.

Hey, can you take care of the last details for the party? I just want to go home alone. I feel sick, I text Naomi as I pull out of the school parking lot. Another lie. I'm not sick. Sure, I feel horrible, not physically, but in an "I need to grow the hell up" way. It's 4 o'clock. Mom has dinner ready when I get home.

"The guest bedroom is all set for Sid," she says, handing me a Coke to go with my sandwich.

"He will be glad he has a room to himself," I say, thinking back to his texts.

"Your party all set up?"

"Yeah. Naomi's dealing with the finishing touches," I say, scarfing down the sandwich.

"Naomi! What a sweet girl!" Mom says, looking out the windows in front of the sink.

"Shit!" I say out loud

"Language!" Mom shouts as I get up from the table and run upstairs. I run into Elliott's room and he is sitting on his phone.

"Don't tell Mom!" I say, knowing he has already

seen it.

"You mean, don't tell Mom about your girlfriend?" he says, pulling up my Facebook page.

"I swear, you don't know what you're dealing with here. Don't tell her." I'm trying to show him how serious I am. If this lie reaches home, I don't know what I will do.

"I don't see what the big deal is. She's hot," Elliott says, scrolling through Naomi's page.

Well, Elliot's straight... I think in my head. It's not that I ever thought he wasn't, but when I was his age, I had already kissed a boy and was too embarrassed to ever say a girl was "hot", especially one so much older then me.

"Promise?" I say, sitting down on the bed beside him.

"Okay, fine, on one condition," he says, putting down the phone.

"Anything."

"I'm invited to your party."

"Um, anything but that," I say, knowing it's not a good idea.

"Hey, Mom!" Elliott screams.

"Yes, honey?" I hear from downstairs.

"Nothing, Mom!" I yell back. "Fine, fine, fine, but you have to get Mom to agree to let you go."

"Easy," he says, getting up and grabbing my arm. "Now, get out!" He closes his door behind me.

"Teenagers," I say as if I'm not one of them.

I go into my room and lay down, scrolling on my Facebook. There's so many likes on Naomi's post, but hardly any on mine. Lin and Concha liked it. I'll have to explain to them, later, what this was all about. I'm sure they will get a kick out of it. My situation starts to sink in when I'm alone. I'm, well, gay. I'm slowly getting more and more okay with that. I'm a teenage boy and I can't deny when something turns me on. It's kind of hard to ignore. I'm ready to get drunk at my party and forget who I am for a while.

"Oh, that reminds me!" I say to myself. I pull out my phone.

Did you ever get that ounce? My friend is a total pothead and will be bummed if you didn't :(. I hit send.

Not a second goes by before my phone vibrates.

Gotcha covered! <3, Naomi replies.

My eyes grow heavy. With no social life, I find myself falling asleep around eight. If I was in L.A, it would only be five and I would just be getting home from school. *Time zones are weird* are my final thought before my eyes win and I pass out.

It's my last day as a seventeen year old. I don't feel any different. My stomach is turning with excitement because Sid is already on the plane. It's Friday, but I'm skipping school for Sid. I'm not really skipping because my mom knows about it, but, still, it feels good. Once again, I have a huge to-do list before Sid arrives. I want to show him what it's like to live like royalty for a week. First , I had to go grocery shopping. I bought the basics: Hot Cheetos, Marshmallow Fluff and rye bread. I also got steaks and fancy cheese, anything I could see a king eating in my head. I even thought about buying caviar, but I, honestly, think it's gross.

Next step: weed. I have to go see Naomi and pick it up from her. I know when Sid gets off that plane he is going to need something to calm himself down.

Come on out! I text her as I pull up to Carter's house. Well, Naomi's house. It has always felt like Carter's house, to me, since that first morning with the sausages. Naomi comes out and knocks on my window.

"Here's your stuff," she says without hesitation

"Thanks!" I say, grabbing it and shoving it in my glovebox.

"Now I have to get back to working on your party. It's tomorrow, 9pm, in the old warehouse off 32nd, okay?" she says, walking back to her house. I roll up my window and drive away.

Last step: pick Sid up from the airport. It's about an hour away. It's my first time driving in the new car for so long, so I turn on the speakers and plug in my phone. *Panic! At The Disco, Shawn Mendes* and *Troye Sivan* keep me company on the way there. It's cold outside, but I have the back windows down anyways. The air blows on the back of my neck. The drive feels too short as I pull up to the airport. I check my phone and Sid's plane landed twenty minutes ago. I scan the crowd of people around the sliding glass doors, looking for Sid's floppy hair or his beanie. I look down at people's feet and I suddenly spot them; two mismatched Vans, one pink and one green. They are moving towards me. I look up and there it is: Sid's goofy face.

"My man!" Sid opens the passenger door and hops in. I don't even say hi back before I'm grabbing him and hugging him as tight as I can.

"Sid, Sid, Sid," I say, roughing up his hair as I release our hug.

"Missed you too, Bright." He looks at me and I look at him.

"Long drive, buckle up!" I say, pulling out of the airport.

"Nice car by the way!" Sid says, inspecting the seat belt buckle.

I don't say anything and drive away. Sid and I don't have to talk to get our emotions across. We can be in the same space and know everything each other is thinking.

"So, a girlfriend, huh?" Sid says questioningly.

"Yeah," I say, not looking at him, keeping a straight face.

"'Atta boy," Sid says, looking forward, just like me. I smile. He looks at me and his smile gets bigger. For once, we can talk about girls together..

"So, my big B, your no longer the big V I take it?" I panic and quickly gather my thoughts.

"No, man, I mean, well, yeah, no, wait." My words don't come out right.

"Whoa, slow down. Speak." He says, laughing at my word vomit.

"We're waiting," I say, more calm now.

"That's cool, man. I know you were always a little shy about those things. I respect that," Sid says, nodding.

Sid. He is so nice. The nicest teenage boy I know. Any other guy would make fun of an eighteen year old who is "waiting" to sleep with his girlfriend. It's not like I'm religious or anything, he knows that. He just takes what he hears, accepts it and understands it.

"Oh shit! I almost forgot. Your present is in the glove box," I say, gesturing.

"It's your birthday and you got me a present?" he says, opening it. His eyes light up. "My man! Got a light?"

I hand him a lighter from my cup holder. He grabs some rolling paper from inside his beanie and rolls a joint. I roll down the windows, trying not to make the car smell like The Stoner Shack.

"Want a hit?" Sid says, holding the joint up to my mouth. I take it in and hold it, breathing out without coughing this time.

"A pro." Sid says, clapping his hands and laughing.

Sid tells me about all the things I've missed back in L.A. during the drive home. It makes me sad, but, since nothing terrible has happened, it makes me smile. He is having a good senior year.

We enter the house and Mom is making lunch. I told her to have the steak ready for when we arrive as a "welcome to my new life" present for Sid.

"Smells great," Sid says as he walks in the kitchen. Mom is focused on setting the table. She only sets two plates because she knows that Sid and I probably want to be alone.

"You boys have a seat. The steaks are almost ready."

"Steak? Damn, what's the occasion?" Sid says, sitting down.

"You," I say, smiling. He smiles back at me and then at my mother. Our plates are put in front of us and Mom goes to her bedroom.

"What's our plan before the party tomorrow?" Sid asks, scarfing down his steak.

"I was thinking we could go shopping," I say sheepishly.

"Shopping. Okay, I'm down."

"Remember back in freshman year, when we would just spend all our time at the mall just being idiots?" Sid says as he cuts his steak.

"I almost forgot about that!" I say, remembering all the good times we spent back then. We never had the money to shop, but we still went the mall all the time.

"Anyways! Let's give you the tour," I say, getting up from the table and putting both our plates in the sink. I walk Sid upstairs. Elliott's bedroom is empty since he is still at school. We stop by the guest bedroom and put Sid's backpack down.

"Oh, sick, no sofa for me!" He says, looking at the queen sized bed.

"And here's my room." We walk in and I sit down in the chair.

"Nice mirror," Sid says, pointing to the only other piece of furniture in my room.

"Thanks." I smile. I like my room. It's simple and it's all mine. Sid and I spend the rest of the day in my room. He is on L.A. time, so I find myself falling asleep before him. I doze off as he talks about Lin and Concha. I feel warm on the inside, and it wasn't from the pot.

"Happy birthday to you!" I'm awoken by Sid and my mom. I rub my eyes.

"What time is it?"

"Shopping time!" Sid says in an overly feminine voice. Mom laughs.

"Oh, right." I get out of bed and take my shirt off. "Let me get changed." I grab my phone and run into the bathroom. I have ten missed calls from Naomi but I ignore them. I brush my teeth and rush downstairs.

"A muffin for each of you." Mom hands us each a

muffin wrapped in a napkin.

"Thanks Ms. A!" Sid says, taking a bite.

"Have fun you two!" Mom says as we move towards the door. "I'll drop Elliott off at your party at nine!" she yells as we leave the house.

"Whoa! You invited little Elliott to your party?" Sid says, licking the muffin crumbs off his palm.

"Long story," I say, staring the car.

"I got nothing but time," he says, crossing his arms.

"He's blackmailing me." Sid laughs as I explain exactly what happened.

"What's the big deal with your mom knowing you got yourself a girl? I think she would be thrilled!"

"Exactly," I mumble. We sit in silence for a moment. Sid understands without me explaining. It's complicated.

"The mall is so empty. It pales in comparison to the mall back home!" Sid laughs as we go into the dressing rooms.

"It's a small town thing," I say from the dressing room next to him.

"I feel like a country club boy," Sid yells

"Good!" I laugh.

We both come out in our chosen outfits. Mine is a pair of black ankle jeans and a white button up shirt with a pocket scarf. Sid is in a pair of light grey chinos and a salmon-colored short sleeve button up shirt.

"Would you gentlemen like some accessories with your ensembles?" a store worker comes up to us and asks.

"Yes, please. Shoes as well," I say as she heads off into the shop. She brings back a pair of shiny black dress shoes for me and a pair of brown leather loafers for Sid. She also brings watches for both of us and a skinny dark blue tie for Sid.

"Thanks. We'll wear all this out," I say as she nods and heads to the register. We're handed a bag with our clothes, which we left in the dressing room.

"Will that be cash or credit, sir?"

"Credit." I swipe my card. We walk out of the store and head to the food court. We sit down at a burger place. Sid orders some fries and I get a simple strawberry shake.

"Man, that was weird," Sid says, looking down at his shirt.

"I know. I felt weird about it at first, but I wanted you to feel like you looked like a million bucks tonight." I smile. He half-smiles. "Trust me, don't worry about it." I put my hand on his shoulder. He smiles normally.

"Fries and a shake!" someone from behind the counter yells. I raise my hand and the food is placed in front of us.

"Happy birthday, man." Sid says, dunking one of his fries in my shake. We sit and eat in silence, completely content.

As we head to Carter's house, I start getting excited. He ordered a limo to take us all to the party so we could drink to our heart's content and nobody would have to drive.

"Carter, this is Sid," I say as we walk up to his front door.

"Sid, cute shirt," he says, looking him up and down.

"Thanks," Sid says, nodding and making eye contact.

I'm jealous. He acts so normal around Carter. When I first met him, I couldn't look at him for more than a few seconds without completely turning to mush.

"Your present," Carter says, pulling out a little baggie containing three small, white squares.

"Oh, sick, what we got?" Sid says, holding the bag up to his face.

"Something to make this party even better!" Carter says, smiling.

"One for each of us," Sid says, opening the bag and handing them out.

"Cheers!" I say. We all put them on our tongues.

"Let's party!" Sid yells as we enter the limo.

"Oh wait, where is Naomi?" I ask, looking out the window.

"Have you checked your messages?" Carter asks, confused. I pull out my phone and remember the ten missed calls. There are fifteen now.

"Oops," I say, opening my voicemail.

"On second thought!" Carter takes my phone. "I think it's better if you don't."

"Weirdos," Sid says, fumbling with a bottle of champagne he found in the limo.

"Let me," Carter says, popping open the bottle. We almost down the entire bottle as we start moving. I'm feeling great.

"Your friend must be a lightweight," Sid whispers to me.

"What?" I say, trying to whisper back.

"He keeps pouring us drinks, but he's only on his first glass." Sid laughs. I never noticed, but Carter is really small and skinny. He's also not very muscular, but more muscular than me or Sid.

The limo stops and we all get out. It's calm and dark outside. The building in front of us is massive. It's ten o'clock. We're fashionably late. The music gets louder as we enter the warehouse. The lights are flashing and there are tons of people, all of which I don't know, but Naomi handled the guest list, so I don't know what I expected.

"Holy shit!" Sid says as he screams and runs onto the dance floor. He looks great in his his outfit. The beanie doesn't really go with the whole look, but I like it. I start to feel loose, like my body wants to move. I want to feel other people's bodies on mine.

What feels like minutes, but what must have been hours, pass as I dance and take shots. Girls are dancing on me. I'm sweaty. Sid is sweaty. Carter is at the DJ stand dancing with the DJ. Sid pulls me in close.

"Where's your girlfriend?" He shouts over the music.

"I don't know. I haven't seen her. Let me cal-" I realize Carter still has my phone.

"Shit, man, I gotta find Carter." I walk away from Sid and into the crowd of people. My vision is doubled and I, somehow, get sucked into a new group of people. I start dancing, getting completely sidetracked.

"Hey," a guy says, dancing close to me.

"Hi," I say, smiling.

"You the birthday boy?" he whispers in my ear.

"In the flesh!" I say, dancing. He pulls me into him and we start dancing together. My shirt is half unbuttoned and he isn't wearing one at all. We're both messed up beyond belief and it's amazing. I grab the back of his neck and scratch my nails down his back. I tug on his short spiky hair and pull him in. I feel our lips touch and mine burn. My whole body feels like it's on fire everywhere he touches me.

"Bright?" I hear from behind me.

"Sid!" I say, falling away from the shirtless guy I was just full-blown making out with.

"I got your phone," he says, handing it to me. "Your...girlfriend? She texted you." He says with a confused tone.

"Okay," I say, continuing to dance.

"Okay then!" Sid says, grabbing my arm. We're dancing arm in arm now. I feel good. My body is still hot. We dance for a long time. The crowd dies down and I start to recognize people from my school.

"Where's Carter?" I ask as we walk over to a table and sit down, dripping in sweat.

"He went home." Sid says, grabbing a bottle of water from a tray that a waiter was carrying.

"Drink up. buddy," he says, putting the bottle to my lips.

"Oh, man, that's good," I say, grabbing the bottle from him and chugging it.

"You might want to look at your phone now," Sid says, gesturing to my pocket.

"Oh shit!" I say, standing up, ignoring Sid. "Where's Elliott?" I frantically look around.

"Oh shit!" Sid stands up as well.

I grab my phone from my pocket. I have so many missed calls and texts but I go past them all and look for ones from Elliott.

Mom never dropped me off, she said it looked too

sketchy. You owe me one for keeping your secret. I sit down and sigh.

"He's fine. He's home." Sid sighs after hearing me say that. I continue to scroll on my phone and see that I have texts from both Carter and Naomi, but my vision is still blurry, so I can't read what they say.

"Sid, read these to me." I hand him my phone.

"You sure, man?" Sid says, grabbing my phone from me.

"Yeah, man, I need to know." I hiccup and look around for more water. Sid reads to himself for a second and then hands me my phone.

"Let's go home, man."

"Aww, are you sure?" He helps me out of my chair and my legs feel like jello.

"I'm sure, bud. You look like a wreck." We both get up and leave, getting into the limo. The driver takes us to Carter's house.

"Can you take us somewhere else?" Sid asks.

"I was instructed by the party planner to drop the birthday boy and friend here," the driver says, not looking at Sid.

"Alrighty then, out we go." Sid helps me. "Brighton, man, look at me. Focus." He taps me on the cheek. "I need you to stand up, okay." I hear his words and straighten my legs.

"I feel good. I feel better," I say. I'm walking now, not perfectly, but better than before. We walk up to the door and knock. Carter answers.

"Birthday boy," Carter says, grabbing our hands. "Did he look at his phone?" I hear him whispers to Sid.

"No, he's too messed up."

"I am not!" I say, grabbing my phone from my pocket. I sit down on the step in Carter's entryway and look through my messages.

> *Naomi: Carter and I talked. It's okay.*
> *Naomi: I kinda knew all along.*
> *Naomi: Enjoy your party.*
> *Naomi: Why did you have to kiss him.*
> *Naomi: I saw you at the pizza place.*
> *Naomi: I'm sorry.*

I cover my mouth and look up at Sid and Carter.

"There's more," Carter says, pointing back at my phone.

> *Carter: I'm so sorry, Brighton.*
> *Carter: oh no I'm so sorry. Please don't hate me!*

I quickly open my Facebook app. I have hundreds of notifications. My relationship status is gone and my wall is filled with pictures from the party. One in particular catches my eyes. It's me on the dance floor with my hands around a random guy. I quickly scroll through the comments. They are horrible. I don't even finish reading one of them before I slam my phone down onto the ground. I collapse into myself.

"Delete it!" I cry, "Get someone to delete it!" I feel my heart beating a mile a minute as the tears stream down my face. Carter grabs my phone and scrolls through the post.

"Someone from another school posted it. I can untag you but we can't delete it."

"Just do something!" I cry, hiding my face from Sid.

"Give us a minute?" Carter says to Sid, showing him to another room.

"Did he see?" I ask, grabbing Carter's hand.

"Yeah, Brighton, I think he did." Carter says, grabbing my hand back. I feel myself start shaking.

"Oh no," I cry. My tears won't stop. They just keep coming out.

"It's okay, Brighton." I feel his arms around me and I start to feel the shaking stop. "You're still pretty messed up. You need to relax," he says, getting up from the step.

"Sid," he calls into the other room, "you're staying here tonight. He can't go home like this. I'll have the maid set up the guest room." Sid nods and they both grab me and pick me up off the ground.

"Don't hate me," I cry into Sid's ear.

"Shhh," he says as we walk up the stairs. I feel myself lay down in a bed. Everything after that is a blur.

13

My eyes are heavy and they feel like they are on fire. I open them and feel two warm bodies around me. Sid is on my left and Carter is on my right. I grab my phone but quickly set it down, remembering last night. I sit and wait for Sid to wake up. Carter opens his eyes and our eyes meet. I'm sitting up and he joins me. We don't talk. He just looks at me and then looks at the phone in my lap. I think he remembers last night as well, since his expression changed when he looked at it. We sit there for what feels like forever. I don't want to move from the bed. I want Sid to wake up. Carter sits next to me and doesn't leave. Sid wakes up, rolls over and looks up at us, probably because we were clearly staring at him.

"Morning sunshines," he says, sitting up.

"Hey," I say, looking down at my phone's black screen.

"Well, I have to take a leak!" Carter gets up and runs out of the room. I smile. He sat with me while I waited for Sid to wake up for as long as he could. He was probably dying the whole time.

"Good guy," Sid says, looking at me.

"Yeah," I say, half-smiling.

"Cute," Sid says, smiling. I look up at him. He

looks good, different from how I imagine I look. After the night I had, I feel like shit.

"Yeah." I smile.

"So, that time you kissed me?" Sid says, laughing

"Yeah," I say.

"Good to know," he smiles.

"Don't flatter yourself," I say, blushing.

"No, no, it's fine. I see you have finer taste now." We both laugh.

"So, you saw what's on my phone?" I ask.

"You kinda asked me to read them to you."
I put my face in my hands, embarrassed.

"It's cool, Bright. You know you're my brother." He grabs my phone from my lap.

"May I?" he says ,unlocking it. I nod and try not to look at his face as he scrolls through my Facebook.

"It's not that bad!" he says, showing me the phone. I read one of the comments that's under the picture. *Hot!* it reads. It's posted by Lin. We both laugh before he continues. "Corina basically ripped everyone in the comments a new one."

"Wow," I say, laying my head back down onto the bed."This is real."

Sid lays down beside me. He doesn't say anything. He doesn't have to.

"Hey." A girl's voice comes from the doorway.

"Hey," I say back to her. Naomi is in her pajamas.

"Sid, this is my, uh, ex-girlfriend." Naomi laughs.

"Nice to meet you, ex-girlfriend," Sid says as he sits up. We all laugh.

"Carter said to come get you guys for breakfast," she says, walking away

"She's cool," Sid says, getting out of bed.

"Yeah, she is."

We head downstairs and the usual spread is laid out; a full breakfast buffet. Sid's face looks just like mine did the first time I saw it.

"Well then, if you would excuse me, I see some bacon that's calling my name." he grabs a plate and some tongs.

"I see why you liked him," Carter says, coming up next to me.

"You were listening to our conversation?"

"I don't take twenty minutes to take a piss, Brighton." I blush.

"I'm cute, huh?" he says as he walks toward the buffet.

I grab a plate and fill it with everything. We all take our food back to the guest room and sit on the bed.

"To sausages!" Carter stabs a sausage on his plate and holds it up.

"To sausages!" Sid shouts. Carter and I lose our minds laughing. "What's so funny?"

"I don't ever want to leave this moment," I say, taking in how I feeling.

"I don't mean to burst your bubble, but I leave tomorrow and we need to get back to yours," Sid says.

"I know," I say, biting into a sausage dipped in syrup.

"Gross!" Carter says, looking at my sticky, sugary sausage link.

"Are you kidding? Sweet and savory is the epitome of all food combinations!" Sid says, covering his sausage with syrup as well.

"Maybe you two are meant to be," Carter says jokingly. We all laugh again. I'm happy.

I'm back in my car in my driveway. Mom is home and so is Elliott. Sid is in the backseat, laying down from his breakfast food coma.

"Sid," I say, not getting out of the car.

"Yeah?" he perks up.

"I don't know what's gonna happen when I go inside," I say, trying not to get emotional.

"Your mom have Facebook?" Sid says, confused

"No, but Elliott does." Sid quickly catches on. I open the door and step out of the car, slowly walking up to the front door. Everything seems normal. There aren't any rainbow streamers. That's a good sign, not that I was expecting any.

"Boys!" Mom says, rushing up to us. "You should have called, Brighton!" she says, giving me a stern look.

"I know, Mom, I was at-"

"I already know. You were at that boy Carter's house. His mom stopped by and we had tea. She was lovely. You should thank her for letting you and Sid stay in her home."

"Wow, Mom, that's great." Sid is holding back his laughter. "Where's Elliott?" I ask, looking around.

"Up in the attic, I think," Mom says, walking back to the kitchen sink.

"To the attic!" Sid says, walking up the stairs. "Where is the little blackmailer?" he says as he looks around the corner and into the attic.

"Sid, hey.," Elliott says calmly.

"Hey, man. I heard you tried to invite yourself to your brother's party. Not cool." Sid gives Elliott a noogie.

"Hey!" Elliott yells, shoving Sid off.

"Have you told Mom?" I ask, just to be sure.

"What? About how you broke up with your stupid girlfriend? No. Who cares?" he says, going back to reading his comic.

"Good. Okay then, back to whatever," Sid says, walking back down the attic stairs.

"Well, it's your lucky day, Brighton. It seems like the untagging worked. I'd unfriend your brother just in case, though." He laughs.

"Already done," I say, putting my phone in my pocket.

"I don't leave for," he looks at his invisible watch, "eighteen hours. What shall we do?"

"Get high and eat Hot Cheeto and Marshmallow Fluff sandwiches?" I say, knowing that he would agree.

"To the kitchen!" Sid runs down the stairs.

"What are you looking for?" Mom yells as Sid and I rummage through the cabinets.

"It's for later!" I say, grabbing the jar of fluff. "To the car!" I grab a butter knife for maximum fluff spreadability.

"No running with knives!" Mom yells as we run out the front door. We drive to a nearby park and sit in my car smoking, laughing, and eating.

"I'm gonna miss you, man," I say, looking at Sid as he licks his red spicy fingers.

"I'm only a flight away."

"I was thinking about applying to some colleges in California," I say nonchalantly.

"No shit!" Sid says excitedly

"I haven't thought about that," he says, looking

down at his lap

"Where you're applying?"

"If I'm going." He shakes his head as if he is disappointed in himself.

"Hey, if I can be gay, you can go to college!" We laugh.

"To college!" I say, holding up a Cheeto.

"To being gay!" Sid says, holding up a joint. We cheers.

"Don't tell anyone I'm eating one of your famous sandwiches."

"You know you love them."

We spend the rest of his time here enjoying each other's company.

Sometimes I forget that I'm a big brother. It's not like I forget Elliott exists, but, somewhere in my mind, I lose the fact that he sometimes needs me for things; and that I need him for things too. It's Monday morning. The first school day since my party. I'm terrified. I know school will suck and I know those jerks will start messing with me again. But, all those worries pale in comparison when I remember that I'm a brother. I feel my insides twist for Elliott. Will word get around to him that his brother's a "big queer", as they like to call it in these parts.

"Mom! I'm driving today!" I grab Elliott by his backpack strap and drag him out the front door.

"Stop!" he says, swatting at my hands.

I pull up to the school parking lot and my mind feels like mush, but the words that have to come out just start flowing.

"You might hear some things about me at school today."

"Like what? That your gay?" I shoot him a look. "Just because you unfriend me doesn't mean I can't see everyone's posts about you, Brighton," Elliott says, looking out the window, avoiding my glances.

"If anyone gives you trouble, you tell me, okay."
He looks at me and smiles. Our eyes finally meet and
nothing feels different. "Good. Now get of my car, you're
cramping my style!"

It was easy. Nothing went wrong. A meteor didn't
suddenly come from the sky and destroy everything I care
about and the air around me feels slightly lighter.

"Morning." Carter walks up to me.

"Hey, where's Naomi?" I ask, since they usually
are together in the morning

"Sick... or that's what she told father."

"Oh?"

"Yeah. She seems to thinks everyone will think she
turned you gay."

"Yikes!" I say, walking into the hallway.

"Yeah. So she sent me to make sure everyone
knows it was actually me!" He smiles and walks in front
of me, walking backwards.

"No, actually, I think it was that guy in Paris..."

"Oh, the truth comes out!"

"Everything does eventually!" I say, grabbing his
shoulders and turning him around to walk the right way.

"Get a room!" I hear in Jean's unmistakable voice
echoing down the long corridor.

"You know you love to watch!" Carter yells back. I
laugh.

"Thanks."

"Didn't do it for you," he says, looking down and
smiling.

"You don't think people will give my little brother
shit for this, right?"

"He's in middle school, yeah?"

"Yeah"

"No. Those jerks don't get their homophobic hard-ons 'til high school. It's usually induced by some awkward gym locker room situation followed by a lot of denial."

"No way! You think Jean is gay?"

"I mean, he was friends with Trevor, but no, not really. It's just my mind trying to come up with a logical reason as to why someone can be such an ass." Carter tugs on his shirt collar and walks into home room.

"Now, kids, I know you're not in the mood to learn, since fall break is in a week, but I'm assigning you a group project. Write something, an article, but it must be based on our school. Pick your partner and have fun. I'll choose the most deserving piece and print it in the school magazine." Mr. Briggs sits down at his desk and pulls out a newspaper.

"Dibs!" Carter says, scooting his desk close to mine.

"Not like anyone else was gonna beat you to it." I look around.

"Now, for our project, I say we write an article about the homophobes of our hopeless hallways"

"Catchy name." I laugh at his enthusiasm.

"I know! Just thought of it!" he brags.

"Is it really a good idea to bring attention to ourselves?" I look around at everyone's faces, each of their voices blending into one mummer.

"Well, people are already talking about you since your party, and you did say you were worried about your brother. Think of the future."

The future. I haven't been able to think about that

recently. Time keeps moving and, sooner or later I'll be gone. I don't mean i'll be dead, but I'll be away at college. Well, that's basically the same thing in my mind at the moment.

"Okay. Let's do it," I say.

"Yes!" Carter grabs my hand.

The bell rings and I head to free period. Carter goes to chem and I'm left alone for forty-five minutes. I want to reach out and make more friends, but, with my current social status, it doesn't seem promising. Who wants to be friends with the new kid who happens to be the target of the school's biggest asshole? That's like purposely putting a target on your own back. Carter is great, but I'm alone anytime our schedules differ. As usual, I end up walking to the middle school corridor. It's safe. Nobody knows me, and if they do, they are probably scared of me since I'm a "big bad senior."

"Brighton?" I hear from behind me.

"Elliott, why aren't you in class?"

He holds up a large piece of wood on a string that says *bathroom.*

"Ah. How's it going?"

"The same as usual. Nobody is picking on me because of you. Don't worry." I smile at his nonchalant response. Elliott seems to be maturing. I don't know what it is, but I feel like I can have an actual conversation with him now. Usually with little siblings, it's like they aren't real people until your both, like, in your thirties, but, somehow, Elliott's caught up. It's somewhat comforting, but a little scary to think about.

"Well, I'm glad I'm not causing you trouble, but keep your head up, those kids are the idiots, not you."

"Nothing I can't handle. Don't worry." He smiles.

"Get back to class." I rustle his hair and walk past him.

"Get out of the middle school building! You look like a creep!" he yells back as I turn the corner.

I'm alone again. There's twenty minutes left until my next class. I could leave, but it's honestly too much of a hassle. I contemplate this every day, whether I should risk being late to gym to leave during free period. I would have just enough time to go to the Starbucks at the mall and get a drink, but only if I ran to my car and there was no line.

I end up taking a seat in the school garden and pulling out my laptop. Research for my and Carter's project is harder than I thought. There really hasn't ever been any online documentation of anything even remotely gay at this school. Heck, it's like the school refuses to acknowledge that there are gay students to begin with. It's odd, considering the headmaster's son is one of them. I take out my notebook and write: *Ask Carter about coming out to his Dad? Mom? Sister?* The bell rings and makes me jump. It's crazy how times flies when you're concentrating.

Gym class. Today we are in the weight room. It's every straight guy's wet dream: getting graded on lifting weights. It's probably the only good grade any of them will ever get. I hate it. My arms are like spaghetti and they can't lift anything impressive. I can't even do a pull-up. Carter has muscles, not like ones you would see on a football player, but more like the muscles of a soccer player. He always spends weight days on this weird machine with a bunch of strings and weights. It's impressive, even though he doesn't have it on the heaviest setting. I'm envious.

"Ready?" Carter comes up behind me, already dressed.

"Give me a minute," I say, taking my pants off.

"I'll be in there. Gotta get the bench press before someone else does!"

He goes on ahead without me and I take my time getting dressed. The locker room is already half-empty, with just a few scrawny stranglers left, like me. Bench press. That's new. Carter must be trying to bulk up.

Trying to procrastinate, I peek my head into the gym. Everyone's already locked into their work-out. I can hear the girl's gym class across the hall, listening to some loud hispanic-sounding music. I look in and they are dancing. Brightly-colored leggings and tank tops flash before my eyes. I laugh at the thought of me and Carter dancing like that instead of lifting weights. I turn back to the gym and open the door a crack to look for Carter. He is on his back, lifting what looks like pretty heavy weights. Some junior with curly hair is spotting him.

"Peeping tom!" Someone pushes the door open and I see Jean's grubby hand only inches from my face.

"Sorry. I was just making sure I was in the right place," I say, knowing that excuse won't work. I'm not new anymore.

"No, you knew what you were doing." He grabs the back of my shirt and pulls me through the door.

"Look what I caught, boys!" He pulls me toward the middle of the gym. The coach isn't here, as usual, and Jean's field hockey friends whistle and cheer as he jerks me inside.

"Quit it, Jean!" Carter gets up from his machine.

"Oh sorry, did I upset your little boyfriend?" he says, shoving me to the ground. A case of medicine balls gets knocked over as I fall and one lands on right my hand. I scream as my hand gets crushed beneath it.

"Brighton!" Carter runs over to my aid and lifts the ball off.

"I'm alright. I'm alright," I say, rubbing my hand. It's already looking bruised and my knuckles are bright red. The stinging feeling slowly fades away..

"Look what you did!" Carter walks up to Jean.

"Oh, did I hurt your boyfriend's hand job hand? Oh, what will you do?" Jean pouts his lips like a baby.

"Luckily, both my hands work fine!" In an instant, Carter's fist moves straight into Jean's cheek. The sound of the impact is almost comical.

Jean looks at Carter as he rubs his face. Then, he looks at me. I'm still sitting on the floor, rubbing my hand. Suddenly, I see a foot coming towards me, hitting me right in the stomach. My breath is taken away and, before I know it, I'm in fetal position, gasping for air. My whole body feels lifeless.

"Brighton!" Carter gets down on the floor and rolls me onto my back.

"Kick his ass," I say, still gasping for air.

I look up and see the junior that was spotting Carter walking up to Jean. He is big, almost bigger than Jean.

He walks up, point blank, and kicks Jean straight in the family jewels. He falls to the floor beside me. An unfamiliar hand is held out to me.

"I'm Jack," he says as he puts my hand on his

shoulder to help me stand up. Carter takes my other side.

"Never had a guy kick another guy in the balls for me before." I laugh but it hurts my sides.

"He had it coming," Jack says as he walks me to the door of the gym.

"Someone tell the coach what happened here," he says as we walk off.

"I'll go tell him. You take him to the office and get him some ice," Carter says, running off. I'm able to stand without any help now.

"I'm Brighton, by the way."

"I know. Carter always talks about you." He smiles.

"Oh, so you guys are, like, friends?"

"I'm in his chem class."

"Are all your classes advanced? " I ask, curious as to why a junior is in two of Carter's classes.

"I'm kind of a nerd when it comes to science and I love gym. I requested them to double up on credits."

"You have gym twice a day?" I ask.

"Yeah," he laughs.

"Damn! Jean might wanna have his nuts checked!" We laugh. It still hurts.

"You gonna be okay?" he says, looking at me as I grab my stomach. "A little bruised, but he didn't hit you anywhere bad," Jack says as he lifts up my gym shirt slightly.

"Let me guess, you wanna be a doctor?" I ask as he examines my stomach.

"Sports related physiotherapy, actually," he says, smiling

"Close enough..."

He walks me to the office and I wait for the nurse while he returns to class. I think I made a friend. The nurse asks if I want to go home for the day, but I decline. I still want to ask Carter some questions for our project. I did take her up on her offer to sleep it off in the nurse's office until lunch, though.

"Looking brand new!" Carter says as I walk up to the bench he is sitting on, which is just far enough away from the cafeteria that you can't hear everyone eating.

"Glad I look better than I feel." I gingerly sit down.

"You stayed and Jean left. How insane is that?" he says, taking a drink of his Coke.

"Jean went home?"

"Yes, and good riddance!" Carter shouts dramatically. I rustle his hair. Lifting my arms hurts my stomach.

"Oh, that reminds me!" I pull out my notebook and pen. "I'm going to interview you for our project!"

"Okay, shoot," he says, looking at me with a smile.

"How did your da- I mean the headmaster take it when you told him that you're gay?"

15

"It's a long story," Carter says, shifting into a more comfortable position. "I'm gonna start from the beginning. Take notes on whatever is interesting to you," he says, crossing his legs and sitting up straight.

"When I was in the fourth grade, yes, fourth grade, I had a girlfriend. Her name was Tiffany, or Tif, for short. She was blonde and wore spongebob socks everyday. One day, in the park down the street from here, we decided we should kiss. So, we did. It was horrible! She smelled like fruit snacks and her mouth was all sticky. I broke up with her right there, on the spot. I know. I've always been a total heartbreaker, you don't even have to say it." He laughs.

"Anyways, fast forward to 6th grade. I had another girlfriend; one of Naomi's friends from Girl Scouts. Her name was Amelia. She was also blonde and kinda pudgy. She had a peacock as a pet in her backyard, I kid you not. That's why I started going out with her. 'Cuz, as a 6th grader, I thought that was soulmate worthy. Anyways, we kissed and stuff. It was fun, but I wasn't really into it. We would even make out. It was really wild at the time. The summer of 6th grade, I had been dating

Amelia for about 2 months, and, as a 6th grader, that's like the equivalent to marriage, so it was a big deal. Then, one day, at the pool, I met a boy. His name was Trevor. He was cute and had curly, bleached hair and tan skin. A 9th grader. I started following him around like a lost puppy. He was, like, the coolest guy I had ever met. After a week of being around him, I broke up with Amelia. I knew I didn't like her, let alone girls." He smiles.

"But, you know, because she was Naomi's friend, she went crying to her and begged her to convince me to go out with her again. Naomi came into my room one night and asked me to go out with Amelia again. I said no, of course, since I had already moved on from that side of the dating pool in my mind. She went on for hours, asking me why I wouldn't go out with her and was basically begging me. So, I just flat out said, 'sis, I like boys!' Naomi being Naomi, she made a big deal out of it. She called Amelia and told her I liked somebody else. I'm still surprised to this day that she didn't tell her the whole story. Anyways, summer ended and I went on into 7th grade, where I went through the typical puberty and all that nonsense. 8th grade came. I was a man now, or that's what my dad told me. I was still gay, obviously." I laugh.

"So, what happened next?" I say, vigorously jotting down Carter's words in my notebook.

"Well, Brighton," he says, uncrossing his legs and scooting closer to me.

" I didn't come out to my dad for another year. My mom came first and she wasn't surprised. Moms always know that kinda thing. I insisted that she didn't tell Dad and she didn't. It's crazy to think someone like Naomi came from a woman like her. So, fast forward to freshman year. Dad was going on three years as headmaster and he was trying to crack down on the locker room drug problem. I had caught up with Trevor from when I was little. He was now a senior and I was still obsessed with him, even though he grew a creepy pathetic mustache. Anyways, I couldn't be seen with him around school because rumors that I liked boys had circulated and he was very, very, very in the closet. So, one day during lunch, we decided to sneak off into the locker rooms to hang out."

"Your first kiss!" I say, remembering the story on the bus to New York.

"Be patient. You don't know the second half of that story." I nod and gesture for him to keep talking.

"Okay, well, we usually would just sit and talk, but I was telling him about this movie I saw the night before. It was just some weird, foreign, run of the mill LGBT coming of age film I found on Netflix. I told him, in detail, about how the main character was a jock and they would sneak off to the football field and hookup. This made him so turned-on that he kissed me. It turned into a full on make-out sesh. The kiss felt like it lasted forever. My middle school fantasies were coming true. Then, suddenly, the locker room door opened and the room filled with light. Standing there, in front of me, as I had a boy's tongue down my throat, was my father."

"No," I gasp.

"Yes. He was furious. He thought when he got an anonymous tip that his son and a jock were seen going to the locker room at lunch, that I was selling his prescription drugs to the lacrosse team. Jokes on him, that was Naomi, but I think he would have rather seen me doing a drug

157

deal than the alternative. Trevor got up and ran. Dad let him go, since he was trying to deal with his son: sloppy haired, red faced, sweaty, semi hard-on, you know, the usual. He took me to his office and we had a really weird talk. We have never talk about it to this day." Carter takes a sip of his water, parched from telling that long-winded story

"Never?"

"Not a word. I'm sure him and Mom talked, but I've been left in the dark"

"And Trevor?"

"He never talked to me again, really. Well, not as my boyfriend, at least. He left a note in my locker saying he was confused and to leave him out if it. Now he's graduated and has been dating a girl for a year or so."

"Wow," I say, closing my notebook.

"Yeah, I know."

The bell rings and Carter and I part ways. I have French and he has history. My mind races when I think of his story.

"Moms know these kinds of things?" I whisper to myself in class, recalling Carter's words. Surely not my mom. My mind swirls the rest of the day. Carter is too good at telling stories.

There's a knock on my door, which is unusual, since we tend to keep to ourselves in this family.

"Bright?"

"Elliott?" I say as my door opens.

"What's up?" he says, walking in and sitting at the foot of my bed.

"Nothing." I close my laptop and we stare at each other for a few seconds.

"Are you staying home all day today?" he finally asks.

"No, it's Saturday. I'm going out."

"Where to?"

"Carter and I are going to the school library to do some research."

"Do you need some help? What kind of research?" he pries.

"Well, we're going to be going through the old year books for a writing assignment."

"Oh," he says, sounding disappointed.

"Sorry, bud." I get out of bed and slip my shoes on. Elliott pulls out his phone and starts texting, as usual. For someone who is desperate enough for social interaction to want to help his brother with school work, you have to wonder who he is texting all the time.

The school library looks more like a cafe that happens to have books in it. There are tables, a coffee bar, and it's open on weekend. It's actually a cool place. A lot of local college kids study here on the weekends. I would hang out in here during free period, but the kindergarten classes have reading out loud practice in here at the same time and it's, honestly, hell.

"Hey!" Carter walks up next to me as I'm in line at the coffee bar.

"You want one?"

"Two sugars, no cream, please." He smiles and walks away. I see him grab a seat near the yearbook section. I order for us. Students get free coffee at the library, so I show them my I.D. In a way, it reminds me of home. The barista hands me two very hot cups. I walk over to Carter's table, where he is already flipping through a yearbook.

"1999." He says, deep in thought.

"1999."

"We're starting at the oldest yearbook they have and working our way forward. So far, all I'm seeing is some odd fashion choices," he laughs, taking a sip of his coffee.

"I'll go for 2000." I scan the shelves.

"Oh, did you run into Naomi on your way out?" Carter asks without looking up from the table.

"No?"

"She's having tea with my mom and your mom. It's her punishment for missing school yesterday."

"She was found out, huh?"

"Father believed her but Mom saw right through it. She told Mom she broke up with her boyfriend and she was too heartbroken to see him. She let her skip, but didn't let her get off that easy."

"Aha, found it!" I sit down with the yearbook from 2000, as well as as many as I could carry.

"Nothing in 2000. Homecoming queen was a girl and homecoming king was her boyfriend."

"Same for 2001. Cutest couple was very straight as well. Oh wait!" Carter suddenly shouts, breaking the silence around us. "Look here!" He points at the open book in front of him

2009 LGBT Alliance Club is listed in the back of the book under the list of unpictured clubs.

"Unpictured?" I question.

"They probably didn't have any member to picture, hence why it doesn't exist anymore," he responds.

We continue to look through every yearbook, up until last year's. Carter was attending school here for the last few years, so it was basically just an excuse for him to show me his old yearbook photos, which I didn't mind. Carter's phone goes off with a loud beep.

"It's a text from Naomi. She says to tell you hi and to check your phone," Carter says, closing the last yearbook.

I grab my phone from my pocket. I put it on silent since we are in a library, but I can see this is more of a cafe, and people don't do that.

Naomi: So I was standing behind you brother and I saw some weird stuff on his phone, like, sexy talk. Gross!

"Oh my god." I start snickering.

"What?" Carter grabs my phone. "Oh, damn! Little

brother got himself a girl! I wonder who is it?" he questions as we get up and walk out to the parking lot.

"You wanna come back to mine? My sister and mom are out and Dad's probably golfing."

"Sure. I'm in no rush to hang out with our moms." I get in my car and follow Carter.

He drives a nice car, just as you would expect. His family has money. Our family car is nice, but if I had picked it out myself, I would have gone for something more like Carter's. It's low to the ground, shiny, in an odd color. It's has a hint of silver, but kind of gold at the same time, with a white leather interior. It's pretty, kind of like him.

"Hello?" Carter shout into his house, opening his front door. No response. We head in and go to his backyard. It's chilly out, since it is mid-November. It's not snowing but looks like it could any day now. We sit down on his porch, looking out at the leave on the trees. Some of them are orange, but most have died and fallen to the ground.

Carter's phone goes off. He opens the text and reads it aloud.

Naomi: mom is going on and on to Ms.Anderson about you and how proud she is of her gay son.

He passes the phone to me.

"How do you feel about that?" I ask.

"It's cute. My mom like the little president of Pflag."

"I wonder how my mom is reacting?"

"Thinking of telling her?"

"No. I think I might wait 'til college. I don't see a point." I shrug.

"Wish I had done that," Carter says, laughing.

"Really?"

"No." He laughs again. "I like being free to be my true self at home." We hear a car pull up out front.

"Must be your dad," I say.

"Yeah, we better go," he responds.

"I'm gonna go back home and give Elliott the two degrees on his new girlfriend," I say, walking to the door.

"Oh, keep me updated!"

"Will do!" I shout back into the house.

"Hello Mr. Hall!" I wave to Carter's dad as I pass by him, getting in my car. He waves back and disappears into the house.

"Mom, I'm home!" I shout as I enter my house.

"In here, honey!" I walk into the kitchen and Mom is sitting at the breakfast nook with Naomi and her mom.

"Mom, can I go up to Brighton's room with him?" She practically begs her mom.

"Sure, but we're leaving soon. You've stayed long enough." Naomi scoots out of the nook and we turn around to walk up the stairs.

"Door open!" Mom yells as we disappears into the stairwell.

"Yeah, door open, Brighton," Naomi says, elbowing me in the side.

"So, what exactly did these texts you saw say?" I sit down on my bed. Naomi sprawls out next to me.

"Whoever it is was calling him baby and what I read of his message it was something like *I wish I could see you* and the person replied *me too baby.*

"Ew," I say, cringing at the thought of anyone calling Elliott "baby" besides Mom.

"You think it's someone in his class?" Naomi asks.

"Must be. He doesn't have anywhere else to meet anyone."

"Weird."

"Yeah."

"I was his age when I got my first boyfriend," she adds.

"Did you call him baby?"

"No, I called him sugar bear." I give her a weird look. "It's a long story." We both laugh and my door suddenly opens.

"Naomi, your mother says to come down. She's leaving," Mom says, giving me an eye. "And door open wasn't a suggestion, young man," she says, waving her finger at me. Naomi laughs as she leaves my room. I lay down and wait to hear their car pull away. Now, I have to confront Elliott. I need to know what's happening in my little brother's love life.

"Elliott, get in here!" I yell in the hallway from my bed.

"What?" He comes into my room and slides his phone in his pocket.

"Who's the lucky girl?" I ask, trying not to sound totally lame, being invested in the relationship of an 8th grader.

"What girl?" Elliott says, not looking me in the eyes.

"Your girlfriend," I say, not as a question but as a statement.

"I don't have a girlfriend." He turns around and walks out of my room.

"Sure, whatever you say, bud," I laugh. I hear him

slam his door down the hall.

"Oops," I say to myself. I must have been too pushy. He's shy. It's cute, but it's still weird that he is dating.

"Brighton, can you come down here?" Mom yells from downstairs. She's in her bedroom, sitting at her desk.

"Yeah?" I say, walking in. She puts down the paper she had in her hand and slides her glasses down her nose.

"You're friends with Mrs. Hall's son, right? Carter?" she asks.

"Yeah?" I say, confused

"And you know he is, well-" she pauses.

"He is?" I question.

"Well, he likes other boys."

"Yeah, Mom, I know." I'm slightly annoyed.

"And...you're a boy."

"Yeah, Mom, I know that too," I say, even more annoyed because I know where this is going.

"I just think it would be best if you made some other friends. More than just Carter."

"It's not like I haven't tried, Mom," I laugh.

"Well, try harder." Her tone changes.

"Why? Carter is nice. And I have other friends. His sister is my friend."

"I just don't want you spending as much time with him. You don't want people to get the wrong idea!"

"Got it, Mom." I walk out of the room, trying not to get visibly angry. Who would have thought that Ma, being from from L.A, could be this closed minded? I'm queasy.

17

"I have an idea!" Carter shouts at me as I walk through the doors of our homeroom class.

"Oh joy," I mumble sarcastically.

"No, seriously, I was writing our paper, it's due tomorrow by the way, no big deal, but I realized something when I was writing about the yearbooks!"

"What?"

"We can start up the GSA again!"

"GSA?"

"A gay straight alliance. You know the LGBT club thing I found."

"Oh yeah, the one with no members. My school back in L.A. had one of those, but we called it something else. We called it a... Rainbow Association."

"Yeah, well, I'm sure in L.A. there were enough members to make it so straight people weren't needed"

"You have a point," I laugh.

"So, I was thinking we could start it backup so next year, when we're gone, we leave something behind to make the school a better place."

"I like that idea. Plus, I do need a club for my college applications," I ponder.

"Yeah, and that." Carter laughs awkwardly.

"First, let's finish this paper so we don't fail English and we can actually leave next year," I say as I grab my notebook.

"Good point." Carter takes his pencil from behind his ear, jotting down who knows what. The bell rings and Mr. Briggs comes in.

"Work on your projects. I know none of you worked on them over the weekend!" He takes a seat at his desk and reads his newspaper, as per usual. I sit as Carter writes in his notebook.

"My mom, when your mom left on Saturday, She gave me a whole speech about how I need other friends because you 'like other boys.'"

"Oh really?" Carter says, looking mildly offended.

"Yeah. It was super awkward but I
m kinda relieved. It showed me my mom's true colors, you know."

"You're welcome!" Carter winks at me. I can tell he is trying to cheer me up. I know that he knows what it's like to have a less than supporting parent.

"Speaking of this weekend, did you ever talk to Elliott?"

"Oh yeah! He's so embarrassed and he tried to hide it"

"Aw, cute! Young love." Carter blushes.

"Have you ever been in love, Carter?"

"No, but I think I thought I was been in love. You?"

"Same." We smile at each other, spending the rest of the period finishing our paper. We hand it in. It's the first time in my life that I've ever finished something that early. Carter made it fun.

The next few days come and go. The days seem to just be flying by recently. Planning for the GSA is in full swing now. Carter is skipping chem again, which he has been doing a lot recently, and I have a free period. With newly designed posters in hand, Carter walks through the hallways. I have the tape as we plaster them on any surface they will stick to. The posters are medium sized with simple, big, black letters reading *Gay Straight Alliance, Support your fellow classmates* with a rainbow stripe going across the top and bottom.

"Should we hit the middle school hallway?" I ask as I tape a poster to locker room door.

" I know I would have liked to see this when I was their age."

"Okay! To the middle school building we go!" We take off running down the hall. I'm having fun. I feel like I'm living my life the way it should be. Time goes by so quickly that Carter and I are almost late for our next class.

"Jack!" I say, walking into the weight room.

"Hey guys!" He high fives Carter and slaps my back.

"Did you see?" Carter hops on the elliptical.

"The posters? Nice." Jack says, grabbing a weight. I sit on the floor, rolling a medicine ball around in a circle, trying to look busy without actually doing any work.

"I tried to start a club once."

"Oh yeah? What kind?" I ask. Jack doesn't seem like a "club" type of guy.

"An Acapella club. You know, singing without instruments."

"You sing?" I ask.

"I did when I was a freshman."

"What happened?" Carter asks, slightly winded from working out.

"The choir teacher totally red-lighted the whole thing. Said it would interfere with her class. Looking back, I'm glad. I'm not good enough to sing without any music, but still, it was rough at the time. Good luck to you guys!" Jack walks off and gets on some weight machine a field hockey guy just gave up.

"Will Carter Hall and Brighton Anderson please report to the Headmaster's office. Carter Hall and Brighton Anderson, please report to the Headmaster's office," chimes over the loudspeaker. Carter and I look at each other. I get up from the ground and hand him a towel for his face.

"What did we do now?" Carter says, wiping the sweat from his forehead.

"Boys, go ahead and get changed. You won't make it back for more gym and we don't want you to be late for your next class," Coach says as we walk past him on our way to the door. I get to the locker room and notice the poster I put up earlier is gone.

"Carter, the poster." I point to the door.

"What? Are you sure we put one here?"

"I'm positive. It was the last one we put up before going to the middle school hallways."

"You're right!" Carter storms into the locker room. "This has my dad written all over it." He rips off his shorts.

We change and rush to the office. Carter is angry and I try to calm him down before we have to deal with his dad.

"Boys." We walk into the headmaster's office and see Mr. Briggs sitting next to Mr. Hall.

"We have a few things to address with you. Your essay." He gestures to Mr. Briggs.

"I loved it, guys, really great work," Mr. Briggs says in a less-than-happy tone.

"So, we're not in trouble? Did we win?" Carter says, less angry now, sitting down in his dad's office chair.

"Not exactly, son. I have to approve everything that's printed in the magazine and this just isn't appropriate," he says.

"I knew it," Carter says from beside me.

"Sir, in all due respect, what parts are inappropriate?" I ask as if I don't know he is just being a completely closed-minded old person.

"Mr. Anderson, I'm going to be honest with you as my son's friend and a valued student; the topic of the article, homosexuality, would not be befitting for all ages of our school to read. The magazine's for everyone, not just seniors."

"So, you're basically saying there are no gay kids?" Carter interrupts.

"They are kids. They are still developing. If we expose them to this, parents could get angry. Please work with me." I can tell he is trying to be careful with his words.

"Will we still get credit for the work?" I ask, trying to make some light of the situation.

"Yes, of course!" Mr. Briggs stands up. "It's an amazing piece, boys. It's well written and very informative. I'm the teacher and you guys taught me a lot about my own workplace."

"See Dad-" Mr. Hall clears his throat."-I mean Mr. Hall, people could really learn from this!" Carter jerkily responds to his dad.

"What about our club!" I shout, louder than I meant to.

"What?" Mr. Hall asks, startled.

"Yeah, you can say the article is too risqué, but what about taking down our GSA poster?"

"I don't know what you're talking about, but I did no such thing." Carter sits down and thinks. I think he believes his dad and so do I

"Gay straight alliance, right?" Mr. Briggs interjects.

"Yes. Carter and I wanted to start up the one that this school had back in the day, but make it an official club this time with actual members."

"Well, I applaud you guys in trying to do that, but did you not read into how to actually do it?" Mr. Hall asks, confused. Carter and I exchange looks.

"Uh, no," Carter says as his dad rolls his eyes.

"You have to have a teacher sponsor to start a club. Someone who will let you use their classroom and volunteer their time."

"Crap," Carter says.

"Language, young man," his dad claps back.

"Sorry. Well, we didn't know that."

"Excuse me," Mr. Briggs chimes in. "If you don't mind me offering, I know students are usually supposed to find a teacher themselves, but I would sponsor the GSA."

"Mr. Briggs, that's very kind, but you don't have to feel obligated. My son, he-"

Mr. Briggs interrupts, "I don't feel obligated. I want to, sincerely."

"Thank you, sir!" Carter jumps up and shakes Mr. Briggs' hand. The bell rings.

"You two get going. Come to my room at lunch and we'll talk more, okay?" Mr. Briggs gets up and opens the office door.

My next class glides by. My mind was elsewhere. I feel odd about the principal being so weird about our article, but I'm more worried that he is Carter's dad. As I walk to Mr. Briggs' class, I can't help but think that if my mind is still stuck on what happened, Carter's must be twice as jumbled.

"Boys, have a seat. I have some snacks and water bottles if you want some," Mr. Briggs says as I walk through the door. Carter comes in right behind me.

"Sir, thank you so much for this," Carter says as he sits down and grabs a bottle of water. I eye a bag of mini Oreos.

"I'm thinking we will start the club every Thursday once we get back from break," Carter says as I give into my craving and snag the bag of cookies.

"That works for me, boys!" Carter looks at me and I look at Mr. Briggs. "If my son were still in school, he would have loved this."

"Your son?" Carter asks, grabbing a bag of mini Oreos for himself.

"My son is about 5 years older than you two. He is gay. He married his partner last spring!"

"Oh, congrats!" I say, taking a sip of Carter's water.

"He was always given a hard time in school. I

always thought it was just because he was shy, but your article, it really opened my eyes to this whole thing. I even gave him a call and we talked about it. So, when you started talking about trying to stand up with this club, I knew I had to do something."

"Thanks, Mr. Briggs. I promise you, we'll try to make this club a success!" Carter smiles. His teeth are a bit black from the cookies

"And if you do that, I'll be the sponsor for as long as there are members." We all smile at each other and chat the rest of lunch away about informal club stuff.

It's fall break. Most teenagers would love the opportunity to avoid responsibility for a week and relax in the comfort of their own home, but, as we have established, I'm no normal teenager.

"Wake up! It's already past noon!" I hear Mom scream from the kitchen. I've already been awake for hours, but I'm in my room, pretending I'm alone. The second I emerge from my sanctity, the day starts, which means it will end, and, potentially, end badly. I've been thinking that a lot lately. I keep avoiding Mom. It's odd because I love her to death, but something has been making me feel anxious recently. I feel like I'm lying to everyone all the time and, of course, today is the day of all days, where family is impossible to ignore: Thanksgiving.

"Elliott!" I yell, walking down the hallway to the bathroom, knocking on his door and few times as I pass by. He's usually an early riser, but has been really distant and sleeping all day. That might be all in my head, though. It's hard to tell.

I turn on the shower and hop in. My body feels warm. The soap gliding over my skin and the water washing away the suds is so peaceful and relaxing. It reminds me of all the times my friends and I went to the beach back in L.A., and of all the times we broke into the school passed closing and swam in the school's swimming pool. It's times like this, when I have no schedule, that I start to miss my old life.

I walk downstairs and take in the unmistakable smell of Mom's sweet potato casserole with maple syrup; me and Sid's favorite growing up. It's salty and sweet combo is one for the heavens.

"Smells good!" I say, sitting down at the breakfast nook, drying my hair with a towel.

"You should hurry and get dressed, we're gonna be late! And where is your brother?" Mom says, frantically looking in the oven.

"Can we please just stay home, Mom?" I say in what I wish was a sarcastic begging tone. I'm actually serious, though. I've lived in this town, heck, this state, for a few months, and today is the day I get to meet the people, the reason, behind why I'm here: Mom's family.

I know the basics. She has a few brothers, my uncles, and her parents are still alive. Grandma and Gramps, as we have been instructed to call them. Besides a few random names Mom has thrown around since getting here, I don't know anyone else. To Mom, they are family. To me, they might as well be my random classmates, or the person behind me at the supermarket.

"Your family is very excited to see you and your brother. We're going. Go get dressed," she says, pulling the casserole out of the oven and quickly pouring mini marshmallows over the top.

I walk up the stairs and my eyes meet Elliott's as he enters the bathroom. I hear the shower start. Elliott is at the age where he takes extremely long showers, if you know what I mean, so I take my time getting dressed.

A tie? I think as I open my closet. I don't own one. I probably should. I pull out the outfit Naomi picked out for me, what feels like, ages ago. The white shirt makes me smile. I wonder what a Thanksgiving looks like at the Hall house. I sit down on the bed, my white button up only half-on. I grab my phone and look through my contacts. *Is it rude to call someone on a holiday?* I think, even though I'm already pressing the button to call Carter.

"Hey!" I say as Carter answers my video chat.

"Oh, the decency!" he says, laughing, referring to my half-on half-off shirt, revealing my bare chest. I adjust.

"Good morning," I smile.

"More like good afternoon," he says, looking at his wrist. He is actually wearing a nice watch.

"You have plans for today?" I ask, noticing he is dressed up pretty nice.

"Just the usual dinner with the fam, but with turkey and dress suits. You?" I look at him and then down at my outfit. His shirt looks almost identical to mine, but ironed and clearly newer.

"Dinner with the relatives," I scoff.

"Oh, you mean THE relatives?" Carter laughs. He knows my feelings about them.

"Boys! Let's go!" I hear Mom yell from the living room.

"I gotta go," I say, looking at Carter

"Have fun! Eat some extra turkey just for me!" Carter says.

I hang up and slip on my pants, running down stairs while buttoning my shirt. Elliott walks out of the bathroom dressed and ready to go. We all hop in the car

176

and start the twenty minute car ride to what I can only describe as my own personal nightmare.

"This is your uncle's house!" Mom says as we pull up to a large, typical suburban home. It has white shutters and blue paneling. All that's missing is a white picket fence.

"Did you come here a lot as a kid, Mom?" Elliott asks from the backseat.

"I lived here for a while when I was Brighton's age."

"You lived here when you were in high school?" I say, surprised. I always assumed Mom grew up in L.A.

"I only moved out west when your father went to college. If it wasn't for him, I don't know if I would have ever left this town," she says with a sad note to her voice as we all get out of the car. Elliott grabs the sweet potato casserole and we head to the front door.

"Welcome!" We're greeted by a very tall man wearing bright green board shorts and sunglasses. I feel overdressed.

"You must be Elliott and Brighton! Come give your uncle some love!" he says, pulling me and Elliott in for a hug. His body is wet. I pull away.

"Oh, sorry! I was just in the hot tub. Did you bring a suit?" He gestures to a back patio door just past the entryway.

"Come on in, come on in," he says, walking away. I walk in and untuck my shirt a little.

The house smells amazing, like everything you think of when you think of Thanksgiving. The sweet smell of pie, accompanied with the smokey smell of a turkey that's been cooking for hours, wafts through the air. I find a couch in the living room and take a seat. Sitting across from me, watching some football game on TV, is an elderly man.

"Gramps?" I say, trying to get his attention.

"You must be Cherie's young man." He stands up, making a few grunts on the way there.

"Good to meet you, son," he says as I stand up and go in for a hug. He pats me on the back and goes back to watching his game. I've never had this many hugs in a short period of time before. It's odd. Dad's family was not really big huggers, so I guess I'm not used to it.

"Dinner will be ready in ten minutes! Make your way to the table," I hear a shaky voice yell from the kitchen. I peek in through the entry and see an old woman, presumably my grandmother. Mom is standing next to her, unwrapping her casserole. I make my way to the table and sit down next to Elliott. My uncle is sitting on the other side of me, now less wet.

"Shall we say grace?" A man says from across the table. He's probably a cousin or great uncle. My gramps chimes in.

"Brighton, son, will you do the honors?" Everyone looks at me down the long table. My throat feels tight and my hands begin to sweat as my uncle and Elliott grab them. I'm not religious, not in the slightest. Neither is anyone in my family, to my prior knowledge.

"Dear lord," I say, hoping that's the correct way to start this. Nobody seems to have flinched, so I continue. "Thank you for this food we're about to eat and thank you for bringing us all together here today." I pause. I hadn't thought about what I was going to say here after that. "Thank you. Amen." I finish and look around the room. A few giggles come from across the table. I feel my face turn red.

"Pass the sweet potatoes!" Elliott says to break the silence. A big bowl is passed down the table. My plate quickly fills with delicious food and we all start to eat. I hear conversations come from here and there between Mom and other people. She seems happy.

"So, what room was yours when you lived here, Mom?" I ask, looking around the house. It seems rather small on the inside.

"I shared a room with your father upstairs," Mom says hesitantly.

"Dad lived here?" Elliott says, surprised, scooping more potatoes onto his plate.

"More like your father was allowed to stay here for a little while. He didn't live here." Grandma scoffs at Mom. The air feels tense.

"You lived here to!" my uncle exclaims. I look at him swiftly

"No, I'm pretty sure I've never even been to this state before a few month ago, let alone this house." I laugh, assuming he is confusing me with some other niece or nephew.

"No, I remember it clear as day. You were in your mom's belly right in this house! You would keep her up all hours of the night, kicking her from the inside!" he laughs. Nobody else seems to be laughing.

"Pass the turkey," Gramps says as he fills up his plate with a second helping.

"Tom, please." Grandma says, taking the turkey plate back from Gramps. My uncle chimes in once more.

"Your mother lived here right after high school,

you see, her and your father. I took them in because my old man had a horseshoe up his ass and wouldn't have a, you know, pregnant nineteen year old daughter." His tone is more tense this time.

"Tommy, that's enough!" my mom says, looking around the table. I follow her glance. Everyone is looking at me and her.

"Sorry, but it's true. Don't be so easy on them, sis," he says. He seems to be a bit older than my mom, but more immature.

"Can I be excused?" I say, looking down at my almost empty plate. Only a few questionable dishes I regret selecting are still there.

"Sure, Brighton," Mom says, smiling at me.

"Me too?" Elliott says, getting up before Mom answers. Elliott pulls his phone out of his pocket, walking out to the back porch. I follow.

"Texting your girlfriend?" I say mockingly. He ignores me and keeps looking at his phone. The sliding door opens behind me and my uncle steps outside. He has a towel around his neck and a pair of swim trunks in his hand. He throws them at me and gestures inside.

"Change," he says as he takes off his shirt.

I reluctantly go inside and put them on. They look like they're straight from the 80's. They are decorated with a neon color-block print in a pattern that looks like it was taken from the carpet of a movie theater. Walking outside, I'm greeted by the cold fall, almost winter, air on my bare chest. I quickly hop in the hot tub, creating a bigger splash then I meant to make. Elliott gets some water on him and, annoyed, goes inside.

"Don't blame your mother for you not knowing

any of us," he says, looking off into the backyard. The leaves from the trees fall to the ground every few seconds.

"I don't," I say, trying not to make eye contact.

"It was your grandpa; my dad. He has always been stubborn. It really took his sister's death for him to open back up to your mom." I pause for a second, deciding what to say. He starts talking again before I have the chance to come up with anything.

"I love your mom. She's always been my rock. But, when I fell into a hard money situation when you were just a baby, I had to choose our parents over her. She was all alone in California. Sure, she had your father, but I'm sure you know how that was. I stopped helping her, basically just ignored her, so my dad would finish paying for my college." I nod. I've never had an adult talk to me like I was also an adult before. It's very odd, but I feel like I could get used to it. I can see where Mom got her value for a good education from. It runs in the family. I can't say it will continue. I don't think I could ever pretend Elliott didn't exist just so I could go to university.

"As long as you don't get anyone pregnant this year, I think my dad and you will get along!" he says, jokingly pushing my shoulder

"Oh, don't worry, I won't" I say a bit too confidently. I blush and turn away from him. I'm starting to say things Carter would say. Mom pokes her head out the sliding glass door.

"Brighton, it's getting late. Let's head home!" she says as she walks away from the door, grabbing her empty casserole dish from my grandma. I hop out of the hot tub and grab one of the towels sitting on a lounge chair.

"Go ahead and keep the swim trunks. They

haven't fit me in years," Tom says, patting his stomach under the water.

I walk into the house with my towel around my waist and begin putting on my shirt. Mom has my pants in her hand and is standing by the door with Elliott.

"You can wear those out," Mom says, opening the door and swiftly making an exit. We all get into the car and drive home. It's only about 7, but Elliott heads to his room right as we get home.

"Turkey makes you sleepy," I say to Mom as we both sit in the living room, trying to make excuses for Elliott's recent stand-off attitude. We sit in front of the TV. It's not turned on but we are both staring at it. I break the silence.

"Your brother was cool," I say, looking down at my, now dry, swim trunks.

"We got lucky with him. He could have turned out like your grandpa," she laughs. "You know I love you, right?" Ma continues.

"I know, Mom." I smile. I can tell she's worried about what I learned today. I knew Mom had me young, but I never really realize until today that she was only a year older than I am now when she was pregnant with me.

"I promise I won't get anyone pregnant, forcing you to disown me and make me live with Elliott" I say jokingly. She laughs.

"I love you no matter what, you know," she says, more serious this time. I suddenly feel anxiety start to bubble up in my stomach.

"Well, I'm gonna go change." I stand up from the couch and head to the stairs. My thought race, thinking too deep about what my mother just said.

"No matter what?" I mumble to myself as I walk up the stairs, officially ending my Thanksgiving.

"Hey, cute boy!" Carter says, walking up behind me, entering my room from the hall.

"Where's Naomi and Jack?" I say, grabbing my backpack off my bed and stuffing a extra blanket into what space is left.

"They're downstairs talking to your mom," he giggles. I grab Carter's hand for a split second as I pass him and walk out into the hall and down the stairs. My mom greets us.

"You boys be careful out there. Did you bring seasick medication?" she says, motioning to my bag.

"Yes, Mom, I packed everything you said I needed."

"Well then, you kids have fun! Jack, it was nice meeting you. It's so nice of you to let my son and his friends accompany you on your boating trip!" she says, grabbing his hand.

"No problem, Ms. Anderson. It's no big deal. I could always use the company. The fish aren't very talkative!" He laughs. Jack has a weird sense of humor. We all leave my house and Jack hops into the driver's seat as we begin our drive to the docks.

"One night away from my dad is just what I need.

" Carter says as he gets comfy in his seat in the back of the car.

"Things been weird?" I ask, remembering the last time I saw Carter and his dad together was when we talked about the whole club thing.

"The usual. He ignores my witty comments referring to my sexuality and I continue to make them," he jokes. I can't help but feel bad for him, but it's not like I can relate to the whole dad thing, or the whole *I'm out to my parents* thing.

"Oh, by the way, Jack, Brighton plays for my team," Carter shouts.

"Carter!" Naomi laughs from the front seat.

"And I'm straight!" Jack laughs as well.

"Me too!" Naomi looks at Jack.

"Keep it in your pants you two!" Carter slides between the two front seats, sticking himself between them. I grab the back of Carter's shirt and pull him to look at me. We stare at each other for a second and then our glance breaks. I see Jack looking at us from the rearview mirror and I feel embarrassment wash over me.

We arrive at the docks and it's already passed lunchtime. Jack begins fussing with the boat, pulling odds and ends from the water placing things in... places. It's a large white boat, like you see rich people using in the movies, but, despite its size, it's rather humble. It's not too big and not very flashy, just a simple white fishing boat. It suits Jack.

"Head on down. There are only two bunks, so we will have to share," Jacks says, smiling at me.

"Dibs." Carter grabs onto the strap of my backpack and pulls me toward the the stairs leading down to the boat.

He places my backpack and his duffel bag on the bed and pushes me down next to them.

"Oh, isn't this nice? Us four *friends* hanging out on a boat," I say, emphasizing the word friend.

"Yes. I know. Friends." He sits down next to me on the bed, looking defeated. I feel the boat kick into motion. The sudden movement causes Carter to fall over onto me and our faces are suddenly close to each other. He goes in for a kiss on the lips but misses with another bump and ends up kissing my forehead.

"Do you kiss all your friends?" I ask him, laughing.

"Only the cute ones," he says, rolling over and blushing. I get up and grab his sleeve, motioning him to come up to the ship deck.

Jack is already getting a fishing pole ready, since he actually came here to fish, and Naomi and I sit under the shaded part of the boat, looking out at the ocean. We're anchored just off the shore in a designated fishing zone. Carter is under us in the kitchen, cooking something for dinner. Jack wanted us to wait and see if we could cook what he caught, but we all silently agreed we couldn't wait that long, nor really wanted to eat seafood that fresh.

In the end, he didn't actually catch anything big enough to eat and ended up throwing everything back.

"Dinner is served!" Carter says, bringing up a pot full of ramen noodle and some sloppy sandwiches.

We all look at the food placed in front of us and begin to dig in. We're all so hungry at this point, so we don't say a word all throughout dinner.

The sun is setting and it's getting chilly on the

water.

"Coffee anyone?" Jack says, getting up from his seat.

"Yes please, no cream and 2 sugars," Carter says, looking back at me to see how I would react to his coffee order. I remember it from the day at the library, but I would never tell him that.

"Naomi? Brighton?"

"No thanks!" I say. Naomi shakes her head no as well. He emerges a few minutes later with two cups of what is probably instant coffee. We sit and talk about nothing in particular for a while, just enjoying the sea and each other.

"Well, look at the time!" Jack says, looking at his phone. "Gotta wake up early tomorrow. The fish don't wait for nobody!" He gets up, setting his half-empty coffee cup on the table in front of us.

"I'll follow. I'm feeling a bit queasy." Naomi says, getting up, looking a little off balance.

"I have medicine for seasickness if you need it!" I shout as they both disappear into the bottom of the boat.

I shiver a little bit and Carter looks in my direction. I look away.

"Why do you do that?" he says, scooting closer to me, filling the gap Naomi left.

"Do what?" I say.

"Look me in the eyes, Brighton," He says, grabbing my chin gently with his hands. I look at his face. I haven't looked at him this clearly in a long time. His freckles and his grey-green eyes are highlighted in the moonlight. The reflection from the water is making his pale skin glow. I feel myself turning red and my body getting hot. I try to look away but his hand is still on my chin.

"Carter, you know I-" I stop and look down at his hand resting on my leg.

"You can't? Or you don't want to?" Carter turns away from me, looking out at the sea.

"Well, I can't say I don't want to, but I also don't know if I want to," I say, sounding more confused than I wanted to.

"Jesus, Brighton, figure it out!" Carter exclaims in a more hostile tone.

"Wow, nice." I say, getting up from my chair. He grabs my hand.

"No, wait, no, that's not what I meant." I sit back down next to him as he tugs on my arm.

"I'm sorry, Brighton. I just don't understand you." he says, avoiding my eyes.

"Don't worry. I don't understand me either," I say, grabbing his hand. He looks at me and smiles.

"You're not like normal teenage boys," he teases.

"Neither are you." I ruffle his hair with my hand. It feels intimate, like I shouldn't be doing it. His hair is soft and the warm red tones glisten as my fingers run through it. He returns the action

"You know, you need to get your roots done. Your natural brunette hair is showing," he laughs, slightly pulling on the stands of my scraggly blonde hair.

"I thought about changing the color back to dark!"

"No, I like it. It's grown on me," he smiles, getting up and walking to the stairs. "You coming?" I get up and follow him to our bed. We both lay down and close the curtain behind us. Naomi and Jack have their curtain closed and I can hear a faint snoring. "My sister is such a loud sleeper!" Carter jokes. It's clearly Jack making all the noise. I laugh, but try to keep my voice down.

"Goodnight, cute boy," Carter says, pulling the blanket up on both of us.

"'Night," I say, closing my eyes and drifting off to sleep.

"Brigh-ton" I'm woken up by the feeling of someone touching my body. I roll over and Carter is curled up in a ball, shaking.

"Oh my god, are you okay?" I take my arm out from under the covers and grab his shoulder. His skin is ice cold.

"Here, let me grab my extra blanket it's in my ba-" I'm pulled back into bed before I'm able to sit up. Carter wraps his arms around me and scoots his body close to mine.

"I'm so cold," he says, snuggling his face into my chest.

"It's okay. Here, have more of the blanket." I shove more of my covers onto him.

"Brigh-ton." He keeps pausing halfway through my name because of the cold. He puts his hands around the back of my neck, his face now directly in front of mine. His cold hands against the warm nape of my neck sends shivers through my whole body.

"It's okay," I say, looking into his eyes. They are red from the cold sea air. He slides one of his hands off my neck, down into the covers and onto my chest. The chill from his fingers makes me squirm.

"Is this okay?" he asks as he grabs my hand and puts it on his chest. I can barely feel his breathing. It's really shallow. My heart is beating extra hard.

"Are you okay?" I'm startled by the way his body feels compared to mine.

"I'm gonna be," he says as he starts to kiss my chest. His lips are warm compared to his hands.

"Brighton," Carter says with more strength as his hand moves further beneath the blanket, grabbing my face with the other.

"Shhhh, Naomi and Jack are right there," I say, trying to keep his voice at a whisper.

"Brighton," he says, even louder. "Brigh-" I cut him off with my lips, pushing them against his. His hands start reaching for me.

I take my lips away and put my finger on his mouth, lightly giggle, and tell him to be quiet. I hear some rustling from Naomi and Jack's room and look over at Crater. He has started to shiver less. I roll over, my back facing away from him in an attempt to go back to sleep. He grabs my head and turns it over my shoulder to face him and he kisses me slowly for a long time. He lets go and I roll back over onto my pillow. I pretend to sleep for the rest of the night, but my own heartbeat keeps me up. I check every hour or so to see if Carter is shivering. I end up getting the extra blanket from my bag and draping it over him, just in case.

It's odd waking up to the sound of the sea and the cawing of seagulls in the morning. Carter isn't in bed when I wake up. I must have drifted off to sleep some time in the early morning.

I walk over the the bathroom and knock on the door. It's locked and I hear the sound of the sink running inside. I sit down on the bed, waiting for it to open. I wait for a while and the sink is still running. I knock on the door again, getting impatient.

"Hello? Naomi?" I ask, knocking, assuming she is doing her makeup or something. The door opens and I'm dragged in.

"Morning!" Carter is drying his hair with a towel. The bathroom is humid.

"What are you doing in here?" I ask with a slightly snarky tone.

"My hair was crazy from the humidity. I had to wash it in the sink; it's too cold to actually shower," he says, throwing the wet towel onto the ground.

"Get out!" I say, pushing him toward the door.

"What's the hurry?" he says, grabbing the front of my T-shirt with his wet hands.

"I have to pee and you need to get out; I've been waiting. Other people are on this boat, you know!"

"No, actually, it's just you and me. Naomi and Jack went to get breakfa-"

"Tell me later!" I push Carter out the door and close it behind me.

"Okay then," Carter says. I hear him walk away from the bathroom door.

I emerge from the bottom of the boat after the longest pee of my life and see that we are docked by the pier.

"Did you know we were back?" Carter says, looking at my embarrassed face.

"No." I sit down next to him and cross my arms.

"I wouldn't have ignored the first knock on the door if we were still out at sea. I thought whoever it was left and went to one of the shop's bathrooms. Please don't be mad at me?" He grabs my hands and I pull them away.

"Where did they go to get breakfast?"

"McDonalds. They are bringing us back something."

"Cool, thanks," I say, trying to cool my attitude.

"Didn't sleep well last night?" Carter giggles at me and grabs my leg. I feel my face turn red.

"Sorry." I get up and adjust myself. I need some water. I walk over to the cooler and pull out a bottle of water and toss one to Carter.

"It's fine, Brighton, no need to be weird. We didn't do anything," Carter says, opening the bottle and taking a long sip. I don't know why I'm acting like this. I feel like I have a mental block stopping me from doing what I want. Like if I do, the whole world will fall apart.

I thought about me and him last night, all night. I couldn't stop after I touched him. I thought about us getting married and living together and how my mom would walk me down the aisle at our wedding. How come, when I'm face to face with him, all I wanna do is crawl out of my own skin and into a hole, or become invisible to the world?

"Brighton?" Carter calls my name while I'm getting lost in thought.

"I need some time to think," I say without thinking.

"Talk to me. Let me help," he says, as he stands up and walks towards me. He grabs both my hands to comfort me. I pull away.

"Deja vu," Carter says as he turns away. I see his eyes well up as he turns his back towards me. I'm brought back to my first day of school, when Carter grabbed my hand. I feel like I'm going backwards: not growing up, not almost graduating from high school, not an 18 year old. I'm stuck as my old, insecure self.

"I'm sorry," I say as I walk away. I don't even have words to describe how I'm feeling to myself right now, let alone the words to console him.

"We're back and we brought the goods!" I hear Jack yelling as he boards the boat. Naomi is quick behind him.

"I'm starved." Carter turns around. His voice cracks as he wipes his eyes. Naomi makes eye contact with me. My eyes are on the brink of tears as well.

"So, I threw up in the water cooler last night!" Naomi exclaims, pointing at the water bottle in Carter's hand. I drop the bottle of water I'm holding and look over at her.

"Just kidding! It was actually in Jack's suitcase." She laughs.

"She's not kidding about that; it was horrible! I can't believe you guys slept through it!" He sets the McDonalds bag on the table. The sweet smells fills the sea air around us. I think back to last night and remember hearing some sound from their room around the time Carter and I were, well, you know.

"Yeah, I slept through the whole night. I didn't hear a thing!" Carter says, looking at me. His eyes are still red.

"Same," I say, looking back at him. I'm glad we decided to keep last night a secret, even though nothing actually happened. I don't know why I don't want them to know, but I'm glad.

20

I feel like I need to ask Carter for advice on how to be with Carter. Who else can I ask? If I ask Sid he would probably say something along the lines of *Aw yeah man, get it! That's my boy!* and, as much as I love the encouragement, I need more than that right now. I did some thinking on the way home from the boat trip, in bed that night, as well as all day and night yesterday. I've been thinking a lot. My head feels like it's going to explode. I just need to word vomit all over someone, but I have nobody. Well, that's not true. I have people, but not anyone who will really understand. It's the morning of the first day back from from fall break and I've even thought about asking Mr. Briggs for advice. But, no matter what way I put it in my head, there is no good way to ask your English teacher for advice on why you're embarrassed to do things with another guy. I don't even think his own son would ask him those kinds of questions.

For the rest of the semester, Carter has free period the same time as me. We planned it this way so we could use it to work on club stuff in Mr. Briggs' office. His class during that period is a study hall for freshman, so he has no problems with us popping in and out as we please.

"Have a good last day of break?" Carter asks as he

spins in Mr.Briggs' desk chair.

"It was alright. You?" I sit down and open up my notebook.

"Naomi and Jack were over the the whole day. I just moped around." He shrugged.

Mr. Briggs walks in and hands us a piece of paper.

"Your club is officially approved and I'm officially the faculty sponsor!" We both look down at the paper and it is indeed signed and dated by Carter's dad, the principal. Mr. Briggs leaves and closes the door to his office, returning to his freshman class.

"Wow, it's really happening!" I look down at the paper, smiling from ear to ear.

"Nope, switch with me. He gave me your sheet." Carter hands me his paper. It's double layered, like a doctor's office receipt.

"Crap," I say, looking at the bottom of the paper Carter handed to me. I hadn't noticed before, because his dad is the headmaster, but there is a parental consent line at the very bottom of the page. Mr. Hall had already signed Carter off, for obvious reasons, but my mom still needed to be clued in.

"Just fake it," Carter says, digging through a box of snacks Mr. Briggs keeps in his back office.

"So, not only am I lying to my mother about a huge part of my life, now I'm falsifying documents and forging signatures?" I exclaim. My stomach aches. I feel guilty enough already.

"No, you're not. I am!" Carter grabs the paper and, before I can stop him, there's a pen in his hand and he's scribbling away. "Just give this to Mr. Briggs tomorrow. He will never know!"

I look down at the paper. It's pretty convincing. Had I not known it was Carter who wrote it, I could have sworn it was a girl's handwriting

"So, Thursday, meeting numero uno!" Carter exclaims as he starts to slowly spin in his office chair.

"Yep!" I nod, looking down at my notebook. Carter, Jack and Naomi's names are the only ones written in it.

"And the only members are us, my sister and Jack," Carter sighs.

"Yep…"

"This sucks!" He slams his fist down on the desk, stopping the movement of his chair. "I'm hoping after our first meeting more people will join."

"Do you know anybody who might be interested?" I ask, intrigued. I don't know much about Carter besides what he or Naomi have told me. I want to know about him more than anyone.

"Well, let's see, before you got here, my dating pool was, well, hmmm-" he looks up, pretending to do calculations, "-zero."

"Ahh, I see," I nod. He laughs. "What about girls?"

"If there are any, they aren't out." He shrugs his shoulders. "There was one girl who was out when I was a freshman. She was a senior, even had a girlfriend. I remember everyone giving her hell. Even my dad would get her in trouble for PDA when, as you probably have figured out, that's not a problem with the straight kids at this school. It was one of the reason Trevor kept telling me not to tell anyone I was gay. It's kinda sweet, looking back at it. Kinda."

"Damn." The bell rings.

"But hey, we could get some straight members," Carter laughs, picking up his backpack and walking to the door.

"I would have joined the club as an ally had I not gotten drunk on cheap champaign at my 18th birthday party, did drugs with my gay best friend and my stoner best friend from L.A. in a limo and stuck my tongue down the throat of some random guy from another school.

"You really are from L.A. That sounds like the start of a horrible Netflix original movie." Carter laughs as we head out the door, waving goodbye to Mr. Briggs.

"Come support our school's first middle school choir concert this Wednesday! Tickets are for sale in Ms. Cron's office," chimes over the loudspeaker.

"Crap! At lunch, come with me to the middle school building," I propose to Carter.

"You want to go to a middle school choir concert? You really are gay!" he laughs.

"No, I have to go and buy me and Mom a ticket. Elliott joined choir," I explain.

"Oh, yeah, sure, no problem." He smiles at me. "Maybe I'll even get a ticket and we can call it a date," he jokes.

"It's a date," I joke back.

"*It's a date,*" I hear someone mock behind me as I'm shoved away from Carter by some big, sweaty body.

"Get lost!" Carter yells as Jean walks into the boy's locker room.

"Out of all the gym courses he could have taken, he follows us to swimming," Carter scoffs, going into the locker room.`

As I follow Carter inside, I'm greeted by speedos,

everywhere. I can't tell if this is a good or a bad thing. Carter has a light green, almost mint-colored speedo. Mine is bright orange. The coach says it's required for us to wear them for "aerodynamic purposes", but, in reality, it just feels like a cruel joke.

"Boys, gather around!" The coach comes into the locker room. "I've just got word the school will be going into lock down. This is not a drill. You will all have to go and sit in front of the lockers in silence." He goes into his office and turns off all the lights, locking the locker room door.

"Does this happen often?" I whisper to Carter from across the way. He is sitting directly in front of me, leaning against someone else's locker. A few kids around the room shush me.

"It's never anything serious, probably just a tornado," Carter whispers back, which is followed by more shushes.

I look down at my backpack sitting next to me. My phone is inside. I'm glad I charged it last night. I open up my phone to see a note I had written to myself about Carter and how I felt about him. I feel my face turn red as I reread it with him sitting only a few feet away. I close the note and open Facebook. I have a few messages from Sid and the others back home from earlier this morning. I look around. Carter is looking at the ground, tracing the lines in the tiles with his fingers. I turn the brightness all the way down so I don't get in trouble. My phone vibrates in my hand, which startles me.

Brice: hey

Me: Do I know you?

I look at the small profile picture beside his typing

bubble.

Brice: *You don't remember me?*

I don't reply immediately.

Brice: *Birthday boy.*

Me: *Oh hey…*

I feel a sick twinge in my stomach as I remember what happened the night of my birthday.

Brice: *So you go to St.Annes?*

I look down at my phone. I'm not the least bit interested, but, for some reason, I keep responding.

Me: *yeah haha*

Brice: *Nice, that's not too far from me.*

I look up from my messages to see Carter blankly staring at me from across the room. He nudges my leg with his foot.

"You have your phone?" he asks, pointing to my hand.

"Yeah. You don't?" I ask, pointing at his backpack.

"I already put it in my locker with my clothes." He gestures over to the row of lockers behind us. "You got service?" He opens his hands for me to give him my phone. I toss it over to him.

"Gonna text Naomi and see if she knows why we're in lockdown." He looks down at my phone and looks back up at me. "Here." He slides the phone back over to me.

"What?" I look at the phone and see a message notification on my screen.

Brice: *We should meet up again sometime ;)*

Some people hush us again.

"Wait! Carter," I say, trying to regain my composure. "Carter, I-" I reach out to him.

"Shhhh!" he says, looking away from me. I open my phone and text Naomi for him. She responds quickly, which is normal for her. I hold up my phone to Carter to show him her response.

Some sophomores were caught smoking weed in the bathroom ;-;. Carter laughs. Almost immediately after getting the text, the loudspeaker chimes twice. The coach stands up and tells us that we're free to go to our next class.

"Hey, wait up!" I say as Carter hurries down the hall. "I'm going to get tickets to Elliott's choir thing. You're coming with me, remember?

"You sure you remember?" he says, still facing forward.

"What's that supposed to mean?" I sprint to catch up to him.

"You know what it means."

"Forget about that stupid guy. I don't even know him!" I say, knowing that's only half true.

"I'm not good enough for you, is that it?" Carter comes to a stop right outside the cafeteria doors.

"You have no reason to be mad at me; we aren't going out. If I wanted to talk to other guys, I could, you know!" I'm yelling at Carter now. I don't want to yell at him, but all my emotions are bubbling up. "I don't even know you!" I instantly regret my words, but I keep talking anyways. "You know about my old friends and my old life. You know so much about me, but-" I stop and look at Carter's face. It's blank. "No, wait, I-" He turns around and walks into the cafeteria.

I feel bad for what I said, but a small part of me also feels relieved. It's not that I like having Carter mad at me, but I feel like I can breathe again without worrying about him and me; us. Yet, when I buy the tickets to the choir show, I get three. Two for me and my mom, and one for Carter. I'm pathetic.

The next day, I'm pulled from sleep by my brother's loud voice.

"Do,Re,Me, FA, SO, LA, TI, DO!" echoes down the hall from his bedroom.

"Shut up!" I yell as I throw a pillow over my head. This has been the routine since he joined choir: wake up, warm up vocals, take a forty minute shower, then rush me to get ready because choir is his first period. Elliott isn't the worst singer, but if I have to hear him sing Silent Night one more time...

"Be nice to your brother!" Mom yells from downstairs. I don't know why she is encouraging this so much. She must be fed up with the constant carols as much as I am. But, I guess a mother can deal with this kind of thing, or maybe she is just hoping his enthusiasm will die down after the show is over tonight. I walk to the bathroom and barge in without knocking. Elliott is standing and looking in the mirror, half-dressed.

"Out. I need to shower too, you know." I shove him out of the way. A small box falls out of his hands and tumbles to the ground.

"Ooooh, what's this?" I say, grabbing it right before his fingers touch it.

"Give it back, Brighton!" Elliott yells as I open the small velvet box.

"Earrings. Girl's earrings!" I mock, opening and closing the little box.

"Give it!" he shouts, ripping the box from my

hands.

"You know, personally, I would go for more of a classic stud for you," I joke. He rolls his eyes as I push him and his little box of earrings into the hallway.

"Elliot's got a girlfriend!" I sing as I close the bathroom door.

My heart has been pounding all day today. Carter has been ignoring me during every class. In gym, he even went through the trouble of going underwater and swimming laps every time I tried to start a conversation. I'm still hoping he shows up at the show tonight. I mean, I don't even want to go to this thing except to be with him.

It's last period. Math: my worst subject. The time is passing achingly slow. In less than thirty minutes, I can go home and change, and then, possibly, go on a date. My first real date. It feels good and kind of innocent, like there is no way anything is wrong with two people who like each other going on a date to a choir concert, especially a Christmas holiday concert. That is, if he even shows up. I put his ticket in his gym locker today. He didn't say anything when we were changing, but I have to hope he is over the whole "facebook message" thing. I've ignored the guy. I've texted Carter a thousand times that I've ignored him.

"And make sure you bring your old textbooks back this week. It's your last call for refunds!" the teacher spews as the bell rings. I hop out of my seat and rush to the parking lot. I pull out my phone and text Naomi.

Update in my little brothers teen romance saga: he bought her earrings, little gold and pink hearts. I send the text and put my phone away.

Once I'm home, I open my closet. All my clothes

are nicely hung on hangers; Ma's doing, of course. I want to choose my outfit carefully. I'm going to be at school with my mother. I don't want anyone to have any reason to say anything to me; a.k.a I'm not going to wear that pink V-neck I borrowed from Carter and never gave back because Jean likes to call me a "flaming flamingo" whenever I wear pink. I doubt the hockey player would be caught dead at a middle school choir show, but you can never be too careful. I settle on a nice pair of grey slacks, some navy blue suede shoes and a white short sleeve button up. I'm not even sure this is a formal attire thing, but I know my first date with Carter sure is, even if we were only half-joking when we called this a date.

"Ten minutes to curtain," the overhead speakers in the auditorium chimes. It's a huge place, but only the first few sections are being used tonight. My mom is sitting close to the front so she can film Elliott. I told her I was gonna sit further back so I could see better. I texted Carter his and my seat number. Now, I wait.

"Five minutes to curtain," chimes overhead. My foot has started tapping anxiously without me noticing. I'm a wreck and I'm sweating like a pig. I feel like I'm the one who's about to go on stage and pour my heart out. I keep track of the time on my phone.

6:45 P.M

Elliott goes on at seven. Maybe Carter thought I would only be here for his performance.

6:55 P.M

The 6th grade choir is performing some foreign Christmas song I've never heard. My mom is pacing up and down the front aisle. She seems nervous but excited. My heart is racing as I scan the crowd looking for Carter.

Elliott has taken the stage with his class. The low hum of prepubescent voices is filling the air. My mom is standing in the aisle, filming with her phone. The songs ring over in my head. I know the words just as much as Elliott because of how much he practiced at home. I feel a bead of sweat drip down my forehead, down my nose and onto my hand. I look down and see a pair of legs standing to my right. I would know those pants anywhere. They're nicely pressed and expensive. I look up and Carter is looking at the stage. He sits down next to me and I smile to myself.

"I'm glad you came," I lean over and whisper to him.

"I'm here for Elliott," he says in an unexpected tone.

I don't care who he's here for, or why. This is my chance to make up for the misunderstanding between me and Carter and show him that I'm not some confused little kid. I decide to not be me for a bit and do what I think Carter would do if he were me. I grab his hand.

He looks down for a second, then he goes back to watching the performance. My heart is beating and I wonder if his is too. I don't know if he has ever held hands with a boy in public before, or if he has had a boyfriend. I don't know anything about him, but that doesn't matter right now. I feel like the string keeping us together is going to snap if I don't do anything.

"Carter," I say turning towards him, no longer in a whisper. He turns his head to face me.

I grab his face with the hand that's not holding his and go in for a kiss. My heart beating and my mind racing. I hope he can't feel how sweaty my palms are. When my lips are only a few inches away from his, he pulls his hand out from from my grasp and his head away from me. I awkwardly fall forward and quickly re-adjust so that I'm facing forward again. Before I know it, my eyes are wet with tears and I don't even know why. I look and my mom is still distracted, as are the people around me. Nobody saw me being horribly rejected, but I don't think I'm feeling embarrassed, really, I'm feeling hurt.

The last song finishes and Carter and I stay still. I'm not up for walking. I feel like any movement will set the waterfall in my eyes off and I don't want to explain that to my mom. The lights grow brighter and Carter looks at me.

"Tell your mom I say hello, and that my mom says hello." He gets up and walks past me.

I feel like my insides are going to come out of my ears. It's not that I was rejected, it's that it was Carter. I feel horrible, like I'm living a weird fever dream. I stand up and walk down the aisle and out to the parking lot. My mom and Elliott are already in the car by the time I get there. My head is spinning and I feel sick.

The morning after my heart break, or what I'm calling a heart break, I feel like hell. My throat hurts and my whole body aches. I'm thinking that this is more than just a case of teenage heartbreak, I'm actually sick. I feel like every step makes my head pound and it just won't go away. Normally, Mom would let me stay home if she knew I was this sick, but I don't think I can let my own thoughts race wildly all day with no answers.

"Hey!" Naomi says, walking into Mr. Briggs' room. I wave, slumped over in my desk. "Jeez! You look horrible! Are you okay?" she asks, sitting in the empty desk beside me.

"Just a cold. I'm fine." I sit up and adjust my hoodie back onto my shoulders.

"Well, I have even more bad news. Well, not really *bad*, just news. Interesting news." She scoots her chair closer to me. "Your brother didn't give those earrings to his girlfriend, he is a big teacher's pet," she says with a big grin on her face.

"What do you mean?" I ask, intrigued.

"The middle school choir teacher is also the girl's varsity volleyball coach. I had to drop off my uniform from last semester and I saw them: the gold earrings with pink hearts. She was wearing them," she exclaims.

I laugh a little bit, thinking about how weird my little brother is and about how weird it would be for me to give Mr. Briggs a pair of cufflinks or something.

"My brother has always been a bit off," I say. We both chuckle. Carter walks in and takes a seat in this desk in front of me. The back of his neck has a few freckles on it and I find myself connecting them with my eyes, like a puzzle.

Class ends and Mr. Briggs has me and Carter stay behind. He asks a few questions about our club, and about the first meeting and about the members. Carter handles all the talking and I linger behind both of them. I feel floaty from my rising fever and I'm constantly aware of my scratchy throat. We part ways for free period. I make my way over to the library and get a warm cup of coffee to try and mend my throat. I wander through the shelves of books, drinking my coffee and trying not to think about my bodies aches and pains, trying not to think about

Carter, basically trying not to think about anything.

Since we're taking swimming this semester, we have extra time to get ready and put our swim gear on. I take my time getting to the locker room. Half the boys are already at the pool when I get there. Me and some underclassmen are changing and, much to my dismay, Jean is standing in the middle of the locker room, buck naked. I mind my own business and keep my head down as I walk past him, quickly changing into my speedo. I walk to the door and I'm stopped by a single finger being slipped into the back of my already too tight speedo.

"Hey, what the f-" I say as I turn around.

"What's up, little man?" Jean says, pulling me back by my suit.

"Leave me alone. I'm not in the mood today, Jean," I say, struggling to walk away. My head feels like jello.

"Oh, what's wrong? You look even more like a little pussy today!" He wraps his elbow around my neck, putting me in a light chokehold as we walk over to the pool room.

As we walk through the door, my vision starts going in and out of focus. I feel like my brain is pushing on all part of my head. I look around, trying to meet Carter's eyes. He has to be in here. I look around frantically as my feet move closer and closer to the pool and my legs get limper and limper.

"Jean, let him go!" I hear a voice yell. I think it's Carter's at first, but then I recognize it. It's Jack. He is in this class too. I almost forgot.

"Oh, what? Your defending him now? What, are you butt buddies?" He squeezes my neck tighter and rubs his knuckles roughly against my skull.

"Cut it out!" Jack shouts as he shoves Jean backwards. I'm thrust from his grasp and lose my balance.

"Brighton!" I hear my name yelled from behind me. It's Carter's voice, but it's faint. I turn around

"Oh, look, your boyfriend is here," Jean shouts as I feel his hands press against my back, giving me just enough of a push to fall head first into the pool. I hear a few screams as the water crashes around me. Then, I hear nothing at all. My arms won't move and neither will my legs. Even if they did, it's not enough to stop me from sinking fast. I feel a hand grasp my ankle and another grasp my shoulder. Then, everything turns black.

"Brighton? Brighton, can you hear me, bud? "

"Carter?" I say, opening my eyes. I'm greeted by the kids in my class looking down at me. I'm on the ground and Jack is hovering over my face. I choke up some water and roll over onto my side. Everyone backs up.

"Okay! Nothing to see here!" I hear the coach's faint voice. "What happened here?" he exclaims when he sees me on the floor, still gasping for air, trying to catch my breath.

"Jean almost killed Brighton," I hear Carter say. He standing up for me and saying what I want to say, but can't right now.

"I had to do CPR, sir. Can I go get the nurse?" Jack says, standing up from his place on the ground next to me.

"Yes, good job. Hurry." The coach pats Jack on the back as he runs out of the pool gym.

One of the other boys hands me a towel and another offers me his hand. I'm lifted up off the ground.

Carter, Jean and the coach are talking while I'm helped over to a bench.

"Carter?" I say as I sit down. One of my classmates walks over to him and gestures over to me. "I'm sorry," I say once he's in front of me. He doesn't stop walking, though, and grabs me with all his weight.

"Don't you scare me like that, you asshole! W-what the hell would I do in this place without you?" I feel him shaking and his words have a squeak behind them. I pull away and look at his face as he starts to cry. I grab him and hug him again.

"Don't worry. The CPR thing with Jack doesn't count as a kiss. You're still my favorite," I joke, my voice sounding horrible from the chlorinated water in my lungs.

The nurse comes in with Jack. Carter and him help me walk to the nurse's office. They call my mom to pick me up and I go home for the day.

21

It's Christmas time in Connecticut. The view outside my window blinds me each morning as a new layer of snow blankets the ground. It's a week until Christmas and there are only a few days left of school before break.

The week after the pool incident felt like a dream. I was gone for most of it. I was stuck at home, sick with strep throat and a pretty nasty head cold. Ma was called into the headmaster's office. Luckily, Carter told his dad that him and Jean were the ones who were fighting, and that I jumped in to break it up, which is why I was the one thrown in the pool and not his son. That's is the story that reached Mom, anyways.

When I went back, Jean was on a three day suspension. Tomorrow is his first day back and his first day as an official member of the GSA. It was Carter's dad's idea. I would have preferred a more brutal punishment, like being pantsed in front of the whole school, or being forced to pick up garbage on the side of the road, but Carter didn't push his dad on his punishment. He was just happy I was okay, and so was I.

While I was home, I spent my boring hours

looking up colleges and applying online. It's kept my mind from wandering and thinking about Carter and how I couldn't see him. It was also good because I was able to choose my top three schools. It's not a surprise to anyone that they are all in California. It feels nice to have gotten one major life choice out of the way. Now I have bigger and badder things to tackle, most importantly, the boy I think I might love. A month ago I couldn't even hold his hand, and now I'm talking love? I might have actually suffered brain damage from my short stint without oxygen.

This is different from the boy in Paris. It's different from my brief crush on Sid. This week I've been away from Carter and it made me realize that I don't want to be away from him. I want him to be all mine. Now I'm at a standstill, because I don't really know how to tell him all that without sounding like I'm some crazy lovesick physco. I've gotten way ahead of myself and I let my mind wonder about the future and university for a moment. I need to make Carter feel like he is wanted because, until now, I've done a pretty bad job at doing that.

It's the first period on the Thursday before winter break starts. The halls at school have been decorated with generic winter and holiday-themed posters for anti-drug campaigns. There has been a lot of anti-drug talk around here ever since those those sophomores got high and caused a lockdown. It makes me think of all the times I moved the trash can in front of the door for Sid when he would smoke at school. Sometimes, I even miss the smell, even though it always made everything in the small boy's bathroom smell absolutely horrible. If I get lung cancer when I'm old, I'm blaming those days.

Sid's not having the best holidays. His grandma fell while trying to decorate for Christmas and has been in and out of the hospital since. It takes everything in me not to hop on the next flight to L.A. to give him a big hug.

"Hi," Carter says as he sits down in front of me, turning around in his chair slightly.

"Hi yourself," I say as I brush my arm against his hand resting on my desk.

"You look good. Like, somehow younger," he laughs.

"Yeah. A week in bed and all you can eat chicken noodle soup will do that to you," I laugh, having a flashbacks to all the soup. It was nice at first, but, God, after five bowls you really start to think that the soup is what's making you sick.

"How are college applications going?" I smile. I'm happy that he remembers me complaining about how long and repetitive all the forms were.

"They're okay. I'm hoping to hear back from SFSU next semester. What about you?"

"Is it bad that I haven't decided yet?" He winces.

"I mean, we only have a half of our senior year left and most people in our grade have already started their applications, at least," I ponder, looking around, wondering if anyone else here will get accepted into my top school.

"San Francisco, huh?" he questions.

"Far enough from L.A. to feel fresh and new, but close enough to not feel like a different country."

"Like Connecticut." He seems bothered.

"At first," I smile, "you make Connecticut better

than L.A. or San Francisco".

"I love that you think that." My heart skips a beat when he says love. For a second, it felt like he was going to say he loved me.

"Class, settle down, settle down!" Mr. Briggs comes in, holding his cup of coffee in one hand and a newspaper in the other. "Today, we are going to be watching *The Polar Express* because it's the holidays and what not."

The whole class explodes with joy. I'm not surprised. Mr. Briggs always gives us what we want right before break.

He brings one of those big rolling TVs out from his office and begins playing the DVD. The room is silent. Some people are watching the movie and others on their phones. Carter and I are only half-watching. I trace his hand on my desk while he rocks his chair back. It feels like we're talking with only our hands. I trace his fingers one by one, comparing them with mine, looking at all the lines and folds.

"I want to spend Christmas with you," I blurt out, a little louder than anticipated. I hear giggles from all over the room.

"That's the spirit, boys," Mr. Briggs jokes. I feel my whole body turn red.

"Deal." Carter turns around and I grab his hand. The idea struck me then, as his fingers laced with mine. A ring. Not for a proposal of marriage, but a proposal of something. That we are something. That we're dating?

When it's time for lunch, Carter has to leave for lunch duty for "picking a fight" with Jean. It sucks, but it also was super sweet of him to take the fall for me. Well, the fall for my mother for me.

"Hey loser!" Naomi comes up to my table and sits down. The cafeteria has been serving classic holiday meals all week: ham and potatoes or pumpkin mash and pot roast. Today is a lovely sweet potato quiche and pineapple ham. It's not my favorite, but it's better than chicken noodle soup.

"I need your help tomorrow!" I say as I pull her in close.

"Shoot."

"Mall. Tomorrow after school."

"Done. My house or yours?"

"Mine. Don't tell your brother where you're going."

"Got it." She smiles and winks at me.

Naomi is the only one who knows I have fallen hard for her brother. One night last week, after a few doses of cough syrup, I ended up spilling my guts to her through a very long-winded, sloppy text. She responded with the longest keyboard smash of the century before promising to keep it a secret between us.

The last bell rings and it's time for something that could either be really nice or super weird: the first new and improved GSA club meeting. Carter and I arrive first, setting up drink cups of orange tang and bags of mini Oreos. Next, Mr. Briggs shows up with a rainbow flag that he drapes over his desk. It's a cute gesture.

"Welcome!" Mr. Briggs yells as Naomi and Jack enter the classroom.

"Swanky," Jack says, gesturing to the rainbow flag and juice

"Hey! It's a start," Carter laughs.

"Don't you mean: gay, it's a start?" Nobody laughs at Jack's joke, as per usual. Except Jack. He loses it.

"What happens if Jean doesn't show up?" I ask.

"I think my dad would have to extend his suspension. He could not graduate," Carter contemplates.

Just as I start to think about how that is more like the punishment I had in mind, he walks through the door and plops down in a desk in the far back of the class.

"Mr. Porter, I hope you're aware that this isn't after school detention. You will be expected to participate." Mr. Briggs motions him to sit in a desk closer to us and the others. He gets up sluggishly and loudly slams himself into the desk.

"Okay. Ladies, and Jean, welcome to the first meeting of the GSA. I had a whole speech prepared just in case someone who wasn't in my immediate friend group, my sister, or Jean showed up, but basically, I'm gay, some of us are straight, we're not that different, let's all get along" Carter says as he grabs a cup of orange tang and takes it like a shot.

"I read online it's important to share orientation and pronouns," Mr. Briggs chimes in.

"Okay then, I'll start. Carter, gay, he/him."

"Naomi, straight, she/her."

"Jack, probably straight, never liked a boy but also never tried! He/him."

"Brighton, uhh, he/him, gay."

We all clap. Mr. Briggs clears his throat. "Mr. Porter. Jean." He gestures for him to go.

"Jean. I'm a guy. I like girls."

"Very good, Jean," Mr. Briggs chuckles under his breath.

"Now what?" Jean asks suddenly.

"Well, now we just talk!" I say, looking around at everyone.

Sitting in a classroom with all of my friends, plus Jean, talking and laughing, makes me miss high school, even though I haven't even left yet. I'm not even close to leaving, but still, I feel like these will be the memories I look back on and miss when I'm old.

"Is this the Gay Straight Alliance?" A small voice comes from the doorway.

"Yes, it is! Come on in. We just finished introductions!" Carter says.

A small girl with short shoulder-length hair sits down next to Carter and me. She doesn't look familiar. She's probably a freshman.

"Name, orientation, pronouns?" Carter smiles at her and asks.

"Hiya! Hailey, she/her and undecided!" she shrugs.

"Cool!" Carter puts his hand on her shoulder

"Welcome!" I say, smiling at her as well, admiring her for actually showing up. When I was her age, I would have never had the guts to come here. Heck, even a few months ago I wouldn't have dared to appear. The rest of the meeting goes by smoothly and I leave feeling a little warmer inside.

The next day, school drags on. Usually, I love the feeling of knowing exactly how long I have to be somewhere, but today, I just wanted the schedule to fall apart and for every class be over. The last period of the day, the bell, the drive home: my heart was pounding. Naomi is going to be here soon and I'm going to go buy

Carter the first gift I will ever get him. In my mind, I'm fantasizing about what will happen in the many years to come. I'll get him more gifts, and maybe, one year, I'll get him a dog as a gift, and then I can get him and our dog presents. The fantasy gets a little out of control when I start to imagine our future child.

"Here's that wrapping paper I took." Elliott pops in my room and throws the green and red striped roll across the floor."I'll be downstairs," he says, closing my door.

I walk over and pick up the wrapping paper and lay it gently on my bed. When I get home, I'm going to wrap whatever present I end up getting for my mom and Elliott, so I figured I would snag the whole roll before Mom used it all up.

"Hmm, tape," I ponder out loud. I walk over to my door and open it. "Elliott, where is the tape?" I yell into the hallway. It echoes down the stairs.

"I don't know. Look for it!" he yells back. I can hear that his mouth is muffled, like he is stuffing his face.

I walk down the hall into his room. The door glides open at first but then gets halted by a large pile of dirty clothes. It smells like a locker room in here: sweaty and stale. Dirty dishes are piled up on his side table. This is so unlike Elliott. I scour for the tape, picking up dirty towels and looking underneath them. I'm startled by a sudden chime under a piece of clothing in the corner. The tone is unmistakable. It's his phone. I scan for the glowing light and grab it. I've never been much of a snoop when it comes to my brother, partly because his life was never that interesting, until recently. I unlock his phone easily, since I am the one who set it up and put the original passcode on it many months ago. He has all the social media apps that any teen would have in this day and age, but I don't care about that. I want to find out more about his girlfriend, or whoever he has been texting so religiously recently.

I see a contact in his text messages whose name is just a bunch of hearts, nothing else. I open it and begin to scroll. I don't see anything weird, just some casual conversations about generic things, like what we had for dinner and what we did for the holidays. Elliott texts like any straight, white male. He speaks very casually and uses the typical emojis, and nothing he says is too deep in thought. Heck, he texts me in almost the same way as he texts this girl. Her messages seem a bit odd, though. She says things that I couldn't even imagine Carter saying to me, or my dad saying to my mom when they were together. I almost cringe at some of the texts.

You're my everything. You are so special.

It feels weird for an 8th grade relationship to be at this level, but it's not like I can judge. My relationship history isn't what you would call "normal," by any means. I hear footsteps coming up the stairs. I throw the phone back down and cover it with an old t-shirt.

"A girl's here for you." Elliott says, walking into his room. I'm standing by his bed, hoping I don't look like a deer in the headlights.

"Did you find the tape?" he says, looking at me.

"Just find it and leave it in my room!" I say, fast-walking out of the house.

"You're not gonna guess what I just did," I say to Naomi, slightly out of breath as I get in the passenger seat. "I just did the worst thing and snooped through my brother phone."

218

"Oh, god. Did you see his nudes?" Naomi jokes.

"Worse. I read his romantic texts."

"Oh, the joys of young romance," she swoons.

"No, seriously, they were...like this girl must be super weird." I shake my head as we pull out of my driveway.

The mall is only a quick drive from my house, but the drive gives me enough time to sike myself out of every small detail of Carter's gift. I start freaking out about the size, the color, the finish. This ring has to be perfect. I manage to find small gifts for Elliott and Mom. Nothing I got them is too personalized or special, they're more practical.

Naomi and I head over to the jewelry store. It's lights shine brightly through the glass windows, the display cases glimmering with diamonds and gold. I scan one half of the store and Naomi looks through the other. The rings go on in rows, all so perfect and pristine. My eyes are drawn to a small silver band. It's delicate, but leaves an impression at first glance.

"Naomi!" I shout across the store. This catches her attention, as well as the attention of a store employee.

"Find something you like?" A woman wearing a pants suit and white gloves approaches me.

"Yes. Can I see that one?" I point at the ring. She grabs it and removes it from the case, gently setting it down on a silk lined tray in front of me. I'm almost hesitant to touch it.

"Are you buying for your girlfriend? Because this is actually a men's band." She gestures to Naomi.

"No, this is for my-" I pause for a second, unsure as to what I could label Carter as. I continue, "-my boyfriend." I wait for a response.

"Oh! How lovely!" the woman chimes. "Well, this band is a great choice. It's 14 karat white gold with a simple, sleek design. It's also very well priced."

"I'll take it!" I pick the ring up and bring it close to my eyes, taking in all its shimmer and shine.

"You wouldn't happen to have the ring size, would you?" the woman questions as she gestures for me to give her the ring.

"Ah, yes, Naomi did you-" She shoves her hand in her pocket and pulls out one of Carter's rings.

"Straight from his bedside table. He wore this everyday last year." She hands the woman the ring.

"Okay, I can have this sized up and ready for you in about an hour." Naomi and I head over to the food court while we wait.

"I know what my brother is getting you for Christmas," Naomi blurts out as we sit down with our shakes at a semi-secluded table.

"I don't wanna know!" I take a sip of my shake. It's strawberry, my favorite.

"My lips are sealed," she says, taking a sip of her shake as well. As we wait for the rings, I plan out, in my head, how I want to give it to him. I think about where I want to be and what I'm going to wear.

"Can you drink and shop?" I ask Naomi as I stand up from the table. She grabs her shake and follows behind me. I walk up to a store that is more than a little intimidating. The store clerks are wearing suits and there is security at the entrance.

"May I help you with anything?" I'm greeted by a man.

"I need a suit, tie, shoes and all the extras," I say, trying to sound confident.

"Yes, sir. Follow me," he says as Naomi and I shuffle behind him. He pulls me into a room with a curtain and takes my measurements. It all feels so special.

"What's the occasion?" he asks as he tugs on my pant leg to get a tighter measurement.

"I have a very important date," I say, trying to stay as still as possible.

"They must be one lucky person," the guy says as he unwraps the yellow measuring tape from my leg and stands up to measure my arms.

"Yes, he is," I say as I hold my arms out to the sides.

My body feels stiff, like I'm a pasta noodle that hasn't been cooked. The suit jacket glides on like it was made for me, but it's snug enough to make me feel like my poster is correct. I went for a light grey suit. Well, I should say the store worker decided I would go for it. I paired the suit jacket with a navy blue button up shirt, black skinny tie, black shoes and black socks. I feel like I cost a million bucks. And I should, because this is going to be one of my biggest purchases yet.

"You ready?" I shout to Naomi from behind the curtain. I walk out and strike a pose, one I imagine a Hollister model would if he were in a suit.

"I'm proud to call you my ex-boyfriend," Naomi squeals. I hear the store worker who helped me laugh. I quickly change back into my clothes. They feel different from when I had them on before, like I'm half-naked or something.

With my suit and the ring in hand, I have Naomi

take me home. After dropping me off, she hurries back to her house to put Carter's ring into place before he notices it's gone. The tape I needed is sitting on my bed. All my other presents are nicely wrapped and I feel like everything is starting to come together.

It's Christmas Eve. This is the best I could get in terms of holiday time with Carter. His mom and dad plan to have a big family dinner on Christmas, while me, Mom and Elliott will continue our family tradition of eating gooey orange-flavored cinnamon rolls and opening presents. Today is going to be fantastic. I slept with the ring on my bedside table. I found myself waking up every few hours to make sure it was real and that it was still there. I hope he likes it. Hell, I hope he loves it! Now the time has come to take Carter to the seaside park. I'm bringing a canteen of hot chocolate and some mugs. It's cold, but most of the snow has melted from last week's storm, so it's not completely far-fetched to have a picnic this time of year.

I'm all dressed in my suit, with two pairs of thermal underwear underneath to keep me from freezing. My hair is a fresh shade of blonde, just how Carter likes it. I grab the ring and slip it into my pocket. As I open my door, I catch a glimpse of myself in the mirror. I look like I'm going to prom. Thank god Mom and Elliott aren't home. I know that if they saw me looking like this, the array of questions they would ask would never end.

"Hey ther- whoa!" Carter jumps into the car. He is bundled up, a large yellow scarf surrounds his face and is situated right under his red nose. "You look amazing!" he says, scanning me in the driver's seat. I try to keep my face from turning as red as his nose.

"You ready?" I look at him and smile. He doesn't know where we are going. I just told him to dress as warm as possible.

The drive to the seaside isn't long, but it feels like it's dragging on. The radio is playing *Death of a Bachelor* on repeat and it calms my nerves enough so that I'm gently humming along.

"You like this band?" Carter asks, turning up the volume so that he can listen more clearly.

"A lot. Back in L.A. I went to all their shows"

"Next time he comes here, we should go together." Carter smiles at me.

"It's a date." I continue to hum along to the song as the seaside grows closer and closer. I feel Carter's eyes on me every few minutes, casually glancing in my direction. I can't tell if it's because of my outfit or my hair. Maybe he is as nervous as I am.

"We're here!" I say as I turn into the parking lot. The sky is a dark grey and the sun is floating just above the horizon. "Thought I would take you somewhere that reminds me of home." I get out and hurry over to the passenger side and open his door.

"The ocean. I love it." He steps out and takes in a deep breath of sea air. He grabs his arms and shivers."Won't you be cold? I mean, you look hot but..."

"Don't worry I thought about that" I pull up my sleeve and reveal my many layers of thermal underwear.

"Sexy," Carter laughs.

"I also brought this." I reach into the backseat and

pull out the picnic basket and thermus. Carter grabs the blankets I packed and we head for the shoreline.

"And we're all set" I say as I lay the final blanket down in the sand, placing the last blanket over our legs.

"I'm all cozy now." Carter snuggles close to me. I open the basket and pull out two red velvet cupcakes and two mugs.

"For you." I hand him a mug and pour in the dark, steamy hot chocolate.

"Why, thank you." he says, bringing the cup up to his lips and taking a long, slow sip. We sit and watch the ocean. The waves crash on the sand and the sound of the ocean foam fizzing away with each fading splash echoes in my ear.

My cup is almost empty and the ring in my pocket feels like it's getting bigger and bigger. I set down my mug and take Carter's mug from him. He turns and faces me.

"I have a present for you. But first-" I stick my hand into my pocket and pull out the ring, hiding it under the blanket. I take my hands and put them on Carter's face. He flinches as my cold hands touch his skin.

"Sorry," I giggle nervously. He takes his hands and brings them up to his face.

"Told you it was cold," he laughs, rubbing my hands. I take a deep breath. The cold sea air feels harsh against my throat.

"I came here, to this state, miserable. And, before I even arrived, you came into my life as the cute freckled redhead on my flight. I've been so confused this whole time about you, and about me, mostly about me. You truly are something so special, Carter. To me, you're the most special. I don't really know how to say it but I lov-" he leans in and kisses me, long and hard. I can feel the slight scratch of some stubble on his upper lip and smell the hot chocolate on his breath. Just as he pulls away, I reach under the covers and grab the ring, placing it in the palm of his hand. He looks down for a second and then opens the box.

"I love you too," he whispers. He smiles as he opens the little box and I grab the ring.

"I'm not sure what finger to put this on. I had Naomi borrow one of your rings for size," I laugh. He directs my hand to his index finger and I slide it on. It fits perfectly and I feel like I can finally breathe.

I feel a warmth come over my body as Carter falls into my chest. His arms wrap all the way around my body and I feel hot puffs of air on my neck as he breathes.

"Well, how am I gonna top that!" he says, backing up and laughing. "I didn't get you anything!" he says in a serious tone.

"Oh, that's okay." I half-smile, trying to keep my cool. I feel my face tense up and I try to hold back giggles.

"Naomi!" Carter says, looking at me as I start to laugh.

"You really are a bad actor," I laugh as he looks around, astounded.

"How much do you know?" he asks, defeated.

"Nothing. Just that you got me something, I swear." I grab onto his arm and shake it.

"Well, she lied. I didn't really get *you* anything, as much as I got *us* something." He smiles.

"What?" I say, confused. He reaches into his inside jacket pocket and hands me an envelope. I open the folded piece of paper and read it out loud.

"This is to confirm your booking of four days and three nights at our resort for the dates of-" my voice fades off. "-San Francisco!" I shout.

"I figured we could use it as a trip to see colleges, but also get out of this small town for a while. Just to be us." He smiles right as I go to kiss him. My lips graze his teeth and we both stop to laugh.

"Merry Christmas, Brighton." I fall into Carter's lap as we watch the sun sink down into the dark reflection of the ocean. It's so peaceful.

"Hey!" Someone shakes me from my sleep. My eyes are crusted shut and my mouth is dry. The light from the sun is too bright and my eyes take a second to adjust.

"Get up! We have to go!" The blanket that was covering me is thrust from my body and a wave of sand falls over me. I stand up and realizing what had happen.

"You fell asleep?" I say as I pack up the picnic basket

"So did you!" Carter says, hopping around, trying to put his shoes on as he runs to my car.

"What time is it?" I hop into the car and quickly turn the key. Carter looks at the clock as I back out of the parking spot.

"Almost six. The sun must have just come up"

"I didn't tell my mom I was going out last night. She wasn't home when I left." I press on the gas, speeding down the empty freeway.

"I thought I would be back before my parents noticed," Carter says, hunching over the front seat and shaking out his shoes.

I floor it to Carter's house, faster than ever. Living

in L.A. and driving on the crazy streets has finally come in handy.

"Good luck!" I say as he hops out of the car. I wait for him to get in the front gate and then quickly drive away.

I'm praying as I approach my street that Elliott is old enough to not wake up at the ass crack of dawn on Christmas anymore. I turn the corner to my house and I am greeted by not one, but two cars in my driveway, one completely unfamiliar. I park beside it and walk up to my front door. I open the door quietly and set my bag down, trying to be as quiet as possible. I turn the corner into the living room.

"Brighton Anderson, where the hell have you been?" I look up. My mother and Carter's father are sitting on my sofa.

"Crap," I say under my breath. "Listen, I can explain." I quickly walk over and stand in front of them.

"And I assume my son is already home, thinking he successfully made it without me knowing?" His dad stands up. I nod.

"Thank you for calling me Ms. Anderson. I'm sorry for any trouble my son may have caused you." He shakes my mom's hand and heads toward the door. I reach for my cell phone to text Carter, but it's dead.

"Are you going to tell me where you were all night? And of all nights on Christmas Eve? And dressed like that?" Mom gestures to my clothing. I almost forgot that I'm dressed head to toe in a penguin suit.

"Mom, I would love to talk, but I have to pee!" I run past her and into the bathroom upstairs, frantically looking for a phone charger.

"We are not done, young man!" I hear my mom walking up the stairs. *Come on, come on.* My phone finally turns on and I dial Carter's number.

"Hey, your dad was just here. He is coming home! What are you gonna tell him? He knows you were with me?" I get no response. "Hello?"

"I'm sorry. I presume this is Brighton Anderson? My son's going to have to call you back." Carter's mom hangs up the phone. I walk out of the bathroom and my mom is standing in the hallway.

" Are you going to tell me what you were up to all hours of the night?" Her arm is blocking my way down the hallway.

"I was out with some friends, at the beach. We were too tired to drive home, so we slept in my car. My phone was dead, so I couldn't call." I avoid eye contact.

"You were at the beach dressed like that?" I totally forgot about the suit, again.

"Yeah." I nod. I can't think of any way to get out of this.

"What am I going to do with you? You're going off to college in the spring and, yet, you still have no problem lying right to your mother's face."

I'm thinking in my head of just telling her the truth, just blurting it out. *You wanna know where I was? I was with my boyfriend!* It's obviously not the best timing, so I refrain.

"I was at the beach. Check my car. There is sand all over it, and blankets we used when we slept are in the back seat." I pray that she won't actually check because, then, I would have to explain the romantic picnic leftovers.

"Fine. I believe you." She puts her arm down and I walk by her.

"I'm sorry. I'm going to bed. Merry Christmas." I get into my bed and lay down. I lied again. I'm not going to bed. I can't stop thinking that if my mom was this angry, Carter's dad must have been ten times worse.

23

"So, I'm grounded for the rest of break…"

"I'm sorry. I love you?"

"Why the question?"

"Because I'm not sure if you wanna hear me say that right now, since I'm the one who got you grounded."

"I would stay grounded forever just to have spent that night with you."

"Shit, my dad's coming. I'm not allowed to have my phone. I'll text you later. Love you too!"

I feel responsible. He says it's okay, but I still don't like it. His dad was not okay with him staying out all night on Christmas. I don't think it helped that he was with me either. I'm sure even the rumors at school get around to the principal. I'm having trouble at home as well. Ma has been on my case for the past few days. Christmas and the day after were all fine and jolly. She was high on holiday spirit, but now I feel a lingering sense of doubt from her whenever I speak. I still haven't asked her about going to San Francisco. Hell, I don't even know if Carter will still be able to go. He booked it for the last four days of break and I would have to miss a day of school because of flights and travel. Mom hates it when I miss school. But, would it really be missing school if I'm going on a trip to visit what I hope will be my new school next year? Here's hoping.

"Absolutely not."

"But Mom, it's for my education." I sit down at the bar in the kitchen while Mom cooks my and Elliott's lunch. "I already can't see my friend for a week because you called his dad. Now you won't let me go to see my future school? It's for my education!"

"Don't try to blame me for your poor decisions, young man." She flips the grilled cheese in the pan angrily.

"But Mom!"

"No *buts!* You still haven't explained to me the large purchases on your credit card. A jewelry store? A suit? I don't think this Carter boy is a very good influence on you."

"He has nothing to do with this! He wants to go to SFSU as well. He invited me. It's not a big deal."

"Oh, I think it's a big deal when my son starts talking to me like this. I'm putting my foot down. You're not allowed to see this boy anymore."

"Mom."

"Brighton."

I put my head down on the counter. She doesn't realize what she's doing and that makes it even worse.

"Here. Eat." She slides the sandwich over to me."Elliot, lunch!" she yells up the stairs.

"Not hungry!" he yells back down, muffled by his bedroom door.

"Well, looks like I'm your lunch date today." She

sits down next to me.

"Thanks." I grab the sandwich and take a bite.

"You know, I'm only trying to do the best I can with you, Brighton."

"Then let me go to San Francisco."

"I'm sorry. For now, it's a no. Maybe I can take you later. Me, you and Elliott can take a trip back to Los Angeles and then road trip up to San Francisco!"

"Mom," I beg. Maybe she would consider it more if she knew I would be going with the person I love and want to spend the rest of my life with. That would probably just make things worse, though. She continues to eat her sandwich in peace.

Carter: What did she say?

Me: Besides no, she says I'm not allowed to see you.

Carter: Me?? Why???

Me: Idk? She says your a bad influence or whatever.

Carter: Oh shit, she knows. She has to know.

Me: You think? No, there is no way!

Carter: Try to figure it out?

Me: I have nothing better to do...Ask your dad if you can still go. I'll work on my mom <3

Carter: Love you.

My texts with Carter take up most of my absent mind. If I'm not thinking about him, I'm thinking about my mom. Sometimes thoughts of my dad float across my mind and takes up my time. I'm also always thinking about Sid and his grandmother as well as Lin and the others back home. I think about how I haven't seen them in a while, other than the occasional few minute long FaceTime calls. My problems seem so small compared to the world's problems, but here in Connecticut, they are consuming me. I need to get out for a little while.

Carter:So I told my dad.

Me: You told your dad???

Carter: That were going out...

Me: shit....really?

Carter: I wanted to explain where I was.

Me: Well, thanks for asking me....

Carter: He basically already knew.

Me: So?

Carter: he wants to talk to your mom.

Me: Shit.

Carter: Yeah. Shit.

Me: My mom said no anyways.

Carter: You're just going to give up?

Me: No...idk....what's your dad gonna say to my mom??

Carter:Not sure...

Me: Ask him?

Carter: I'll try. Gotta go!

I fall asleep waiting for Carter to text me back about his dad.

"Brighton." My eyes open as my mom enters my room with a basket of laundry.

"Hey." I wipe my eyes and sit up in bed. The sun is shining through my window and emphasizing the dust floating in the air.

"So, I talked to your friend's father." My yawn turns into a full on coughing fit.

"Oh," I say, settling down onto the backboard of my bed, clearing my throat. "What did he say?"

"Well, he asked about your vacation. He didn't seem know that I said you couldn't go." I pull the covers over my head and sink down into the blankets. "But-" I perk up at that beautiful three letter word. "He says his son won't be able to go unless you go with him."

"And?"

"And, well, I'm still not happy about the two of you hanging out so much..."

"Thank you, Mom!" I jump up out of bed, forgetting that I'm only wearing my boxers.

"Maybe buy some pajama before the trip. You don't want to be giving him any opportunities." She sets my basket of clothes down and leaves.

Me: You did something

Carter:????

Me: My mom just said I could go?!?!

Carter: Oh, that!

Me: Your dad didn't tell her?

Carter: Yeah, I went to my mom, told her everything

Me: And she talked to your dad?

Carter: Yup.

Me: So, you can't go without me, huh?

Carter: He didn't leave out any of the details I told him.

Me: I'll see you tomorrow for New Years Eve?

Carter: Tomorrow.

I smile at my phone, like an idiot.

24

"A new year, a new me," but I call bull. You can't tell me just because the calendar changes that I'm supposed to, somehow, improve as a human being. Changes happen all around me, all the time. The reason I'm not so keen on them happening this New Years, is because everything is perfect.

I'm getting ready to go to a party at my boyfriend's house for New Years Eve. Jack is coming, as well as my mom and Elliott. Carter's parents invited a lot of friends and neighbors. I'm hoping there will be fancy hors d'oeuvres.

I stroll up to their front door, dressed in a simple white button up and chinos with some casual sneakers. My mom is wearing a long blueish dress. Elliott is dressed,well, like Elliot: messy.

"Ms. Anderson, boys, come in." We're rushed in by Carter's mom. She brushes my back with her hand as I walk through the door. "The other kids are upstairs on the deck." I walk past her, toward the stairs.

"Cute boy!" Carter runs to me as I walk through a set of french doors that lead to the outside. There is a fire pit going with chairs around it. He grabs me and spins me around. I run my hands through his hair.

"We were playing never have I ever to pass the

time. Want in?" Carter grabs my hand and leads me over to the fire and sits me in the chair next to his.

"Naomi, it was your turn. Brighton, put up ten fingers." I spread my fingers wide and hold them up above my shoulders.

"Okay. Never have I ever kissed Brighton," Naomi says as she put a finger down. Carter and Jack follow her.

"Jack?" I question.

"I count the kiss of life!" he says, referring to the CPR in gym.

"Sis, you're supposed to say thing you haven't done in order to win."

"It was too good not to call out that everyone here has kissed your boyfriend," she laughs.

"Okay, my turn. Never have I ever been to California." Jack looks at me and I put a finger down. Carter does as well.

"You have been?" I ask.

"I've been in the airport?" He laughs.

"That counts!" Jack shouts.

"Okay, hmmm. Never have I ever been arrested." Carter looks around. I slowly put down a finger.

"Gasp!" Jack says.

"Spill." Naomi's leans forward in her chair

"Freshman year. Party at the beach. Friends were major stoners. Cops came. You know, the usual," I joke.

"My bad boy. Your turn." Carter turns to me.

"Never have I ever.....cheated on someone."

I look around and nobody puts down a finger. I'm relieved when I see Carter's hands stay still. The game goes around a few more times. My hands have the most fingers left. Carter has the most fingers up after me, then

Naomi, then Jack. It's my turn once again.

"Never have I ever had an STD." I look around. Nobody flinches.

"Never have I ever had sex." I stare at my own fingers for a second, then I look up. Naomi and Jack are both down to one finger now. I turn to my right and count Carter's fingers. They are the same as before. All six fingers are still pointing strong.

"Okay then. Sorry Naomi, never have I ever done drugs." she laughs, dropping her hands to her knees. Carter and I each put down a finger as well.

"Carter?" I look at him and he looks back at me. We stare at each other for a few seconds.

"Well, I'm down to call it quits for now if you guys wanna keep going." Jack's voice trails off as he walks away.

I bring myself closer to Carter's face, my mouth close to his. "So are there snacks?" I barely get the words out before laughter starts to bubble out of me.

"Follow me, ass." He laughs and grabs my hand, guiding me down the stairs. When we get to the bottom of the stairs, I let go of his hand.

"My mom's here," I shrug. He gives me an understanding smile.

I look around. The snack table is surrounded by a bunch of middle-aged people with tiny plates. I sneak my way in and manage to grab a few fancy looking sausages and some odd smelling cheese.

"Want to go sit in my room and eat your sausages?" Carter laughs. I follow him through the crowd of people and into a small hallway. He opens his door and quickly jumps back.

"Holy shit!" He slams the door behind him.

"Oh my god, what? " I'm startled by his sudden reaction.

"Holy shit, Brighton." He opens his door slowly and I peer inside the room. There are two people laying on his bed. I step forward.

"Holy... Elliott." I step back and Carter closes the door once again."What did we just see?" I ask, blinking a few times to make sure my eyes aren't deceiving me.

"That's messed up." Carter shakes his head.

"So, did we just see my little brother doing god knows what with some random woman?" I lean against the wall beside his door.

"That wasn't some random woman, that was Naomi's volleyball coach." Carter leans against the wall beside me.

"No way. No, that couldn't be." I turn toward him.

"One way to be sure." He goes up to the door and opens it again. The two are sitting on the edge of the bed now.

"You. Get out of my bedroom." He points to the woman. She stand up and passes us, not making eye contact. We both go in the room and shut the door. I hand Elliott my plate. I've lost my appetite.

"Jeez, what do we do?" Carter paces in front of the bed while Elliott sits and quietly picks at the food on my plate.

"We have to tell someone." I'm pacing along with him.

"You can't tell Mom!" Elliott stands up from the bed.

"Sit down. Jesus." Carter lightly pushes Elliott

back onto the bed.

"What time is it?" Elliott asks, patting his legs, looking for his phone.

"Almost midnight? I don't know." I grab my phone out of my pocket. "Crap. It's, like, legit almost midnight, like, in a few minutes."

"Damn it!" Carter says, turning to Elliott. "You stay here. Don't leave this room. We will be back." Carter grabs my hand and closes his bedroom door behind us. He takes me all the way up the stairs to the deck. We emerge into the group of twenty or so people who are standing around outside, peering into the sky.

"10, 9, 8, 7-" people chant, looking down at their watches and phones. Carter grabs my face.

"-5, 4, 3, 2, 1"

My lips press against his as he tilts me slightly backwards. He stops quickly and wipes his mouth, looking around.

"Look!" I point in front of me at Naomi and Jack, who are full-blown sucking face.

"Did you know about that?" Carter looks at me, flabbergasted. I shake my head.

The first boom goes off as the sky fills with colors. The fireworks are being reflected onto the chilly surface of Carter's pool.

"Now follow me." Carter grabs my hand as we walk into the crowd. He grabs his father's shoulder and gestures for him to follow us.

"Go find your mom. I'll catch my dad up." He takes his dad down the stairs as I scan the crowd for my mom. I catch a glimpse of the top of her hair as she moves toward me.

"Mom, you need to come with me." She walks right past me and ignores me. "Mom?" I follow her down the stairs. "Hey Mom?" I grab onto her shoulder and turn her around to face me. She is crying. "No, Mom. Mom, it's okay. Elliott's okay." I try to pull her in for a hug and she pulls away.

"How could you do this to me?" She turns around and walks away.

"Me?" I question, confused. Elliott walks up behind me and taps me on the shoulder.

"You tell my secret, I tell yours." He shoves past me. My knees stiffen under me.

"Mom. Ma. Mom." I run past Elliott. "Please, Mom, look at me." I step in front of her and she stops.

"I don't even want to look at you." She tries to step aside. My eyes begin to fill with tears.

"Mom, please don't. Mom, I'm sorry. I don't know what to- I love him."

"I don't want to hear about that kind of thing!" She shoves past me and walks out of sight. Elliott stops in front of me.

"Carter is talking to his dad right now. You're going to be okay. You don't understand now, but we're helping you and you're going to feel really bad for what you just did." I fall to my knees in the hall, my face in my legs, crying. It won't stop. I feel Elliott walk away and another body approach me.

"Brighton, hey." I feel a hand on my shoulder and I look up. It's Carter.

I can't speak, so I just fall into him. He looks around confused and hugs me back.

"Get me outta here," I manage to get out.

"Okay. Okay. Let's get you into my room." He helps me up. I feel the eyes of everyone around on us.

"No, get me far away." I shake my head, tears continuing to fall down my cheeks. He walks with me and sets me down on his bed.

"Come on, it's okay." He picks up one of his shirts off the floor and hands it to me so I can wipe my face.

"It's not okay. It won't ever be." My eyes dry for a second before welling up again. "She hates me!" I cry.

"Who? Who hates you?" He gets down on his knees so that his eyes are level with mine.

"My mom. She hates me, Carter." I grab onto his shirt.

"Shit, where's your brother?" He looks around his room, realizing that we are alone.

"He told my mom about me. About us." I look up at him, my whole face feels like a swollen balloon. He sits down next to me and hugs me. I lean my head on his shoulder, my tears leave little dark marks on his light blue shirt.

"It's gonna be okay, I promise" Carter strokes my hair and I sob into him for a while. I fall asleep in his arms.

25

My throat is dry. My head is pounding. I feel hungover and broken.

"Morning," Carter sits down next to me on the bed and hands me a cup of coffee.

"What time is it?" I wipe my eyes. My tears from last night have dried and left a layer of crust around them.

"Almost ten." He pulls the covers higher onto my lap.

"What did your dad say about Elliott?" I take a sip of my coffee, trying to take my mind off my own situation.

"He just said he'll take care of it." He shakes his head in disappointment. A teacher sleeping with a student is the worst, especially when it's someone as young as Elliott. I look around the room.

"What are those?" I point to a few suitcases in the corner that were definitely not there yesterday.

" Well, we do have a flight in a few hours." He laughs. I perk up.

"I totally forgot about San Francisco!" I turn to him. "I don't have my stuff!" I say, looking down at my coffee, swishing the liquid in the cup around.

"I have enough for both of us." He takes my cup and sets it on the bed side table.

"But my mo-"

"Needs time to think," he says, cutting me off. "It took you so long to accept yourself. Heck, I had to give you a lot of space, so you should give her some time too." He puts his hand on my shoulder.

"But Ellio-"

"Shh, he's fine. He might feel like shit for outing his own brother, but he will be fine." He puts his other hand on my shoulder and looks me in the eyes.

"We're going to San Fransisco." My eyes widen. "We're going to San Francisco!" Carter yells, ripping the blankets off me.

"I guess you were right. I do need to get away from this town and be me for a bit." He smiles at me.

I spend the rest of my morning getting ready with Carter. I get to use his shampoo and wear his clothes, including his underwear. I've never felt closer to another human being.

"*Last call for flight 192a to San Francisco International Airport.*" I hear echo faintly from the terminal as I take my seat next to Carter. I open my phone and look at my messages, opening up my last text conversation with my mom. It was nothing special, something about what I wanted for dinner this week. I begin to type:

Mom, I know you're not happy with me right now and I know your mind is thinking a hundred different things. I know what it feels like. I've thought them all and thought them 10000 times over and there is no other answer. This is who I am. I'm gay. I wish I could have told you myself, when I was ready, but just know that it's okay. I'm okay. I'm on the plane to San

Francisco and I'm hoping to hear from you before I get back.
Love, your son

"Passengers, please prepare to taxi to the runway," the stewardess says over the speakers.

"Send," I say out loud. Carter looks down at my phone and then back at me. I press the power button and my screen goes black.

"You know they don't make you turn your phone off anymore, right? Airplane mode,"Carter says, laughing.

"Shut up." I lean my head on his as the plane slowly jerks into motion.

I'm finally in San Francisco. The immediate vibe I get is different from that of Los Angeles. It's, somehow, smoother here. I have no other way to describe it. The overcast rolling in over the hillsides and the mixture of street performers and well-dressed business men occupying their own little part of the city add to the aura of the city. We arrive at our hotel and it's really fancy and probably stupid expensive. I wouldn't expect anything less of Carter.

"It's a bit late. Shall we order in?" he asks, taking his shoes off as I lay on the bed. I'm a little smelly from our long day of traveling.

"I don't mind. Room service or take out?" I sit up, eyeballing the bathroom for my shower.

"You pick." He unbuttons his shirt and I give him a look. "Oh, I was gonna shower while you order," he says, taking of his pants, gently folding them and placing them on the desk.

"I was gonna shower while you ordered," I say, getting off the bed.

"After you," he says, starting to put his shirt back on.

"I'm not that hungry right now. Maybe we can

shower first?" I walk up to him and brush his shirt sleeves off of his shoulders.

"You sure?" he asks, even though he is already walking toward the shower. I close the door behind him and start taking off my clothes. The room begins to fill with steam as Carter jumps into the large, white-tiled shower before me. I look in the mirror as I take off my remaining clothes.

"Coming in!" I announce quietly as I scoot past the shower curtain, letting the warm water cascade over my face. I close my eyes as I feel Carter's hands caress my back. I turn around, letting the water fall onto his head. He runs his hands through his hair. The water makes it look darker, almost brown. His freckles glissen as the water runs down his cheeks. The moisture on his shoulder and chest creates a mesmerizing glow. I feel the desire to touch him, to feel his body under my fingers. I'm frightened by my own thoughts, but I'm also intrigued. Carter must be thinking the same thing as his hands run through my hair. They are soapy. The smell of his shampoo rushes to my nose. It's familiar and makes me feel comfortable. I lean back, letting the water rinse the soap from my hair. Carter rubs my body as the soapy water runs down it. I feel his hands wander. My body feels weak to his touch. My mind races as feelings of pleasure reach every inch of my body. I mimic Carter's movements, reaching and grabbing at his body. His is face close to mine, but just far enough away that it leaves me wanting more.

"It's okay," he says, bringing me closer His hands reach lower. I feel myself shiver as the cold air outside the shower blows in. My body goes stiff from the sensation.

Carter laughs gently as I lean into him, going limp in his arms. The water washes the final bit of soap off both of our bodies. I sit outside of the shower for a while, feeling myself slowing coming back down to Earth. Carter finishes his shower while I sit in silence with the stupidest smile on my face.

"Yes, two quesadillas and a side of sour cream, 2 milkshakes: one strawberry, one vanilla, and a side of fries." Carter hangs up the phone to room service. "They said it will be about half an hour," he says snuggling up in bed beside me. I'm turn on my phone for the first time since the flight. Carter snatches it from my hand and sets it on the nightstand. I don't fight back.

"Let's just be together," he says, grabbing the laptop from his bag and opening up the SFSU website.

"What are you doing?" I say, peering over as he navigates the site.

"I don't think I even have to wait 'til tomorrow to see the school. If you're there, it's perfect."

I feel a small sense of guilt wash over me.

"I wanna be with you too. But if you would rather go somewhere else, please don't go to a school just for me," I mutter, trying not to dampen the mood.

"Thanks for worrying about me, but, honestly, this is the best thing for me." He pauses. "My dad always assumed I would go to his alma mater because he went to Saint Anne's and it's their sister university, and I always thought: yeah, I should go there 'cuz it's what he wants. I never wanted anything to do with college." He looks at me and rubs his hand on my knee. "If, for some reason, you were to hate me and never talk to me again tomorrow, I would still want to go to this school," he reassures me. I grab the TV remote and put on the food network. We both watch in awe, drooling, waiting for our food to arrive, hand in hand.

"Morning sunshine!" I'm woken up by the sound of the hotel curtains opening swiftly. The light shines bright in my eyes. I reach for my phone to check the time, but remember it's still off and set it back down.

"It's 7 A.M!" Carter says, grabbing his shaving bag from his suitcase and walking to the bathroom.

"7 A.M?" I lay back down, grabbing for my phone and turning it on.

"I'm on Connecticut time," he laughs, entering the bathroom. I hear the sink turn on and the shaving cream spew from the canister. My phone turns on and pings a few times, all of them texts. I check and it is, indeed, 7A.M. I brace myself before opening up the messages. I see one from Sid. He is thrilled that we're in the same time zone. Even though he is in the hospital with his grandmother again, he still remembers to text me often. There is another from Naomi asking how our flight was, but no reply from my mom. I set my phone back down and plug it in to charge.

"Give her some space," I say, getting out of bed. I keep repeating what Carter told me yesterday to keep myself sane.

"What?" Carter asks as he peeks his head out from the bathroom. I gesture for him to go back in and he does. I walk over to the the door and lean in. He kisses me, getting a bit of shaving cream on my chin.

"Can you grow a beard?" I ask, looking at him as he slides the razor down his face.

"A very light ginger beard that only shows up in

the sun." He laughs as I rub my face with my hands. It's impeccably smooth. He watches me as I do it. "I love your face." He brushes my chin with the back of his hand. The space between us feels different, like we've become one. It's truly amazing.

A few BART rides and a taxi later, we have arrived at the entrance of San Francisco State University. The campus is large and hilly and filled with lots of grassy common areas for students. The buildings are really angular, like they were designed to look like mountains. We stop at a local sandwich shop on campus that the taxi driver recommended. All the sandwiches on the menu have super interesting names. I go for the *Adam Richman*, which is just a fancy chicken sandwich. Carter got the *Handsome Owl* and it's made from some very odd vegan meat with a spicy wasabi sauce. I take a bite and I am instantly pleased with what I ordered.

Our first stop was the university's music department. My choice. SFSU might be know for its film department, but I'm more interested in music and how it's made. I'm not sure if anything will come out of studying music production, but it's a start for me and my college career. After exploring the department, we head to the building where Carter's major would be. To my surprise, he stops in front of the writing block of the university, as well as the library.

"I didn't know you wrote?" I ask him as we wander through the library, looking at the rows of books. Each row holds about ten times the amount we have back at our school.

"I don't. Well, I should say I have not, yet." He continues. " I always felt like nothing in my life was worth writing about, like I did not matter, but I always felt the passion. I figured I should explore that while it's still there." He smiles and I smile back. He's similar to me. We both aren't certain about anything when it comes to our futures, except that we love each other.

We head back and rest at the hotel a bit.

"Tomorrow's our last night here, then we leave early the next day. We have to leave by 5 A.M." He sits up in bed.

"I don't want it to end!" I sit up next to him, dramatically putting my arms in the air.

"We're both eighteen, you know," he proclaims.

"Yeah...?" I question, taken aback by his sudden statement. .

"We're in a big city. There has to be some eighteen plus clubs." He looks at me, excited.

"Like a gay club?" I laugh, questioning him.

"Yeah, why not?" He pulls out his phone to see if there are any nearby.

I have never once thought about going to a gay bar, even living in L.A. Even though West Hollywood was only a short drive away, it never crossed my mind that I would be connected to it in any way. Maybe it was because I was too young or too closeted, but I'm suddenly filled with anxiety and excitement.

"There are a ton in The Castro," Carter says, confused.

"Oh, that's like the gay area!" I chime in.

"Huh?" Carter questions.

"You've never seen it, like, in a movie? It's where a lot of important stuff happened back in, like, the 70's for gay rights." Carter shrugs in response. "Have you ever

251

been?" I ask, intrigued. He looks confused. "To a gay bar?" I push further.

"No, I live in Connecticut," he laughs.

I'm suddenly realize that Carter isn't the experienced guy I saw him as. Sure, he is super out and proud and all the jazz, but he is just a small town boy. It's kind of cute to see him out of his element. We find a street on Google with a lot of gay clubs and hop into an Uber.

"Here's your stop. Be safe, boys!" our Uber driver says as we scoot out of the back seat. I grab Carter's hand. I feel him flinch for a split second.

"I forgot where we were," he laughs as his grip tightens. We walk up and down the streets outside of the bars, holding hands while we look for one that is eighteen plus. I see Carter's eyes glow as he looks around. I see the various pride flags flying from balconies and in restaurants. People are handing us flyers for themed nights at their bars. Some of them are men, some women, and some are neither. The people here are all mixes of everything you can imagine. Back home, Carter and I are the weirdos who don't fit in. Here, we blend in with the crowd. I untuck my shirt as we walk past a small bar. It's calm on the outside, but we can hear the faint bump of pop music coming from inside. We hand the bouncer our I.Ds. he nods and hands them back. We walk past the curtain into a room of about 50 guys. All of them are dancing and some are shirtless. Most of them are older men in their 40's and mid-50's. Carter and I look at each other and head over to the bar and sit down.

"This isn't what I expected," Carter laughs as we look around at everyone.

"We gotta be at least 20 years younger than

everyone in here." I grab his hand and we laugh again.

"You must be from out of town!" A man comes over to us to strike up a conversation.

"How could you tell?" Carter laughs.

"My name's Sam and this is my husband, Marco." Another man appears and puts out his hand. Carter and I shake their hands as we introduce ourselves.

"What bring you two young-ins here?" Marco asks, sitting down next to Sam.

"This place looked the least intimidating," I say over the music.

Carter chimes in, "At least from the outside!" We all laugh. I'm still holding Carter's hand tightly.

"You together?" Sam asks, grabbing his husband's hand after noticing our clasped hands.

"Yes, sir." Carter replies, rubbing his thumb against my skin.

"Ah, young love! Sam, remember those times?" Marco says as he wraps his arm around Sam.

"How are old you two?" Sam asks us.

"Eighteen," we both respond.

"Wow, so young!" Sam shouts.

Sam is an older, grey-haired gentleman with a face that looks like it's been through the wear and tear of life. Marco has, what I assume is, a hispanic accent, darker skin and curly hair. He reminds me of Grand in an odd way.

"You boys be safe. Don't take any drugs from nobody and take a taxi home, not the train, you hear!" Sam yells at us as Marco pulls him back onto the dance floor.

Carter and I look at each other and smile. I lean in

for a kiss. We get up and leave the bar and The Castro.

27

"I don't wanna." I stubbornly refuse to open the car door.

"It's been almost a week. Your mom has to have calmed down by now," Carter says, nudging my shoulder. I grab my backpack from the backseat. A little rainbow flag pin is pinned to the front. It's a souvenir from our trip. Carter gets out and hugs me before getting in his car and driving away.

I walk up to my front door and open it up. The locks aren't changed and my key still works, so my own imagination's wild thoughts haven't come true.

"Mom?" I shout into the house. I walk into the kitchen and see her cooking something in a big pot. I set my backpack down on the counter.

"Whatcha' making?" I ask, but I know by the smell that it's her homemade chicken soup. She looks over at me and then down at the counter. Her eyes pause on my backpack and the little rainbow pin.

"Please don't leave you things around. It's unsightly." She doesn't make eye contact. I grab my bag and set it at my feet, out of sight.

"Chicken soup?" I ask, trying to sway the

conversation away from me.

"Your brother isn't feeling well. He missed school today," she says, still not looking at me, her tone very distant.

"How is he doing?" I ask, remembering all the things I tried to forget during my trip.

"He doesn't seem to think he did anything wrong. That must run in the family," she replies crudely.

"Well, we should blame that teacher. She shouldn't have gotten involved with a student in the first place. Elliott is just a kid," I bite back.

"You're the one to talk about inappropriate relationships." Her tone is more hostile now.

"Okay, Mom." I give up and grab my bag. "By the way, I had a lovely time on my trip, thanks for asking. The college was beautiful. It's all I could have ever hoped for. San Francisco is amazing," I say. I don't turn back and continue walking up the stairs.

"I'm coming in." I open the door to Elliott's room, my backpack still in hand. "So your sick?" I say, sitting down on the edge of his bed. He looks at me and then glances away. "I'm not mad at you," I say. He looks down at the pin on my backpack.

"I'm sorry, Brighton." Elliott sits up and scoots to the end of the bed and rests his hand on my bag.

"Forget about that. It was horrible and, yeah, I wish you didn't do what you did, but I'm more worried about you." He looks at me, confused. "You know what your teacher did is not okay, right?" I put my hand on his shoulder and he looks away. "Elliott, come on." I shake him a little to get him to look at me. He ignores me and scoots back up into bed. "Mom is making chicken soup." I say, getting up and walking to the doorway.

"I'm not really sick." Elliott says, his voice muffled from under the covers.

"I know," I say, closing the door. I walk down the hallway and into my room so I can set down my things. I open my bag and take out all the papers from the college, as well as the flyers that were handed to me in The Castro. I smile as I remember the trip and remember me and Carter and how it felt to be with him. My face turns red thinking about it.

My phone vibrates in my pocket. It's Lin on FaceTime, so I grab my laptop and take the call on there.

"Hey, long time no see!" I say cheerily. His face is pale. "Hey, what's wrong?" I take my laptop and sit up in my bed.

"Sid's grandmother...it's bad, Brighton," he says. I look past him and see that he is in a strange place I've never seen before.

"Where's Sid," I ask, frantic now.

"He's in with her now. The doctors don't think she's gonna pull through, Brighton. I don't know what to do." Lin is on the brink of tears. I feel myself starting to cry, but know now isn't the time for that. I knew Sid's grandma had been in and out of the hospital since Christmas, ever since "the big fall," but I didn't realize it was this bad. *I never thought she would...* I stop myself from thinking any farther.

"Lin, when you can, tell Sid and his grandma that I'm sending them my best wishes." I try to smile. Seeing Lin like this is hard, but I'm glad it's him telling me about this and not Sid. I don't think I could handle seeing Sid cry, especially when he's so far away.

"I gotta go. My mom is waiting for me in the car. Visiting hours are over." Lin hangs up the call and I go downstairs.

"Can I have some soup?" I ask Mom as I wipe away a couple tears that escaped from my eyes. She hands me a bowl and a spoon.

"M-mom," I say, my voice shaking. "Sid's grandma...she's not going to make it." I start to cry. I feel like I've reverted to my younger self. Mom hands me a Kleenex and continues dishing out soup. "Mom?" I say getting up and walking towards her. "Did you hear me? Sid's grandma is-"

"I heard you." I see her eyes are watery and I go in for a hug. "Brighton, stop, not now, busy." She shoves me off her. She's gentle, but it's enough for me to step backwards.

"M-ma!" I back away. I'm horrified. I can't hold back my tears as they changed from being about Sid to being about this. "Mom, it's me, your son." She doesn't look at me. "Mom." I cry out her name. She grabs a bowl of soup and puts it on a tray.

"Take this to you brother." She motions to the tray.

"Mom, what's so wrong with me that you won't even touch me?" I push the tray away from me. She grabs it and walks to the stairs. Without thinking, I grab my keys off the counter and run as fast as I can out the front door, not even looking back.

Before I know it, I'm at Carter's house. I didn't know where else to go. I knock on the door. I can't call Carter to come down because I left my phone in my room.

"Hello!" The door opens to reveal Carter's mom. I'm suddenly aware of how red my eyes and cheeks are and frantically wipe my face.

Hi Mrs. Hall, is Carter here?" I ask, trying to sound as normal a possible. My voice still sounds a bit stuffy from crying.

"No, I'm afraid not. He and his sister went to pick up dinner for us. Mr. Hall is away on business, so we decided to treat ourselves to pizza!" she says, trying to look at my face. "It's cold out there. Why don't you come in and wait. They should be back soon!" She grabs my shoulder and shuffles me in the house. I take off my shoes before entering since they are muddy from running to my car earlier. I sit down on a couch in the living room and she brings me a cup of hot tea and sits down on the other end of the couch, facing me. "Are you okay, dear?" She pushes a cup of sugar cubes closer to me. I set the cup of tea down next to it and stare at the white shiny cubes.

"Mrs. Hall, were you okay when Carter told you?" I say, grabbing a few cubes of sugar and plopping them in my tea. I avoid making eye contact.

"Told me?" She pauses. "Oh," she exclaims as she realizes what I'm asking. "At first it was a bit of a shock, but I always knew my boy was a bit out there." She chuckles.

"And Mr. Hall?" I question.

"Well, he is a bit old fashioned, but he didn't react all that much. He just ignored it at first."

"And now?" I ask, looking up at her. My eyes are finally dry.

"Well, now he is more accepting. He doesn't make any rude comments about it and let's Carter do his own thing." She smiles at me as I take a sip of the tea. It tastes like flowers and sweetener.

"Carter's lucky" I say, trying not to think about my mom.

"He sure is." She smiles and continues, "he was lucky to find a lovely boy like you to share himself with." I smile back.

"My mom isn't coming around to it. You know, me and Carter." I try to say what I'm thinking, but my brain is all swirls.

"I thought that might be what's going on. Carter told me when he was packing for your trip." I look over at her, my eyes welling up again. "My best friend back home's grandma is sick." My tears leak onto my cheeks and fall down my face.

"Oh dear." She comes close to me and puts her arm around my shoulder. It's warm and her curly, red hair scratches against my face.

"It's okay, dear. Everything's gonna be okay," she says quietly as she strokes the back of my head as I sob into my hands.

The sound of the front door opening catches my attention and I look up.

"Brighton?" Carter walks over and takes his mom's place as she stands up and grabs the pizzas from Naomi.

"Brighton is staying for dinner. Naomi, set an extra seat at the table," his mom announces and heads for the kitchen, leaving us alone. I explain what happened at home to Carter.

"Thanks for the pizza. It was delicious!" I say as I stack three pieces of crust on my plate. Carter grabs one of them and bites into it.

"No problem, dear!" His mom looks back at us.

"Brighton, let's go up to my room." Carter grabs my hand and looks back at his mom. When we get to his room, he closes the door and sits next to me on his bed. "Do you want to stay here tonight?" Carter puts his arms around me.

"Are you sure?" I question.

"My mom actually asked me when we were in the kitchen if I wanted you to stay over. You know, since home is weird right now." I smile at him

"Please." I hug him.

"My mom says she will talk to your mom." Carter pulls my head back and looks at me.

"Do you think it will help?" I ask.

"It's worth a shot, right?" He smiles and we lay back in bed together.

28

It's been over a week since I started staying at Carter's house and enough is enough. His mom let me sleep in his room the first night, but now I'm in the guest room and it's really lonely. Don't get me wrong, I love seeing Carter in the morning for breakfast, but the big bedroom is characterless. It feels like I've been forced out of my own home again. I've held on this long, but the time has come for me to go back home. I just hope Carter's mom can talk some sense into mine.

"Brighton, I'm coming in!" Carter's mom knocks on my door and Carter follows behind her.

"Naomi is already at school. My husband has given you guys excused absences, so don't worry." She smiles at me as I fold the clothes Carter let me borrow in a pile. We decided it would be best for me and Carter to be there when she talks to my mom, and that it would be best if Elliott wasn't there, just for the sake of making it easier on me. I grab my keys and Carter and I get in my car. His mom follows in her SUV.

"You ready?" Carter says, grabbing my hand before we go in. We get out of the car and he let's go. I grab onto it again as we follow his mom up to the door.

Carter and I sit eagerly, listening to our moms talk.

It's almost unreal to see these two worlds combined. My boyfriend and his mom are in my house, and everyone knows that he is, indeed, my boyfriend. There are points where I hear my mom raise her voice, but she quickly quiets down.

"He is your son, Cherie. You think I loved this at first?" I hear Carter's mom say loudly to my mom.

"I know he is my son. But whenever I think about the things he has done, I just don't understand," my mom says.

"You don't need to understand how the mind of a gay man works, Cherie." Carter's mom snaps back. I can't help but laugh a little at her wording. "I didn't love the idea of a gay son at first either. I mean, we all think about our son's wife and kids from the second they are born. But, you know what, I love my son, gay or straight. Heck, he could kill someone and I would still stand by him." Carter laughs at his mom comparing being gay to committing murder.

"Of course I love my son!" my mom claps back.

"Then why has he been living at my house for a week and not home in his own bed? He was so sad, Cherie, I couldn't believe it," Carter's mom says. "He told me you wouldn't even hug him," she yells.

I stand up and walk over to the kitchen, where they are standing just out of sight. Carter walks up and grabs my hand. I look around the corner and my mom is crying.

"Mom!" I walk over to her and put my hand on her shoulder. She places her hand atop mine.

"I don't understand, Brighton. This lifestyle you have chosen, I don't get it." She shakes her head. Carter stands next to his mom.

"Ms. Anderson," Carter chimes in, "when your son moved here, he was terrified of his feelings. I mean, he was making himself sick over the lies he was telling to adhere to the lifestyle *you* want for him." My mom looks up at Carter. "I know what it's like to feel like that. It's the worst. I dont wish anyone to ever feel like that, ever. But, I also don't ever wish anyone to be outed like your son was," he finishes. She looks over at me.

"Don't be mad at your brother." She looks at me as if she never thought of it that way before.

"I'm not, Mom. He didn't mean to hurt me. But what your doing is making what he did a million times worse. This is why I didn't tell you. This exact reaction is what my worst nightmare looked like."

"Is that true?" She looks me in the eyes for the first time in a while.

"Mom, I was scared." My eyes start to water. She pulls me in for a hug.

"I still don't get it," she says, crying.

"I didn't either, not for a long time," I comfort her.

" I read your message when you were on your trip." Mom says, still hugging me. "I love you, Brighton, don't ever think I didn't." She pulls me back and looks at me. I look over at Carter and his eyes are glistening a little. His mom has her arm around him. "I will try to understand you more, son. I can't promise I will be like Carter's mom overnight, but I will try." I give my mom one last hug before walking over to Carter and hugging him. I refrain for giving him a quick kiss because I don't think my mom is ready for that yet.

"Stay for lunch. Please, my treat. I owe you for

taking care of Brighton," my mom says to Carter's mom, pulling her to sit down at the breakfast nook.

"Can Carter and I go up to my room," I ask gingerly.

"Door open," our moms say at the same time. Carter's mom laughs.

"Look at that!" Carter yells quietly as we enter my room. He puts both hands on my cheeks and kisses me hard. I kiss him back.

"You don't know how bad I wanted to do that!" I say as I pull away for air. He smiles at me and I go back to kissing him. My phone interrupts us before we get any further.

"Did you change your ringtone?" Carter says, grabbing my phone, which is somehow not dead, off my shelf.

"No, that's my ringtone for anyone I don't have in my contacts," I say, taking the phone from Carter.

"Hello?" I answer.

"Brighton! How are you?" I immediately recognize the voice.

"Dad?" I say. Carter steps back and looks confused.

29

My father, Bruce Anderson, isn't all that bad of a guy. My mom has a bit of hatred in her heart for him after all he put her through during their marriage, but she did fall in love with the guy for a reason. He as a certain charm to him. Almost everyone who meets him takes a liking to him.

My dad is flying to Connecticut. Word finally reached him that Elliott, Mom and I had left and he quickly booked a flight to come here. He even took time off from his dental practice to see us. I was tasked with the job of picking him up at the airport.

"Why do I have to come with?" Naomi whines in the passenger seat as we drive to the airport.

"Because you didn't have a important chem test today and you get to skip school for this," I answer back jokingly

"True," she says to herself. "How long is he staying?" she asks, looking out the window, tracing Jack's name into the steamy glass.

"It's Friday and I get to see him all weekend. He is leaving on Monday."

"You never talk about your dad," she says with no

tact.

"He was a good dad. He was very strict and traditional, but, you know, he cheated on my mom," I say reluctantly.

"Yeah," she sighs. "I'm gonna nap," she says, leaning her head onto the window.

"Aw, man. I wanted to hear about you and your budding relationship." Naomi perks up.

"How did you know about that?" Her eyes widen.

"I saw you on New Years. Plus, you haven't been the most subtle at school," I laugh.

"We're not trying to get to serious. I mean, school is over in five months. That's not a lot of time." She looks sad.

"So, do you know where you're going to apply?"

"Undecided." She wipes Jack's name on the window away.

"How about SFSU?" I ask hintingly.

"As much as I would love to spend another four years being my brother's third wheel, I think I'll pass," she laughs. She lays her head against the window again and dozes off.

"Well, who do we have here?" My dad says in his deep husky voice as he gets in the back seat. Naomi jolts awake.

"Oh, no, Mr. Anderson, please have the front seat!" She starts to open her door.

"No, no, no! I couldn't take the seat from my son's beautiful girlfriend and, please, call me Bruce," he says, looking at me. Naomi shoots me a look and I can see she is holding back a bought of laughter. I start driving away from the airport and look at my dad in the rear view mirror. His hair is grey on the sides but still dark on top. The hint of stubble on his face is all gray. He is wearing a button up shirt, light wash jeans and a leather jacket. I don't how he's okay in this weather. I feel cold just looking at him.

"Also, Dad, this is Naomi. She's not my girlfriend." I laugh.

"Well sorry, my mistake." He smiles.

"Well, technically, I'm his ex-girlfriend!" Naomi jokes. I elbow her in the passenger's seat lightly.

"Oh, I see then." My dad chuckles roughly.

"So, Dad, where to? Your hotel?" I ask.

"No, no! I want to go to your place to see your brother!" he says excitingly.

"Elliott is at school, Dad. It's Friday." He looks at his watch.

"Well shoot, kid, then what are you doing here?" he asks, concerned.

"I had to pick you up. Mom wouldn't," I explain.

"It's just like her, not putting your school first. You know how important education is," he argues. His response reminds of how my house was before he left.

"I know, Dad, but it couldn't be helped. Anyways, I have an easy workload this semester, so it's okay."

"If you say so," my dad grunts. "And you Naomi?" he asks, less concerned

"I'm just skipping!" she laughs.

"I'm glad she's your EX-girlfriend," Dad jokes. We all laugh.

"Let's stop at a restaurant; my treat! Then we can pick Elliott up at school!" Dad says, pointing at a freeway exit. We sit down at a Denny's right off the freeway.

Naomi and my dad chat about this and that. I tell him about Sid's grandmother's worsening condition and he becomes concerned. He and Sid always got along.

"Pay at the counter when you ready, guys." Our waitress sets the check down in front of me. He looks at the check, surprised.

"Wow, you *have* grown up!" He looks at me sincerely.

"Yeah, Dad, I have." I smile at him. We pile back in the car and drive to the school.

"DAD!" Elliott jumps in the backseat and gives him a big hug. Naomi gets out and goes back to class. Carter replaces her.

"Don't you have one more class?" I ask as he sits down.

"I can miss one French class. It's not like it will come in handy in San Francisco anyways," he says excitedly.

"No way! Did you-" I start as he pulls out a letter.

"I got in!" He pulls me into a hug. In his excitement, he didn't see my dad in the backseat.

"Oh, hello!" He turns around and smiles with a small wave.

"Dad, this is Carter, my friend and Naomi's brother!" I breeze past the introduction. Carter gives me a look.

"What's this about San Francisco?" he questions.

"I applied to a school there and so did Carter, Dad. He got his acceptance letter."

"Did you check the mail today?" he asks excitedly.

"Mom did. Nothing," I say dejectedly.

"They have to send a rejection!" Dad chimes in.

"What?" I respond.

"If they don't want ya', they send you a letter as well. So, no news is good news!" I can tell Dad is trying to cheer me up. I begin driving again and drop him and Elliott off at his hotel.

"You don't wanna stay with them?" Carter asks as we pull away.

"No. Elliott needs to see him more than I do. I told him about the whole thing with Elliott and the teacher. I think my dad should talk to him about it."

"Oh, yeah. Yikes, I wouldn't wanna be there for that either." He cringes.

" Exactly. So, now we have a few hours to kill while they talk." I lean in and kiss him, pulling over into a McDonald's parking lot.

"Yeah!" he says, leaning in. I feel his breath on my lips as he speaks,

"I miss our hotel room," I blurt out as were making out. Our lips pull apart.

"Oh?" Carter laughs. I feel my face go red.

"You know, it's just...we can't really do anything at my house 'cuz of my mom, and, well, your house is never empty," I say, embarrassed, fiddling with my thumbs on the steering wheel.

"Well, this will just have to tide you over then." He leans in and kisses me again.

"That does the opposite of tide me over," I laugh. My phone vibrates

"Oh, Elliott says he is spending the night at Dad's and that we can head back."

"You have plans for tomorrow?" Carter asks as I pull out of the parking lot.

"Just dinner with Dad and Elliott."

"Well then, I'm staying at yours tonight," he smiles. We head back to my house and go up to my room.

"Is your Mom downstairs?" Carter asks as I lay down on my bed next to him.

"She's cooking dinner. She will be busy for at least an hour."

"Good." He bites his lip and rolls over onto me. His warmth radiates through my whole body. My laptop rings in the corner of my room.

"Shouldn't you get that?" Carter leans over. I grab him and kiss him. The ringing stops. I start to unbutton Carter's shirt. It's a light shade of purple today with shimmery gold buttons. My phone starts ringing.

"I should get that." I reach over and grab my phone. It's a FaceTime call.

"Hey Sid. Uhh, can I call you back? I, uh-" I stop my sentence midway as the call finally connects to video.

"Bright." Sid's eyes are puffy and the color has drained from his face.

"No." I feel my arms tingle.

"My grandma, Brighton, she passed away in her sleep this morning." I see Sid break down. The phone moves away from his face quickly. I drop my phone on the bed. My arms and legs start to go numb and I feel dizzy. Carter picks up the phone.

"Hey Sid," he says in a calming voice. Sid waves, wiping his tears away with his sleeve. Carter puts the phone back in my hand.

"Don't you move. I'm coming to Los Angeles," I say as I take the phone, crying.

"No, you can't. You have school and your dad is

271

there." It's just like Sid to be worried about me in a time like this.

"No, you can't be alone. You're all alone," I cry. Carter takes the phone from me.

"Hey, Sid, you have a place to go, right?" Carter's trying to make sense of this situation.

"I can stay with my mom for a few nights, but I can't live there and I don't think I can be in Grandma's house without her just yet," he says, trying to stay together. He is sitting on a bench, presumably outside the hospital.

"You want to come here?" Carter asks nonchalantly.

"What?" I tune back into the conversation

"I can't afford it, man. All I have is the money in my pocket from lunch." Sid looks somewhere beyond the phone.

"I have some points saved up. If you want, after everything is settled there, you can use them to fly here," Carter offers.

"Would that be okay, Bright? Can I?" I see Sid's eyes light up.

"Of course, man. You're my brother, like my mom's third child. She would never shut you out." I grab the phone from Carter.

"I know this is soon but, do you know when they are planning the funeral?" I ask, trying to figure everything out.

"Grandma didn't want to be buried, so we're spreading her ashes on the pier where she met Grandpa." Sid looks away from the camera and wipes his eyes.

"Well, whenever you want, let me know and I'll

get you here." Carter pokes his head into the camera's view.

"Thanks, man." Sid look at us. He finally notices that Carter has his shirt half-open.

"Oh, shit. What did I just interrupt?" Sid lets out a little giggle. I laugh and pull Carter's shirt back up on his body.

"Miss you, man." I say as something distracts Sid from the call.

"I gotta go; my mom's here. She's taking me to hers for the night." He hangs up.

"Life's too short," my dad says as he takes a bite of his steak. We're at Applebees for dinner. Carter tagged along for moral support, since I'm still shaken from the news. "Poor Siddy boy." He shakes his head. "When is he flying in?"

"On Friday," Carter answers my dad.

"Oh, shoot. I'll have just missed him. Well, give him my wishes," Dad says, dipping his fries into his shake.

"Wow, like father like son!" Carter exclaims."This boy does that all the time. He always mixes sweet and savory foods!" Carter mocks me.

"Not true!" I say, pretending to argue with him..

"There is no other way to eat!" Dad chimes in.

"Well, we will have to agree to politely disagree," Carter says, bowing to my father. They both laugh. My dad and Carter are hitting it off. They both seem to have the same sense of humor. Maybe that's why it was so easy for me to get a good banter going between Carter and I when we first met.

"You know, Dad, life is too short-" Elliott's baked

potato arrives and I stop my speech. I sit, thinking. I make eye contact with Carter as he places his hand on the table. I grab it while nobody's looking and hold on tight. Carter shoots me a look and quickly catches on.

Dad looks down at the table of food and locks eyes with our hands. I take my other hand and stir my shake nervously. I feel like dying on the inside. Dad grunts and looks up at us.

"So, uh, did you hear back from that San Francisco school?" he looks up from our hands, looking, instead, at our faces.

"No word yet." I sigh. Carter looks at me with excitement after my Dad's nonchalant reaction.

"It will come!" Dad smiles at us and we finish our meal.

"I'll see you boys tomorrow," Dad says as he gets into a cab. Carter, Elliott and I get into Carter's car and drive home.

"Did that just happen?" I ask as Elliott gets out and goes into our house.

"Yeah, I think it did." Carter is looking straight out the front window.

"Do you think he gets it? Like, that were more than friends?" I think back to just an hour ago. My hand still feels hot from Carter's touch.

"I think so. Like, there's no way he couldn't, right?" Carter replies.

"And bringing up San Francisco like it all makes sense now why I wanna go to San Francisco!" We both laugh hysterically. "Oh, the homosexuals like it in San Francisco. It all make sense now!" I try to mimic my dad's voice as we continue to laugh.

"Kiss," Carter says, pointing to his cheek. I plant one on him and get out of the car. "I love you!" he says, pulling away as I walk up to my house.

It's the next day and, much to Mom's dismay, Dad is back in our house again.

"It was nice seeing you, Dad!" Elliott says as Dad walks into the living room.

"Good seeing you too, kiddo." He rustles Elliott's hair and then turns to me.

"Brighton, I'm proud of you." He sits up straight and looks over at Elliott, then back at me.

"I've got myself two very brave boys." He smiles. "Brighton, walk me out?" he says, as he's walking to the front door.

"Goodbye, Bruce." Mom says from the kitchen as Dad opens the door. He looks at her and waves as I shut the door behind us.

"You and your partner," he grunts uncomfortably, "will come visit me when you're in San Francisco, won't you?" he asks as I walk him up the street to meet his cab.

"Yes, me and my..." I pause. "Carter will come visit you." I smile.

"You happy?" he asks. I nod. "That's good," he says as his cab pulls up. He gets into it, waving to me as he drives away. I walk back into the house.

"Your dad, did you tell him?" Mom asks. I'm surprised she brought up the topic.

"Yeah, he was cool with it," I say, sitting down on the couch. I lay there thinking about the past week and everything that's happened. I think about Sid, my dad and Carter. Everything is coming into place except for one thing: San Francisco. I applied before Carter and still haven't gotten a word from them.

Sid. Sid. Sid. My mind races as the clock on the wall of my math classroom continuously ticks. There are seconds until the bell rings and minutes before I get to see Sid. His ticket was one way. Carter says he can go back with his points whenever he wants or, to be more honest, whenever he feels ready. Sid is a tough guy, but his grandmother was his everything. She took him in when his own mother couldn't and had been his whole family for the past ten years. I don't even want to think about the pain he must be going through or what he thinks at night when he is trying to sleep. The only experience I have had with death is with the class gerbil in 3rd grade. We came in one morning and there he was, in his cage, not moving, stiff as a board. The teacher was, honestly, more distraught than any of us. We didn't understand death. My great aunt's death last year didn't affect me at all, either. I had never met her and my mom never talked about her. I'm lucky. I'm feel terrified of losing someone. My mind races as I think about all the people in my life that I love and want to keep safe.

"You're dismissed!" The bell rings and the sound of paper rustling as people pack their bags is overwhelming. I stand up and dart for the parking lot.

"You ready to go?" Carter says, patting my back.

"Yep. Mom picked him up at the airport over an hour ago. They should just be getting to my place."

"You think he will be surprised?" Carter asks, giddy as can be.

"He should be. We worked our asses off on this," I say as we both hop into my car and take off to my place.

"SID." I yell as I open the front door. There he is, sitting on my couch, eating a Subway sandwich.

"Brighton!" He hops up and we run into each other arms.

"You okay?" I ask, patting his back.

"I will be." He hugs me tighter.

"Wow, should I be jealous?" Carter chimes in.

"Get in here, Mr. Frequent Flier!" Sid grabs Carter and the hug gets split three ways. Sid grabs me and pulls me to the side. "So, man, did you and him, you know, dance the horizontal tango?" He nudges my side with his elbow.

"Now, Sid, you're not accusing me of deflowering our precious little Brighton, now, are you?" Carter jokes.

"Of course not, good sir" Sid speaks in an old English accent and we all laugh.

"You haven't been upstair yet, right?" I ask, excited.

"No. I was instructed to stay here with my Subway sandwich." Sid points to his food on the coffee table.

"Well, grab your footlong and follow us!" Carter yells. Sid looks down at his crotch and then at the coffee table

"Oh, you meant my sandwich!" We laugh as we

walk up the stairs.

"Okay! Open them!" I shout as we walk Sid into the previously empty guest bedroom.

The walls are a faint color of blue, Sid's favorite color, and there is a bed with a few neatly placed pillows sitting in the center of the room. I even tried to replicate his *Nirvana* poster dart board, but used a *Panic! At The Disco* poster instead.

"Oh, man, is this my room?" Sid asks, sitting down in a bean bag chair that I brought in from Elliott's attic.

"We wanted you to feel welcome, so we gave it a makeover," Carter says.

"With help from Naomi, of course" I add in, since she picked out all the furniture and bedding.

"Well, I'll have to thank her, then" Sid gets up and looks around at all the little things we put around the room.

"You can stay as long as you want, Sid," I say, plopping down on his bed.

"I will take you up on that offer." He plops down next to me.

"I'm coming in!" Carter jumps into our laps, his head landing in mine, knocking the wind out of both of us.

"I'm sorry to break up this cuddle fest, but I smell like an airplane toilet. I need to shower." Sid grabs his duffel bag and walks out into the hallway.

"Should we break in his bed." Caster nudges me jokingly

"You're gross." I shove him off me, laughing, before we head downstairs.

"Brighton!" Mom walks into the living room,

279

where Carter and I are watching TV. I quickly lift my head from its resting place on his shoulder. "I forgot to tell you because of all the excitement, but you have two letters!" She hands me two medium-sized envelopes.

"Shit," Carter says looking at the papers in my hand.

"What's all the commotion?" Sid walks down the stairs with a towel around his waist and in a turban on his head.

"I either just got accepted to college, or didn't," I say, not looking up from my lap.

"Shit," Sid says, sitting down next to us.

"Well," Carter says, grabbing one of the envelopes. "This one's from California Berkley." He holds up the first letter. As he lifts it, I see the SFSU emblem stamped at the top of the letter still sitting in my lap.

"Let's open that one first" I say, grabbing the letter on my lap and rubbing it like it's a genie lamp.

"Shall I?" Sid says, taking the letter from Carter. He rips open one side of the envelope and pulls out a thin sheet of paper and reads,

" Dear Brighton Anderson." He pauses. "The admissions committee has met and I am sorry to inform you that we were not able to admit you to University of California Berkeley for the 2019/2020 school year. We had over 9,000 applicants an-" Sid stops reading and puts down the letter. "Berkley is for stuck up rich kids anyway!" Sid says, trying to cheer me up. " No offense, Carter," he jokes.

"I'm just gonna do it." I look down at the letter from SFSU and begin to tear the flap open, grabbing the paper inside. Carter grabs my other hand as I pull out the letter. I read it silently to myself, then out loud.

"It is with pleasure that I inform you of your admission into San Francisco State University!" I jump up as does Carter and Sid.

"You got in!" Carter shouts.

"I got in!" We all jump around like absolute idiots.

"I take it Carter already got accepted as well?" Sid questions.

"Yeah, just last week. We have been waiting for this letter," Carter explains. Sid nods.

"What about you, Sid? Did you hear back from any of your choices?" I question, trying to calm down.

"They all rejected me." Sid picks at his leftover sandwich wrapper that's sitting on the table.

"Oh, Sid." I put my hand on his shoulder.

"It's still early. You can still apply to your other choices," Carter says, trying to comfort Sid.

"It's okay, guys, I'm not upset. I knew it was hard to get into the schools back home, close to Grandma, but now I can apply to out of state schools," he says, looking more sad than anything else.

31

"A double date?"

"Yes! You and my brother, me and Jack!" Naomi says as we make our way to the lunch table.

"I don't know, Naomi, won't that be a little weird?" I say, moving the peas on my plate around with my fork.

"Weird how? We're all friends," she says, taking a bite of the roast beef meal she ordered from the cafeteria.

"I mean, I don't know." I ponder why the idea of a double date with Carter feels weird to me. Is it because it's on Valentine's Day?

"Come on! Jack and I just started going out and, like, it's too early in the relationship to do something special on Valentine's Day," she whines.

"I don't think I've ever been on a date." The thought hits me and spills out of my mouth.

"What? But you're dating my brother!" Naomi sets her fork down on her tray.

"Yeah," I say pondering to myself. Things started off really weird with Carter. We went from being friends, to being who knows what, to being together. I guess the choir concert was a date, but that was an absolute fail. I technically asked him to be my boyfriend on the ocean "date", but we weren't really dating at that point.

"Come to think of it, you never took me out on a date when we were together, either" Naomi breaks my train of thought.

"Is Carter okay with the double date?" I ask.

"No. I'm not asking my brother on a date for you. That's your job," she says, shaking her carton of milk.

"I'll ask him," I agree. Naomi's face lights up.

"Valentine's day is tomorrow, so you have to ask him today!" She jumps up, drawing some attention from the other kids around us.

"He doesn't have any plans for us already?" I ask, knowing that Naomi usually knows everything about Carter when it comes to me and him, even before I do.

"Carter doesn't really like Valentine's Day..." Naomi's words trail off, as if the statement was missing some information..

"How c-" I'm cut off.

"You have to ask him about that yourself." I feel the air in the room get a little bit tense. "Speak of the devil!" Naomi stands up as Carter sits down. "I'm gonna go watch Jack's swim practice," she says, walking away and dumping her tray in the garbage. I watch Carter as he sets down his lunch. It's from home today. He pulls out a few small containers. Most of them are filled with vegetables and with some other mixture of what looks like stew.

"Hey, how come you don't like Valentine's Day?" The words slip from my mouth before I realize what I'm asking. I feel myself tense up as he opens his mouth. He takes a bite of some broccoli and thinks for a few seconds.

"Remember when I asked you if you had ever been in love?" he asks, not looking up at me.

"Yes?" I say, thinking back to that time when I thought love was what I had for Sid, or for the boy in Paris.

"And I said I thought I was?" He look up at me, his face twisted into an intense expression I have never seen before.

"You don't have to tell me if you don't want." I regret asking. I feel like I'm prying into something I don't need to know about.

"It's fine. I want to tell you." He sets down his fork and begins to tell me a story.

"It was two years ago: sophomore year. I had just come out and was feeling comfortable with myself for the first time in, basically, my whole life. It was probably similar to how you're feeling now." He smiles. I smile back.

"Except I didn't have a boyfriend like you. I was alone. Sure, I had my short run with Trevor, but, by this point, he was already so in denial of his feelings that I had given up on him. I never really loved him." I see a wave of sadness pass through his eyes as he pauses.

"But there was this other boy. His name was Grayson. He was on the field hockey team and he was beautiful. His hair was long, like shoulder length. He was the only boy in the school with hair that long, so he stood out. It was always nice too, not scraggly like the other guys on the team. He dressed better than everyone as well. He always wore button ups and nice shoes and, me being me, I saw similar traits to me in him with how he dressed and, overall, cared more about his appearance than most boys. I got into my head that he was gay."

"But he wasn't?" I ask. Carter's storytelling has always been enthralling.

"No, he wasn't." Carter looks down. He continues his story. "Now, you didn't think that I didn't have any friends before you got here, right?" he laughs. "I was actually friends with some of the field hockey boys, including Grayson, and, yes, Jean as well, before he became an idiotic buffoon. I would spend time with them and their mind numbing conversations about sports and hunting everyday just to be around Grayson. This went on for the entirety of sophomore year. I was out, but it's not like everyone knew. If someone asked, I told them, but it wasn't the talk of the school. Then junior year came along. It was the beginning of the spring semester around this time. I had gotten into a stupid fight at home with my dad over something that I don't even remember now. But, back then, any fight turned into a chance for my dad to make a snarky comment about my sexuality, or about fags." Hearing Carter say that word makes my skin crawl.

"So, I texted Greyson to meet up with me. He didn't have a girlfriend, so I knew he wouldn't be busy even though it was Valentine's Day. I was just so lonely in my house. I didn't want to be there and I just wanted to feel something. So, we met up." Carter pauses, taking a sip of his water. The cafeteria is clearing out as lunch period gets closer to ending.

"We decided to meet at the school football field. It's what we use as our track practice now. The school retired their football team before we were even students, but Grayson liked to throw around the ball from time to time with the other guys. So, I didn't object because I knew he liked it.

"I can't imagine you doing any type of sports," I laugh, thinking of Carter in a football jersey.

"Just wait, we'll get there." He takes another sip of his water. The bell rings but we ignore it.

"So, we are throwing the ball around for awhile and I'm bitching about my dad, just letting it out. Grayson could relate because his dad wanted him to focus more on academics and less on sports. So, we both were mad at the world a little bit, then BOOM-" Carter slams his hands down on the table. I jump slightly in my chair. "-the football hits me square in the face at full speed." Carter laughs and rubs his nose.

"My face was pouring blood and my nose had been just *destroyed* by Grayson's throw. He rushed over to me and walked me to the bleachers. Now I'm sitting there, trying to stop my bleeding nose. Once the inside of my nose stopped bleeding, Greyson ripped a piece of his shirt and went really close to my face, trying to make sure it wasn't broken. I was watching his eyes. They were dark, the darkest brown I had ever seen. In the moment, as he was touching my face," Carter pauses for a second and looks up at me, "I kissed him." Carter shrugs, looking off into the now empty cafeteria. I sit on the edge of my seat.

"And you can guess his reaction. It was like someone with a contagious disease had just touched him. He furiously wiped his mouth and spat at the ground, spewing any and every curse word he could think of.

"And you?" I ask, grabbing his hand.

"I was crying my eyes out like an idiot." Carter laughs. "He just threw the piece of his shirt at me, told me he isn't like that, called me some horrible things, got in his car and left. I went home feeling humiliated. The next day at school, I walked up to Grayson and the others, Jean was there by the way, and I was mortified. Grayson told them, all of them. They were horrible, Brighton. They wouldn't stop. They would call me names everyday, especially Grayson. Eventually, they all graduated or didn't care anymore."

"Except Jean," I say, putting the pieces together.

"Yeah." Carter nods.

"Well, it's a year later," I say as I scoot closer to him. "You're not going to be lonely this year."

"Well, of course not. I have you." He closes up his Tupperware container and shoves it in his bag.

"Well, actually, you have me and Jack and Naomi!" I blurt out.

"What?" Carter looks confused.

"We're going on a double date!" I grab Carter's hand and shake it, trying to act excited.

"You know what? That sounds good!" he says, matching my excitement.

"Okay! Get the details from Naomi. You're in her next class. I gotta go; I have a history test!" I get up and dump my plate, realizing we're both very late for our next classes.

"GSA, today after school!" Carter yells as I leave the cafeteria.

The GSA is booming. Sid, even though he is taking the online courses our school offers to graduate, comes down to sit and chat with us all. Jean even joins in the conversations with Sid. They, strangely, have a lot in common. A few girls from freshman year have joined. They're friends with Rachel and they have their own little group where they talk. It's more than I could have ever hoped for.

"Okay, so, we're set on a restaurant and a time," Naomi says, closing the notes app on her phone.

"Naomi says this is your first date!" Jack says, pushing my shoulder. Jean chuckles from behind us.

"No?" Carter says, chiming in

"I mean, kinda," I say, leaning back into my chair. "We have never really gone on a normal date." I continue the thoughts I had from lunch earlier today. Carter thinks for a second.

"Was San Francisco a date?" Carter questions. Naomi and Jack laugh.

"No, that was like a couples getaway. Basically your honeymoon, except you aren't married," Jack laughs.

"A date, guys, like dinner and a movie, walking around the town just holding hands and window shopping. Those are a date," Naomi clarifies. I see Carter making the same mental checklist is his head as me.

San Francisco, walking around The Castro holding hands, window shopping... well, window shopping for a gay bar to go into. We both smile at each other and laugh.

"Time to wrap it up, guys!" Mr. Briggs gets up and sets down his newspaper. "Gotta prepare for my own Valentine's Day," he says, grabbing his wallet off his desk. A thought strikes me. I have to get Carter flowers, or maybe chocolate.

"I gotta go too, guys!" I stand up and walk to the door. "See you tomorrow!" I sprint down the hallway to my car and drive to the store, where I buy the cheesiest panda bear holding a love heart and a small box of caramel chocolates.

The day goes by quickly. Friday always does. The last bell rings and I head over to Carter's house. Naomi and I agreed to have a "girl's evening" before our date to get ready. Once again, I find myself getting invited to "girls events", but I'm okay with it.

"My brother is at the store," Naomi says pulling me into her bedroom. It's the first time I've been in here and it's different than what I had imagined. The walls are white. I thought they would be pink or something, but the overall look is very mature. Sure, there are fluffy things everywhere: pillows and such, the odd, random bra on the floor or, in this case, hanging on the door handle. I sit down on the bed.

"What did you get him?" she says, grabbing a tube of some kind of makeup and putting it on her cheeks. I pull the panda out from my backpack.

"Awwww," she cooes, trying to grab it from me. I put it back into my bag swiftly.

"I want flowers," Naomi says as she sifts through her closet, pulling things out and shoving them back in.

"Jack's a smart guy. I'm sure he will get you flowers," I say, smiling as I pull out my phone.

Naomi wants flower, I text Jack while she isn't looking. I owe him for saving my life that one time in gym. I smile at her and she smiles back, grabbing a dress and slinking it over her half-dressed body.

"What is your friend doing tonight? Sid?" Naomi asks as she shoves random makeup bits into her bag.

"He is staying at home with my mom and binge watching romance movies on Netflix," I laugh.

"Seriously?" she asks, putting on her shoes.

"Sid's never been one to be in a relationship." I try

to imagine Sid buying someone flowers and I can't picture it.

"It's good that your mom has him, then. What about your brother?" she asks, spraying perfume. I'm in awe of all the steps it takes for her to get ready.

"The middle school love heart dance is tonight. He is there with some of the kids from his class, I guess," I shrug.

"Nobody ever found out, huh? About my volleyball coach?" she asks gingerly.

"Nope. Your dad handled it perfectly by keeping the student anonymous."

"That's good. Shall we go?" She stands up and walks to the door, now an inch or so taller than me in her heels.

"You look good!" I say as I spin around

"You do you!" She smiles at me as we walk down the hallway to the car.

"Ladies!" Jack says as he walks up to our car outside the restaurant, flowers in hand.

"Hi Jack" I say. Carter walks up behind him and I get out. Naomi walks up to Jack and takes the flowers. I hear her ooh's and aw's as I hug Carter.

"I've never had sushi before!" Jack says as he opens the doors of the restaurant. The smell of vinegar hits my nose.

"I'll have a California roll," Jack orders, per my recommendation. It's the least sushi of all sushi, in my opinion. I order my favorite, shrimp nigiri, and Carter orders a bunch of raw stuff that, honestly, I can't stomach. Naomi gets teriyaki chicken since she doesn't like seafood. I give Carter a look after he orders.

"I went to japan last spring. I learned to love this kind of stuff," he laughs.

"Carter," I say, pulling the panda bear out of my bag. "Happy Valentine's Day!" I hand him the chocolates and kiss his cheek.

"I love you," he says as he brushes the hair on the panda's head. Naomi and Jack are in their own little world. Naomi is still gushing over the flowers.

"Nice job texting Jack." Carter smiles, watching Naomi.

"Oh!" he says, pulling out a small box from his pocket. He opens it up to reveal a small silver ring. It's thinner than his, but, over all, the same. He grabs my hand and places the ring on my index finger.

"Now we match," he smiles.

"So, is this where you were?" I say, remembering Naomi saying something about Carter being at the store.

"They has to resize it from the floor model. Your fingers are so tiny," he says, smiling as he looks at the ring I gave him for Christmas.

"To us!" Carter raises his glass of oolong tea. I raise my Sprite. Naomi and Jack follow. The night comes to and end. Jack and I switch cars and Carter takes me home.

"Brighton!" I'm greeted by Sid and my mom sitting in the living room. The TV is paused on a movie and they are both hovering over my laptop.

"What's up?" I say, slinking my coat off and placing it on the coat rack.

"Your mom was telling me about her time in New York!" Sid says, turning the computer screen around to show the NYU website.

"Mom, you were in New York?" I question, sitting

down next to them.

"Before I got pregnant with you, I actually got accepted to NYU but didn't end up going." Mom has a bit of regret behind her voice.

"Are you going to apply?" I ask. Where is this whole thing is going?

"Yeah." Sid nods his head, turning the laptop back to face him. His eyes look bright and excited for the first time in a long time.

"I went to New York last year," I say, remembering the trip and all the shit that went down. I would like to go back and actually enjoy the city. I remember my suitcase and my night with Naomi and my kiss with Carter.

"I think you will like New York, Sid. It's a crazy city." I smile.

Senior Prom: the day most girls dream of their entire high school career, or at least that's why my mom says every time I mention school or Carter. I'm not going to lie, I'm excited for prom. It feels like the last milestone of my life in high school and in Connecticut before I leave for my new college life. It's hot here now. It's my first time experiencing this much heat and humidity at the same time. Spring in California is usually just like any other month, mild heat but nothing unbearable. I don't even want to imagine what summer is going to be like. The AC in our house runs whenever the sun in shining, but it's still a bit chilly at night.

During spring break, Carter's mom flew to San Francisco to look for an apartment for Carter. It eventually became her looking for an apartment for me and Carter because the rent is stupid expensive and there isn't really a point in us living separately. She came back with a few places in mind, but I'm letting Carter decide because it doesn't really matter to me as long as I get to be alone with him.

Now that spring break is over and there are a few weeks left of April, my brain is back in the usual grind of school. I already got accepted to my first choice, as did

Carter, but we're still taking classes seriously, unlike most kids in our grade. Ever since spring break, everyone has been running wild. The senior prank that, of course, Carter and I were left out of until it had already happened, was putting a kiddy pool in Carter's dad's office; pool noodles and everything. There was even a fake palm tree. It was truly a surprise to Carter and his dad when they arrived at school that Monday. Naomi apparently knew about the prank, but didn't say anything because she didn't want to be labeled as a blabbermouth. Mr. Hall gave her and the rest of the senior class an earful afterwards.

"He asked you?" I say as Naomi paints my nails, jerking my hand away,

"Stop! You're messing it up!" she says, grabbing a tissue and wiping the smeared blue polish off my skin.

"How did he do it?" I ask as she blows on my fingers. The paint feels stiff. I don't like it.

"I walked out of the P.E. locker room and there he was with about five of his swim team buddies. They were in their speedos and swim caps, butts facing me, and they they all turned around. Prom? was painted on their stomachs in blue body paint. Jack came out in front of them and said 'would you like to go to prom with me?' and handed me a pink rose." She points over to her dresser where the rose is in a small glass of water.

"Lucky," I say as I watch Naomi paint my small pinky nail.

"Carter will ask you," she says, dipping the brush back into the bottle.

"How do you know? What if he is waiting for me to ask him?" I pull my hand away and look at my nails.

They are sparkly and kind of messy.

"You just have to wait," Naomi smiles.

"You know something!" I say, grabbing for the bottle of acetone on her nightstand.

"I might." Her lips curl as if she is physically holding in the secret. She takes her hand, runs it across her lips and flicks it away, throwing away the "key". She's not going to tell me anything. "Twins honor," she says, helping me take off the nail polish that she just put on me.

Carter continued to stay silent the next few days at school. Carter acted the same as usual. I would mention prom and we all would talk about it like it wasn't in two days. Today is the last school day before prom and I'm jumpy. Every time the bell rings or the classroom doors open I become tense. I'm expecting some crazy promposal, but nothing happens. It's the last period of the day and I still haven't been invited.

The school intercom chimes with an announcement about the last chance to buy prom tickets as I start to sulk in my own disappointment. I never thought I would be upset about not getting asked to prom. Back in California, we actually thought it was annoying when all the seniors would be pulling these stunts. But, I guess it's different when you actually know who you want to go with. I tune into the last bit of the announcement: the nominees for prom court. I'm surprised to hear Naomi and Jacks name's in the list. Jack is a junior and, usually, they don't make the list, but he is pretty popular and so is Naomi. The announcer pauses and there is a brief commotion on the loudspeaker. She clears her throat and comes back.

"Carter Hall and Brighton Anderson." The

microphone beeps to signify that that's the final announcement before the bell rings to dismiss class. My mind races. Is this Carter's doing? Did he nominate us for prom king and...queen? I rush outside and find Jack and Carter standing outside my classroom.

"What was that?" I ask as I walk out. Based on both of their expressions, I can tell that this wasn't their doing.

"It was the fucking field hockey team" Jack announces. "I heard them talking about something like this in the locker room before swim practice last week. I didn't think it was you they were pulling this stunt on."

"Carter?" I ask. He is sweating from running to my class.

"I didn't know," he says. I look down and he has a half-disheveled bouquet of flowers in his hand."Will you go to prom with me?" He hands me the bouquet. I take it and stare at him.

"Will I?" I hug him. Jack laughs as people around us begin to look our way.

" Carter, your dad can take you off the ballot, right?" Jack asks as we walk to Mr. Briggs room.

"Yeah, I gue-" I cut Carter off.

"Why not run with is?" I say, smelling my bouquet of flowers.

"You sure?" he asks, picking a petal off one of the flowers that was half-fallen off.

33

Today's the day. I hear in movies that prom is supposed to be the best day of my life, more than a sweet 16 or, sometimes, more than graduation. Up until yesterday, I didn't even think I would be going. Carter took so long to ask me that I thought it wouldn't happen, but he probably thought the same thing about me and got sick of waiting.

Most girls spend weeks looking for their perfect prom dress, while most guys scramble to find the right tux to rent the week of, and here I am, the day of, and I waited so long to get a date that I'm wearing a t-shirt I got in San Francisco with a tuxedo print on it. I matched it with a pair of my nicest black dress pants.

"Brighton, could you please open the door?" Mom's voice comes from the other side of the door and is accompanied by a light knock. "Brighton, please, I want to talk to you." She knocks again.

Ma has never been one to be insistent on anything besides, you know, the whole uprooting our lives thing, so I figure it must be worth a shot to hear what she has to say. I open the door as I grab my wallet off my dresser and lay back on my bed. Mom comes and sits at the foot of my bed, rubbing her hands on her knees as she looks around my somewhat messy bedroom.

"Brighton, there comes a day in every parent's lives when they must--"

"Mom, we don't need to go through 'the talk.'" I interrupt her in an attempt to stop the awkward conversation she was about to try to force me into.

"Brighton Anderson! Would you please just be quiet and let me finish? It's your prom day! I know we haven't had the best relationship over the course of the last few months-" I cut her off again.

"You mean since you forced me to live in another country, almost?"

"You're still in America," she chuffs

"Honestly, it was a bit weird at first, but I think you moving us here was actually a good thing. I got to meet someone who I really like and it feels like home now. I'll always miss L.A. just a little bit, though," I say, looking at the photo of me and Sid pinned to my wall.

"You know, my intention was never to make you unhappy. I wanted to improve your and your brother's quality of life and make things better for us as a family. Ever since your father left, I haven't been able to give that to you. Now we're not in a shoe box apartment and we're not struggling to make ends meet. We have enough money to pass by for the rest of our lives if we manage ourselves right," Mom says, resting her hand on my leg.

"You know I'm happy here, right?" I say to her as I adjust my shirt and clip-on bow tie in my phone's front-facing camera. In my head, I'm replaying all the times this past year I've been a total ass to my mom. All she ever wanted to do was make my life better. "Mom, I love you. I really do. I'm sorry I never say that. Elliott, we still need to work on him. Maybe give him a few years? Even if he got with an older woman, he is still so immature!" I chuckle.

"Don't even joke about that, Bright. That's not something we talk about."

"I think we should. But, Ma, we done here? I love you and I love this moment we're having, but I gotta go." I glance at my watch.

"Oh, yes, of course! Oh, I remember my prom. Your father and I--" I cut her off for the third time.

"Mom."

"Right. Yes. Have a good time, sweetheart!" She leans over to kiss my forehead and walks out of my bedroom. I see Elliott sitting next to the desk in his bedroom, fiddling with his phone. I give him a quick wave and guide myself down the stairs.

"Mom!" I scream, "I'm leaving! I love you!"

"Brighton, wait! I want to give you something!" She runs down the stairs.

"Here! Take this and wear it. It was your father's. When the dance was over he gave it to me. I was super cold when we got to the car and I never gave it back." She hands me a dusty garment bag.

"Mom, it's lowkey creepy that you've kept that even through the divorce." I grab the bag and unzip it. The jacket is a very classy, warm grey color. You can tell it's not new, but it still has a certain charm to it. I throw it over my shoulders and stuff my arms through the sleeves. Mom looks at me with that look parents give you, as if you have done something to be proud of when, in fact, all I've done is put on a coat. I smile at her and she smiles back.

Carter and I agreed to meet at a little mom-and-pop diner in uptown Gilford. It's a fairly new place and Carter wants something to eat before we go. I pull up to the side of the diner because, from here, I'm carpooling with Carter. I begin to blush when I walk in as I think about how Carter is going to react to my outfit. My dad's jacket smells mostly like dust, but there's also a hint of cigarette smoke. It brings back a few painful memories, but I bear it because I think it makes my attempt at an outfit somewhat acceptable. Hopefully, Carter feels the same way.

I sit down at a corner booth. Carter isn't here yet, but I'm also about ten minutes early. I'm not sure how I managed that with the whole "hallmark mom and son" bonding thing that went down, but I'm glad because it gives me a chance to calm my nerves.

My phone pings. As I look at the notification, there's a loud honk. I look up and see Carter in a rental car outside. It's a really nice looking sports car with the convertible top down. He's smiling from ear to ear as he rushes to the door of the diner.

Hey, are you ready?" He stops abruptly."What are you wearing?" He looks at me from afar.

"Uh, well, you asked me yesterday and I, well, I didn't have much to wear, "I scramble. I'm stumbling over my words and he puts his finger up to my lips and shushes me. He comes in closer and gives me a light kiss.

"I'm just happy to be with you. Plus, that sports jacket makes it tolerable." He chuckles and gives me another kiss. "Let's sit and eat." Carter is wearing a dark green suit jacket. It's soft, like velvet, or maybe suede. I noticed it when he hugged me and my chin brushed across his shoulder. There is a tiny scarf with what looks like a little bird on it tucked into his front pocket.

"Oof, I'm stuffed!" Carter exclaims. "I think we should eat here more often!"

"Hey, babe-" I'm trying something to see if he'll catch onto it. Sid calls me Bright, which is a short version of my name, obviously, and I really like that, but when I tried to think of a similar thing for Carter, the only thing I came up with was "Cart", and that isn't a cute nickname, so I'm settling for the overused but still endearing "babe". "-what time is it?" I look at him and he's smiling.

"Uh, it's around eight.... babe." He smirks at me.

"Oh, we're a bit more then fashionably late!" I stand up, brushing the crumbs from my meal off my lap. "We should get going!"Carter grabs my hand.

We drive up to the school. There's nobody outside and I can hear the faint sound of the loud music playing in the gym. Carter parks the car and looks over at me.

"Babe," he's smiling, "you ready to go inside?" I smile at how quickly he started using babe when talking to me. My heart beats a little faster in my chest.

"Well, it looks like we're the only ones just arriving." My hands start to sweat as I look around at the human-void parking lot full of random limos and cars.

"That doesn't matter. All that matters is that it's you, and it's me, and we're here together." He smiles at me and gets out of the car. He walks around to my door. "Let's face the world," Carter says, grabbing my hand and pulling me from the car.

I immediately I see Naomi and Jack as we walk in. They're standing out from the crowd, to say the least.

Naomi's dress is a deep purple color with an array of crystals covering her top half. The rest of the dress flows down from her waist in an elegant yet simple manner. The crystals cast small iridescent rainbows all over the floor as the colorful lights flash around her. Jack's tux is a dark plum color with black accents to match.

"You're late!" Naomi screams across the hall to us. "They're about to announce king and queen! Let's go!" She yanks Carter and my arm into the gym where the main dance floor is.

"Hold on!" Carter jerks away from Naomi and wanders up to the DJ booth. I see him whisper something to him before being pulled away.

The emcee of the prom is standing at the microphone on stage, holding the tiny little envelope with the names of the king and queen.

"Will our prom court please join us on stage!" I look around at the crowd as we all take the stage. My hands shake as we all line up behind the crowns that are sitting on two little pillows on stage.

"And now, without further ado, our very own king and queen are…" A drum roll sound effect comes from the DJ booth which is followed by some scattered laughter in the crowd."Naomi and Jack!" The gym uproars. Carter and I look at one another. "And now, if we can clear the floor for the first dance."

Naomi looks over at us as she walks down the stairs. Carter gestures for her to go as we make our way behind them.

"Let's go get some drinks over here." Carter pulls my hand towards the punch table. This is prom. This is my life.

"So, I guess we're not destined to be royalty," Carter says, spooning some punch into a tiny paper cup.

"They really look amazing," I say, looking over at the dance floor. Naomi and Jack are slow dancing.

As I take a sip of my punch, the song changes. I recognize it immediately. Before I can say anything, my cup is taken out of my hand and replaced with Carter's palm.

"Dying in L.A.?" I look over at him as we make our way to the floor. More people have joined Naomi and Jack now.

"I know you like this band. I looked them up and this song is about L.A., so it reminded me of you."

"So that's why you left me to talk to the DJ." I laugh as he pulls me in to his arms. He soft suit is against my face, my head is on his shoulder and our feet are moving perfectly in motion with the rhythm of the song and the pings of the piano.

This is *my* prom. It's perfect in all its small ways. I close my eyes and take it all in. The gym smells like cheap cologne and sugar. The sounds of people around us laughing and talking begins to muffle into nothing as I tune into Carter's heartbeat. Each bump makes me feel closer and closer to him. There is, truly, nothing more amazing then feeling completely in sync with the feelings and the emotions of the person you love.

34

"It's not gonna fit!" Carter yells as he shoves his last piece of luggage into the backseat.

"It has to!" I get behind him and push just hard enough to squeeze the door shut. "The one time you choose to be an over packer," I joke. Carter grabs my hands as we back away from the car.

"It doesn't feel like we graduated." He shakes his head.

"I feel like I just got here." I turn around and look at the buildings behind us. The setting sun is hitting them just right.

"Well, we gotta get going if we want to make it back home for Elliott's graduation," I say, letting go of Carter's hand.

"Tell me *why* we are driving back to Connecticut instead of flying." Carter leans his body weight onto me.

"Because we're saving money!" I say, putting my hands on my hips.

"No, seriously." Carter looks annoyed.

"My mom wants her car back," I laugh. "Four years is a long time to 'borrow' something, plus we'll fly back to San Francisco in a week. Don't you, at least, wanna see your sister?" I grab the keys off the roof of the car and wipe the sweat from my forehead.

"You mean my sister, who went to college for a year, then went back home just to get married and win the ultimate twin competition?"

"What?" I laugh.

"Whichever twin gets married first is, like, you know, the ultimate winner. She did all the major life events first," Carter jokingly sulks, walking over to the passenger seat. "How long is the drive?" he says, shifting in his seat.

"We're driving across all of the United States! Be more excited!" I turn on the car and rev the engine.

"How long?" The engine quiets down along with my excitement.

"Forty-four hours," I sigh.

"Well, let's get going." He slams his door and we take off into the setting San Francisco sun.

Forty-four hours and many rest stops and Big Gulps later, we're back in Guilford, Connecticut.

"My man!" I hop out of the car and run toward Sid, who is standing next to the front door. Carter runs past me to go to the bathroom.

"Bright!" Sid grabs my hand and bring me in for a hug.

"How's New York treating you?"

"One more year 'til graduation!" He shakes his head.

"Now you know how I feel!" Elliott joins the conversation.

"You still salty that you didn't get accept your first try?" I pull his beanie off his head and put in on mine.

"Not salty, just, well...yes." He laughs.

"And my little brother is all grown up!" I reach up

and rustle his hair. It's bleach blonde now, like mine once was.

"They must put something in the water in Connecticut 'cuz little Elliott is way taller than you, Bright!" Sid closes one of his eyes and pretends to measure the height between us.

"I'm also taller than you, though, Sid," Elliott jokes, grabbing Sid's beanie off my head and putting it on himself.

"Mom?" I question, pointing into the house.

"Not just your mom." Elliott grabs my hand.

"Mrs. Hall!" I say as Carter's mom walks out of the house. Carter follows.

"Brighton, it's been years. Call me Christine." She hugs me, rubbing my back as we part.

"Where's Naomi?" I look past them and into the house, expecting to see her and Jack pop out too.

"They are still driving up from their trip to Rhode Island. They will be back tonight," Carter's mom says.

"See, Carter, you still beat Naomi in some things," I joke.

"What?" my mom questions.

We go inside and sit on the couch. I explain Carter's jealously over Naomi and Jack's marriage. I talk about school and job interviews as well. Mom tells me about a date she went on with the lawyer who first met us at this house all those years ago and how horrible it was.

"I wish your father were still here to see this." Carter's mom looks over at me and him, sitting close, hand in hand.

I see Carter swallow hard, his father's passing still fresh in his mind. I remember the day like it was yesterday. We had just finished our first year at SFSU. Carter was planning a movie night for us and some of his film writing class friends and the phone rang. They said he died of a heart attack. He was in his office late at night and the janitor found him the next morning. Carter was inconsolable. He was pronounced dead at the scene and there was nothing anyone could do. He didn't get to say goodbye and I didn't know how to help him.

"On a happier note, I finished my first screenplay!" Carter stands up and bows before plopping back down next to me.

"Ooh, what's it about?" my mom questions.

"It's about a boy who grows up in a small town," he teases.

"And…" Elliott's eager for more.

"You will have to wait and see when it gets turned into a movie."

"*If* it gets turned into a movie," Carter's mom chimes in.

"Yeah, yeah," he waves her off. We laugh.

"I can vouch for him. It's actually really good," I say, trying sneak in that I have read it.

"You know, I know a kid from my psyche class who made a short film and went all the way to Sundance," Sid chimes in.

" Well, if nobody picks up my film, I'll be sure to give you a call," Carter laughs.

I'm sitting here with my family, my boyfriend and my best friend. We're laughing and talking like nothing matters. The sun is setting and my eyes are sleepy from the long drive. I look around and see the stairs where so many awkward encounter happened and the kitchen where so many meals were eaten, good and bad. I look at Sid and I remember of his famous Hot Cheeto Marshmallow fluff on rye and wonder when the last time was he had one was. His hair is short, like, shorter then it's even been, and he is clean shaven. Even he looks like an adult. Ma looks older, but not in a bad way, just the normal wear and tear of life. It scares me a bit to see her getting older, but I try not to think about that too much.

"I'm going to head up to bed." I stand up. Carter yawns and follows.

"Door open!" both our moms yells. It brings me back to a different time in my mind.

Carter lays next to me in bed. The roof of my room is the only thing that looks the same. The furniture is completely different and the bedding is more "mom chic" than I'm used to.

"Brighton, are you asleep?" I hear Carter's voice as my eyes close.

"No, I'm just resting my eyes," I respond, only half-conscious.

"So, I was thinking..." He grabs my hand and pulls the ring off my index finger. I wake up from his sudden touch.

"What?" I say as he grabs my hand tighter and slides the ring onto my ring finger.

"Will you marry me?" He smiles.

"Whoa!" I fall backwards off the bed.

"Everything okay up there?" I hear footsteps running up the stairs. Multiple faces appear in my doorway. I hold up my hand from my place on the floor.

"Yes," I say, standing up.

"Yes?" my mom puts her glasses on and looks over

308

at me.

"Yes!" Carter's mom runs over and puts her hand on Carter's cheek. "He said yes!" She holds his head while he tries to shake it up and down, grabbing his own ring and switching it.

"What's all the hubbub?" Naomi and Jack walk up behind the crowd pulling a suitcase.

"I said yes." I hold up my hand. The ring Carter gave me five years ago glistens in the light. He holds up his hand as well.

The rings are finally on the right fingers.

Acknowledgments

This book was carefully worked on and crafted by not only myself and my co-author, but by a wonderful group of people who all cared about this little universe we created. Thank you to our editor, Kelly McCasland, for putting her time and effort into editing this book. Thank you to all our early readers, who's criticism really helped this work blossom into what you have before you. Thank you to the people in my real life who inspired some of the interactions between the characters and some of the events that took place in their lives. Your part may be small but, in a big way, it brought these page to life. Thank you to my co-author, Jacob Jensen, for jumping in head first on this wild idea of mine to write a book.

CPSIA information can be obtained
at www.ICGtesting.com
Printed in the USA
FSHW021956300119
55382FS